Mountain Home

by

Harley Herrald

Published and Distributed by:

Granite Publishing and Distribution, LLC
868 North 1430 West
Orem, Utah 84057
(801) 229-9023 • Toll Free (800) 574-5779
Fax (801) 229-1924

ISBN: 1-930980-25-6
Library of Congress Catalog Card Number: 2001091572
Printed in the United States of America

Page Layout and Design: Myrna Varga • The Office Connection – Orem, Utah
Cover Design by Tammie Ingram
Cover Art by Jennett Chandler

*To Mary . . . With whom all
things can be and without
whom nothing will be.*

Chapter 1

Sitting here on the side of the mountain, I can see down into that beautiful valley—the valley that has become my life these past years.

Scanning the complex of buildings that had, once, been only a cabin and a small barn, I marvel at how much has happened. My life has turned from that of an out-of-work cowboy to one of hope and meaning.

I remember that day when I had first seen that valley. I was broke, hungry and three hundred miles from anyone I could call friend; and very aware of how little I meant to the world.

I rode into the valley, the first time, to kill a bear, that was killing a man I had never seen. That single act set into motion a chain of events, the last link not, even yet, forged. It was there, at that site of death, I first met my Clatilda. Then, the widowed plural wife of Jethro Bailey, the man killed by that bear.

Her courage, that day, was a wonder, and continues to be a strength to me.

As I look out upon the valley I feel a sense of awe at what I see. I, personally, take no pride in the ranch, even though it is a grand thing. I merely happened by at a time when this grand plan had already been set in motion. I was not its creator, more its shepherd. Just a big, dumb cowboy who grabbed a star as it flew by, and found myself, years later, glad for the ride.

I know in the back of my mind, that Clatilda has been the steady hand bringing all this together. She has certainly guided me into a life I would never have imagined. She, of the honest, quiet, strength. If our children have any admirable qualities, I pray they will be her honesty and courage.

Our oldest son, William, is, in truth, not ours. He is the product of the marriage of Jethro Bailey and Clatilda's "sister wife," Jennifer. He was born a few months after Jethro was killed. His mother died giving birth to the boy. Clatilda raised him as her own and after she and I were married, I became the only father he ever knew. I believe he was seven or eight before he ever considered the fact that Clatilda and I were not his real folks. Even then, he seemed unimpressed by having two sets of parents. He just put Jethro and Jennifer away, as an old, cherished memory.

Looking down into the valley, I remember the mighty changes in all our lives since that terrible day I killed that bear.

Few are privileged to look back upon a single event, and be able to say at what precise moment in time their lives change to become what they are. I could.

I am now on a path to reach a point that, those years ago, I would not have been able to see, let alone understand. I had no ambition, at that time, beyond finding a riding job before I ran out of everything and wound up riding the grub line. I would not, then, have even thought about the purpose or direction of my life. My ambition stretched toward two meals every day, a warm place to lay my head at night and twenty-five or thirty dollars at the end of each month. That was all I had ever known, and felt it not to be a bad way to spend my life.

Again, as I look out over the valley, toward the farm of my friend, Seth Blalock, I can't help but grin, to myself. Today I might ask him for any thing, or ability, he had, and have every expectation of immediately receiving that for which I asked. A few years ago I had promised him I would run him out of this valley, or kill him. Now, his children call me, "Uncle Will." His wife, Anne, *I also consider a dear friend.*

My horse began to fidget, as we had been sitting still too long. I was not, however through with my reminiscing. Where the next few years might lead, I could only guess. But, at least now, there was a plan to my future. Maybe, just maybe, I will continue to be blessed, as I have been the past few years.

I watch as William comes out of the big barn with his pony. I hope he is not coming to look for me. I am too comfortable in my solitude. He turned instead toward the small graveyard where so many, now, are sleeping. He stops, on a small knoll and picking a handful of wild flowers, he remounts and turns, once again toward the graves, I remember such an afternoon, a few years ago when I had found him at that same place. It seems like only yesterday. . . .

Chapter 2

I was coming home from helping Seth Blalock assemble his new potato planter when I saw William standing at the fence around the graves holding his horses reins in one hand and a clutch of wild flowers in the other. I turned my pony and rode up the hill to stop beside him.

"Pa," he said as I stepped off my horse, "did you know those folks very well?"

"No, son," I answered, "I never knew Jethro at all. The bear had done him in by the time I got to him. As for Jennifer, I saw her very little, as she was sick all during the fall before you were born. One thing I can tell you about her though is that she was a strong lady. Strong like your Ma is and honest in the way she faced life, just like your Ma."

"Do you think it's wrong that I don't really feel any love for them, Pa?"

"No, son, I don't think it's wrong not to feel love, but remember what your Ma said. We don't mean you should do other than respect their memory. Cause, boy, don't ever forget, those two folks are responsible for giving you the life you now enjoy."

"And, William, speaking of the life you enjoy, did you get a deer?"

"No, sir, I saw two does, but both had fawns, and I figured we could just eat something else tonight."

"That's good thinking, son, your Ma would have us both cleaning her chicken house for a month if you'd knocked down a doe with fawn."

We both mounted and rode the short distance home. Anna Laura met us at the barn door.

"Pa, mama wants you inside right quick! Sarah is real sick, and mama wants you to go to town for Brother Terry."

I flipped my reins to William and broke for the house. When I went in, Clatilda had Sarah on the kitchen table and was bathing her body.

"Will, it's like it was with William, when he was a baby. She started with a fever about noon and she just keeps getting hotter."

"Let me bathe her for a minute while you take a break," I said, stepping around the table.

"Will, I'm worried. She seems hotter now than William ever was, and I've been bathing her with cold water for almost two solid hours."

As I reached for the rag from Clatilda, and slipped my hand under Sarah's head and shoulders, she stiffened and seemed to twist back and forth, suddenly.

"Will, she's convulsing!" Clatilda said as she scooped up the baby and held her close. Sarah seemed to be jerking as if she wanted down or turned.

"Will!" Clatilda practically shouted. "Go get Seth. This baby has to be blessed, and now!"

I went through the door, not caring whether it stayed on its hinges. William was just turning my horse toward the corral. I shouted for him to bring the house to me. He turned and seeing me running, jerked the horse around, and flipped the reins over the horse's neck. I leaped to the saddle and jammed my spurs harder than I would have tolerated another doing; even to his own animal.

I went around the barn and toward the Blalock's house, in a flurry of dust and barking dogs. As I rode toward the Blalocks, I thought of how badly Clatilda had wanted Sarah. We had both wanted more children; and, after Anna Laura, we tried for a bigger family. Robert had been still born and we had despaired until Sarah came along. If anything happened to this little girl, Clatilda was going to be nearly inconsolable.

I swirled into Seth's dooryard just as he stepped out his door with two milk buckets in his hands.

"Seth, I need you now!" I said. "Get up behind me I'll explain on the way."

Typical of Seth, he said nothing, just dropped the buckets to the ground where he stood. He stepped into the stirrup, I had vacated, as he swung up behind me. My pony crow-hopped a little but I had no time for such and jerked the animal around and gigged him hard again, with my spurs, and he, good honest animal he was, lined out for home.

All I told Seth on the way was that Sarah was sick, and we had to bless her, and right now.

We swept up right to the door, and Seth was off one side of the animal, and I the other. As I stepped through the door, I came upon a scene that is burned into my soul for all eternity. Clatilda stood in front of the table with the baby clutched to her breast while huge tears coursed down her face.

"Will," she said as I stopped suddenly, "our baby's gone. She's gone, Will!"

I stepped over, taking both my wife and my daughter into my arms.

Seth, behind me, said, "Are you sure, Clatilda?"

"Yes, Seth," Clatilda's voice was muffled against my shoulder.

I heard the door close, and immediately, the running hoof beats of my pony.

It seemed only a few brief moments before Anne Blalock came through the door. She, ever so quietly, stepped to Clatilda's side and seemingly, with no effort, gently turned Clatilda toward the bedroom. She looked at me and with only the slightest nod and movement of her eyes turned, and escorted Clatilda into the bedroom, closing the door behind them.

At first, I was more than some put off by this, but then I thought how very little I could do for Clatilda, or Sarah, now. This was a time for Anna and Clatilda to gather themselves and care for the last needs of my daughter. Clatilda and I would have our time to grieve together and my time . . . well that would be later.

I turned to Seth. "Seth, will you please take my pony and ride to town for Bishop Terry and his wife. Tell him I would also appreciate it if he would bring John too."

Seth said not a word, just turned, and soon I heard my horse loping out of the yard.

It was almost two hours later that Anne found me in the barn. I had William and Anna Laura with me as I worked on, yet another, casket. This time I cleaned the wood with little but my own grief.

"Will, I believe Clatilda would like you with her, now. I will take the children home with me. Bishop Terry and his wife just got here. So, I will go see to my brood. Seth and I will be back shortly."

I didn't much want to go into the house, particularly with Bishop Terry and his wife there. Somehow, this seemed a time to be alone. I knew Clatilda did not find this to be true. I knew she would want those around her whose love and respect she felt. I went into the kitchen to find Bishop Terry sitting at the table and his wife, Ruth, and Clatilda standing in front of the kitchen stove. Clatilda was stirring a pan, and Ruth stood with her arm across Clatilda's shoulder.

Bishop Terry stood and stepped over to grasp my hand. There were many things said, by all, in the next few minutes, but all I remember was Clatilda. Quiet, moving competently around her kitchen, seeing to the needs of those of us whom she considered her charges. She had only one question, and that was to ask of William and Anna Laura. When I told her where they were, she wordlessly, turned back to serving those few in the kitchen, which soon, also included Seth and Anne.

I excused myself to tend to my evening chores. As I stepped out the door, Jess Turner and Hester came into the dooryard. The horses hitched to their buggy, showing the results of a hard run.

Hester stepped, unassisted, from the buggy and briefly touching my shoulder, went directly into the house. Jess just reached and took one of my milk buckets, and with nothing said, followed me into the barn.

William had brought the milk cows and the two goats we now kept, into the barn before going with Anne.

Jess and I went to our tasks, and by the time we'd finished it was full dark. As I was checking the lanterns in the barn, Jess stepped over beside the small unfinished casket.

"How many of these have you made since coming amongst us, Will?" he asked quietly.

"Including the one John Terry had me build when his boy was killed, this will make five. And, I have to tell you, Jess, I weary of the task."

"It's no wonder, friend. May I help you complete this one?"

"No, this is a job I'll do myself. It's not that I don't appreciate your offer, but I'll finish it myself."

Jess said nothing, just turned and snuffing one of the lanterns while I put out the other, stepped out the door and led the way to the house.

Clatilda took my hand, and led me into our room after I'd placed the milk on a table.

Sarah was in her crib dressed in her finest, and looking the angel she had always been. It was difficult at first to look at her but I couldn't keep my eyes from her sweet face.

"Once again, Will, you have a casket to build."

"It's almost complete. I can have it done in another hour. When have you decided to bury her?"

"I have told Bishop Terry tomorrow afternoon. Is that all right with you?"

I looked at this woman, this wife of mine. Once again I wondered at her strength.

"Yes, ma'am. That will do."

We started to leave the room, but I stopped Clatilda laying my hand upon her shoulder. "And once again, my lady, it will be me who will bless the grave."

Clatilda turned, placing her arm around my neck, and buried her face against my shoulder. For a few moments she was wracked by deep sobs.

Sarah was buried on a beautiful late summer afternoon. It seemed the entire valley turned out. We had decided not to go into town and then all the way back out to our place. Bishop Terry conducted the service in the ramada I had made of the original brush arbor. Most everyone brought some chairs in their wagons and buggies. The rest stood.

I wondered how we would ever feed such a crowd but I had forgotten the providence of Mormon women. When it was all over, our table was still covered with food.

Chapter 3

Hours of grief turned, slowly, into days and weeks of longing.

We helped Seth and his boys harvest their potatoes and once again, he had a bumper crop.

Clatilda and I had decided to cull and sell our herd that fall so that by early September I had a good-sized trail herd ready.

We discussed, back and forth, where to sell our cattle and it was decided we would get the better price if I could get the cattle to Denver City. The length of such a drive worried Clatilda and, frankly I'd have been happier if I could have started in July, early August, at the latest. I brought the matter up in Priesthood meeting one Sunday, and Jess Turner strongly advised against such a venture. John Terry offered to take part of the herd, which he would then, carry over the winter, and butcher, for sale through his store. But, when I told him the number I would have for sale, what he said he could use accounted for less than ten percent of what I'd be selling. He saw his purchase was of no help.

Unfortunately, my intended trail drive took up most of our meeting time and went on outside the church.

There were several young men who wanted to go on the drive but when I told them of the time involved and possible route, that number thinned considerably.

Clatilda and I discussed it on the way home, that evening. She advised I wait until the next summer. I told her I didn't want to carry that many cattle through the winter. I had a strange feeling that there was some urgency in my selling off a large part of our herd. It wasn't the money, for the past few years had been good to us, indeed. I still refused to take part, or even take notice, of the income from the store. But from time to time Clatilda would try to draw me into a discussion of the disposition, of what she referred to as, "our store money."

I talked to Seth that Monday, and he offered to go and bring Daniel. But, I refused, saying one of us, from our valley, being gone for the eight to ten weeks necessary for the drive, was enough.

Monday afternoon I went in to see Bishop Terry and found him at John's store. He and John both seemed eager to see me. John said he had talked to one of his customers from over east of the settlement, and was told there were several young men in their area that would jump at the chance to earn money this time of the year. Most ranches had laid off their summer help, and many of these young men had several years' experience working cattle.

John agreed to ride over to the small settlement with me, the next day, and introduce me to his customer.

Clatilda accepted the news with mixed emotions. She was happy I might be able to find enough men to help on the drive, but was saddened by the prospect that it would actually take place.

I picked up John Terry at his house before daylight the next morning, and by noon we were setting in the cabin of his friend, Gilberto Medina. Senor Medina had sent two of his boys to neighbors to advise them of our presence and possible jobs for their friends. Senora Medina was most gracious and treated us to a dinner fit for a king. Her food was abundant, spicy, but very good.

By mid-afternoon there were six young men seated around the

Medina's table, all eager to go a droving. I agreed to hire all six for the drive to Denver City and Senor Medina agreed to bring along his wagon, which he would convert to serve us a chuck wagon, of sorts. I told the men of my plans to take orders for goods to be purchased in Denver City, and that this would provide them work and wages on the return trip, helping me with the pack train on which I would return the merchandise.

It was agreed they would all meet me at my home the following Thursday, thus giving Senor Medina an extra day to ready his chuck wagon. John and I went back that afternoon. It was long after sunset before I got back to my house.

All the way home a plan had been forming, and I was anxious to discuss it with Clatilda.

I told her that now that I had such a crew, I planned to take most of our herd to Denver City, keeping only twenty or thirty young cows, and a couple of my best bulls. Clatilda sat for a moment, staring at her folded hands.

"Will, why are you doing this?"

"I don't rightly know, except I have an almost overpowering urge to sell as many head as I can. I know we have plenty of hay and water to carry the whole herd. But, Clatilda, I feel that I have to rid us of these cattle. It sounds strange, even to me, because I know that just as soon as I get back, I'm going to start right over trying every way I can to build up our herd again."

"But you are sure this should be done?" she asked.

"Yes, and as I said, I can't give you a good reason. It's just something I feel should be done."

She leaned back in her chair and looked right into my eyes in that way of hers.

"Well, cowboy, don't think that just because you sell off all of your cows, you're going to spend the winter loafing around in my kitchen."

I was sorry, then that I would be leaving in a couple of days, for this was the first sign I had seen of my dear sweet, ornery, Clatilda, since the day we buried Sarah.

She said nothing more, but when I came back after completing my chores, she had a piece of apple pie with cream on the top and a big mug of hot chocolate. That evening, Clatilda and I, once again, picked up the strings of our lives to re-weave whatever tapestry we could.

I had William, Seth, his sons Daniel and Aaron come help me the next day to gather together the herd I intended to sell. I kept only eighteen cows, but I had four good, young bulls I couldn't let go. Seth was curious and asked why I was effectively selling off my entire herd.

"Seth," I began as we rested our horses, "I don't rightly know. Except I've got this hunch I should sell as many as I can do without."

"Man, you're not going to be much of a rancher with that little dab of cows. Why, I've got half that many and all I have is a few milkers, and a few I'm feeding out to butcher."

"I know, and I don't have a real good explanation."

"What is it, Will, the Spirit talking to you?"

I looked at him for a moment then chuckled, "You know, Seth, you're probably right. I've been too busy worrying about my so-called hunch to look at what probably is the fact of the matter."

Seth and I went in for dinner, leaving Daniel, Aaron, and William to keep the herd bunched.

I told Clatilda of my conversation with Seth, and my feeling of stupidity for not recognizing the source of my promoting to sell the herd.

"Will," she said, "I came to that conclusion last night. I rewrote my list of things I want you to get for me, in Denver City. It's lying there on the table. You'll find it much longer than before."

I remembered, then, something Bishop Terry had said about the women and how they, "God bless them," keep us men on track.

I didn't say anything to Clatilda; she looked too smug as it was.

Daylight, the next morning, found my yard full of horses and young vaqueros. I had told the young men that I would be able to furnish each an extra horse from my remuda. But, they would be wise, if they had them, to bring an extra horse. Each brought two plus the one he rode.

Chapter 4

Shortly after noon that first day of the drive, we were east of the settlement, and still trying to settle the herd. It had been long since I had been involved with a trail herd of that size. We had tallied through one of the stack-yard gates. We had five hundred thirty-two cows and thirty-four horses. I had brought my entire horse herd. I knew we would need them.

It was late in the afternoon of the second day, when we turned the herd in on Medina's north pasture. It was easy to see why Senor Medina wanted the cattle there. The ground was poor and badly in need of the fertilizer the cattle would leave.

Medina had his wagon set up. He had gone to Terry's store the previous day, as I had told him, and picked up the supplies he would need, charging them to my account.

As I laid down that night, I regretted my decision to have William stay with his mother. Two reasons had prompted my decision. One was school was to start in the settlement the next week, and the second was, I wanted Will to be on hand to help Clatilda and Anna Laura. The wisdom of both those reasons faded in my wish that I could have him along for the company he would be.

That third day proved to be the most difficult of the entire drive. Grazing was poor and the creeks were mostly dried up. By the time we reached good water, the animals were even fighting among themselves. It took almost a week to get into the eastern mountains. We were crossing at the center of the Greenhorns, and while the trail was not extremely difficult, there was some heavy timber that kept us busy for a couple of days.

Luckily, for the five days it took to get across the mountains to La Veta, we found good grass to bed the herd down upon every night.

I'd noticed by the time we started down the eastside of the mountains toward La Veta that several of the men were frequently having animated conversations. I was never close enough to hear what they were saying until one evening I came in for supper a little later than usual. The two Medina boys, Jamie and Al were in a heated discussion with Leon Vasquez. They were speaking in Spanish, and only glanced at me, as I stepped off my pony. I listened, as I picked my supper. Leon said something about my not being able to understand, so they could talk as they pleased.

I stepped over by the fire where they stood and casually began to discuss the day's events . . . in Spanish.

I explained that I had been raised living next to a Spanish-speaking family. If I wanted to talk to the kids I played with, it had to be in Spanish. There were five of them and one of me. Not much choice.

Leon explained to me that they were concerned about a rancher southwest of Walsenburg. They said he had a reputation for cutting herds that crossed his land. They were all concerned about how I might handle this problem.

"I can only tell you one thing, fellows,' I've worked hard for those cattle, and I owe nothing to anyone. If this man's land is fenced, we will go around. If he has markers, we will go around those; but, if he is just trying to run a sandy, over open range, he's not going to have much luck."

"What if he and his men try to cut the herd anyway?" Al Medina asked.

"I guess, I'm, once again, in the position of being one in many. My question to all of you is, what will you do if this man and his crew try to cut the herd?"

Jamie Medina had been standing quietly by the fire with a cup of coffee in his hands. He tossed the coffee into the fire and looked across at me.

"Senor Jackson, if you say you will not allow the herd to be cut, I guess that ends it. I see no reason for further talk. The herd will not be cut." He looked around at each of the others then turned back to me. "If you will not have your herd cut, we will see your wishes are followed."

With that, he and the others turned to the fire to dish up their suppers. While I had thought I was late, they had obviously waited for me.

I went to the chuck wagon, and from my bed roll I removed my pistol and belt. I noticed all watched as I buckled it on. I had previously ridden only with my rifle on my saddle.

The next morning at breakfast I noted that everyone wore a pistol, even the elder Medina. Some of the rigs were fancy and some were plain. All were wall cared for and all of the cartridge loops, on the belts, were full.

I thought long and prayed hard that day, and the next. I was sure that I would not allow my herd to be cut by some high binder, trying to bully his way to a larger ranch.

I was less than comfortable with what I might be leading my young crew into.

We saw no one that day, or the next, but the morning of the third day, after the warning by my crew, and as we pushed the herd out onto the sloping hills toward the river, we saw a group of horsemen loping toward us from the southeast.

Jamie Medina had been riding close to me for the past two days; now pulled up beside me as we sat and watched the riders come across a rolling knoll.

"It's the Three Star crew," Jamie said.

"How would you know that?" I asked.

"They are the ones who cut herds, senor. Why else so many, and coming directly to us?"

As they came closer, we could see there were five riders, one on a tall black horse. I was aware that some of my riders were turning the herd as they milled and settled down to graze while three rode, then, to stand their horses behind Jamie and me.

The Three Star crew rode up to about thirty feet from us, then stopped. The man on the big black rode another ten feet ahead of his crew.

"Who's leading this outfit?" He demanded.

Before I could speak, Jamie nudged his pony a step or two forward.

"Who asks, senor?" Jamie asked quietly.

"That don't figure to be your concern, Mex.," the man answered bluntly.

"Well, friend, it's sure mine!" I said as I nudged my pony up next to Jamie.

"You own this herd?" he demanded.

"Partner, my friend, here, asked the question, 'who's asking'?"

"The name's Cecil Denton, I own the Three Star, and, mister, you're on my land."

"We saw no fences or no markers," I answered, simply.

"No matter, you're on my land, and nobody crosses my land for free. Most particularly no one pushing a herd of cattle, tearing up my grass and using my water."

I sat, quietly, with my hand resting on the saddle horn. Denton stared at me as if he expected some comment.

Finally Denton spoke again. "Well, what you got to say for yourself. How do you intend to make it right?"

"Make what right, Mr. Denton?" I asked. "I have done nothing I feel must be made right."

"Well, you're sure going to pay for tearing up my range. And, mister, you get smart with me, and you'll pay big!"

I noticed his crew begin to fan out behind him and at the same time, edge forward somewhat. I felt the time for talking was over.

"Denton, we might as well get it straight. I owe you nothing. As far as I can tell this is not your land. If you think I'm going to pay you some kind of bribe, in money or cattle, to cross open range, you're wrong. I'll give you nothing. That's final. Take it, or leave it!"

I noticed one man, on a pot-bellied little grulla, had edged up beside Denton. When I finished, he had a crooked smile on his face. Somehow his smile was not menacing, just amused.

"Well, mister," Denton said, sitting up straight on his pony, "you ain't taking that herd one step further until my boys cut out fifty head! You can take that or leave it!"

When he finished, I had my pistol out, cocked, and pointed at his belly. For a brief moment the action seemed not to register on any one in the Three Star crew, with the possible exception of the man on the little grulla. His smile widened.

"Mr. Denton, you are a very short time away from whoever your maker may be. Now you can do one of two things. You can turn and leave here, quietly, and right now, or you can die, not so quietly, but also, right now. What will it be?"

Indecision was in his face, as was real panic. We sat there for a second until, in the quiet, the cocking of Jamie's pistol, followed by the cocking of other pistols behind me sounded unusually loud.

"Mister, you've made a big mistake. You'll not live to tell this story. In fact, you won't live to make it to Walsenburg and it is less than fifteen miles, over there. We'll leave, but you won't know when we'll be back!" Denton blustered.

"Then, you'll not mind if I take out a little insurance," I said. "Get down off those ponies, all of you, and now."

The Three Star crew slowly dismounted, all except the man on the grulla.

I glanced over at him. "You, too, friend."

"I may, in a minute. First I want to see what comes next."

"That's easy," I said, "what comes next, is that everyone takes off their boots, and socks, if they are wearing any."

"Oh, no!" Denton shouted.

My shot struck the ground a few inches in front of his toes.

"Denton, I can put the next one through your foot or between your eyes, and at this point, I don't much care which. I'll not ask you again. Get barefoot, right now!"

This, as I re-cocked my pistol.

It seemed only a matter of seconds until four men were trying to find a place in the dry grass and ground cactus, to comfortably stand, in their bare feet.

I looked over at the man on the grulla.

"Now, my friend," I asked, "what will it be?"

"You offering choices?" he responded.

"Only two. Dismount, and get barefoot or make your play."

"Well, I'll tell you; whoever you may be, my mama didn't raise no idiot sons to be talking back to no cocked pistols. But, I'll tell you something else; I ain't getting barefoot in that cactus garden, down there. So what do we do now?"

I thought for a moment then I spoke to Jamie.

"Jamie, carefully ride over there and disarm our friend, and we'll take him into Walsenburg. Could be the law there might be interested in this fellow."

Jamie rode around the man and when he returned he had two pistols, a double-barreled derringer, two knives and a Winchester.

"You going to war or just careful?" I asked when Jamie showed me the arsenal.

"When one goes among the Philistines . . ." he said, with the same crooked smile.

I turned to Al Medina, "Gather their horses and boots."

"Denton," I said, "you'll find your horses, boots, and pistolero in Walsenburg. You ever come at me again, you come shooting, cause I may just shoot you on sight!"

I turned away as the groans and complaints started. Some whining, some cursing, both at me, and at Denton. Strangely, Denton was not among the whiners or cursing ones.

We started the herd again, and Jamie rode close to the one on the grulla, who strangely fell right in to helping drive the herd. I watched him closely, and as the day wore on, I was impressed both with the man's consistent efforts to help in the care of the herd, and also in the quickness, and surefootedness, of the little pot-bellied grulla.

It was not until we bedded the herd down on the banks of the Huerfano River that I had an opportunity to, again, speak to our reluctant drover.

I had just sent the two Arellano brothers, out to night-herd, when I turned and he was standing by the fire, staring at me.

"What's your name, my friend?" I asked.

"Don't really matter, does it?" He responded.

"Not much, it's just I tire of saying 'hey you'."

"Some call me Jacob. some, Jake. Don't matter which, to me."

"All right, Jacob. What's it going to be? Do we treat you as a prisoner or otherwise?" I asked.

"What's the 'otherwise'?"

"With your word not to cause any more mischief, we'll treat you as a guest in our camp."

"You'd accept my word?"

I looked at him for a long moment.

"Yeah, Jacob. I think we just might."

"Who are you, partner? I've seen hired guns who would not have had the guts to do what you did with Denton and his crew. But you, I've never heard of. at least not by reputation. Come to think of it, I don't know your name either."

"I am Will Jackson from over west of here. And, as far as facing down Denton, that was no big deal. He was bluffing. I don't play poker anymore, but when I did, I made it a practice to call what I thought was a bluff, every time."

"Why didn't you kill Denton? He intended to kill you. At least he said he would."

"I don't kill people for making mistakes, unless such mistakes harm my family. He'll have time, on his walk, to reconsider the error of his ways."

Jacob just grinned. "Well, Mr. Jackson, if you're willing to take my word for it, I'll give it to you. I'll be a good boy, at least til we reach Walsenburg."

"So be it! Let's eat!"

We started early, the next morning. By noon, we were on the northwest side of the village. Jacob and I rode in and found the local marshal. It took only minutes for him to certify Jacob, not to be a wanted man. He was awed at the tale of Denton and his crew, barefooted on the prairie, and agreed to hold their horses, guns and boots until retrieved.

Jacob and I went to the local café for dinner. I asked him what he would do now; go back to work for Denton, or what?

"Nope," he answered, "I don't much cotton to his kind of boss. I'd always be wondering when he was going to fold again."

We sat quietly, enjoying our meal, when Jacob put down his fork, and pushed his chair slightly back.

"Mr. Jackson, how about I go to work for you?"

I looked at him for a moment. "Jacob, I can offer only a droving job to Denver City, then helping me with a pack train back northward of Alamosa. When I sell this herd, I'll have less than two dozen head left at my ranch and even those could be tended by my young son."

"That'll do, if you'll have me. It's been awhile since any man took my word for anything. It felt pretty good. Maybe I'll just ride along and see what other surprises you might come up with."

"Well, all right, but there is one problem."

"What's that?" he asked.

"Well, Jacob, to tell the truth, it's that animal of yours. Jacob, that is without a doubt the sorriest looking piece of horseflesh I've ever seen. He seems to move well, but with only that one horse, and me, with none to spare, how do you plan to keep up!"

He chuckled. "Yeah, he is sort of ugly, ain't he? But, I'll tell you something, that pony once took me, non-stop, from Fort Sumpter to Santa Fe. And, when we got there, he kicked the hostler at the livery stable so hard, the kid spent a week in bed. Me and Herbert will be there when needed, don't worry."

"Herbert!" I exclaimed.

"Yeah, and don't make fun. He's named for an old friend of the family."

I sat, looking at him, not knowing whether I was being ribbed, or was facing a grinning nut. Either way, over the years I've seldom been more amused than I was then. Herbert!

We rode back to the herd, and Jacob went directly to Jamie.

"I'll trouble you for my firearms, Senor Medina." Jacob said.

Jamie looked at me. I nodded.

Jamie went to the chuck wagon, returning with Jacob's arsenal.

"Next time, senor, be more thorough," Jacob said as he removed another derringer from his boot, a stiletto suspended by a thong down the back of his neck and a short-barreled pistol from in a shoulder holster hidden inside his vest.

Jamie could only stare. Over the years Jacob has several times surprised me, but never so profoundly as that afternoon on the flats above Walsenburg. I can think of nothing Jacob has ever done to more

absolutely prove his honesty, to me, than his revealing those hidden
weapons.

Chapter 5

The drive from Walsenburg toward Pueblo was long, dry and boring.

We were, as I guessed, some twenty miles south of Pueblo when, once again, Jamie rode up beside me and silently pointed toward the northeast. There, coming at a long lope, was another group of riders.

Jamie was on my one side and Jacob the other, when a half dozen men whirled to a stop in front of us.

"Howdy!" spoke one of the riders, an older, grey haired man. "That's a good looking bunch you're pushing."

"We like them," I responded.

"My name's Stanton, Earl Stanton. I own the B-H over east of here. This here's my foreman, Wilson Heath. Wilson spotted your drive this morning and thought I'd be interested. How long you been on the trail?"

"A little over a month," I answered.

"Where you come from?"

"Why do you ask?"

"Mister, don't get your guard up. Me and my boys intend you no harm. I'm in the market for cattle, a lot of cattle, even more than you're driving. Will you sell?"

I felt myself relax, even as a released bowstring.

"Well, yes, Mr. Stanton. If the price is right, I would sell."

"You be in the position to give me a good Bill of Sale?" Stanton asked, looking me straight in the eye.

"They are my cows. We came from a ranch over in the northwest corner of the San Luis Valley."

"You're not, by chance, one of those Mormon folks, up in those two valleys, are you?"

Not quite knowing what to expect, I guardedly responded that I was, indeed, one of those "Mormon folks?"

Stanton gigged his pony up to mine, and with his weathered face wreathed in a wide grin, stuck out his hand and boomed, "Well, now, that's prime! I'm Brother Stanton and what did you say your name is?"

Suddenly, while I thought a quick prayer of gratitude, I took Stanton's hand, introducing myself and the two on either side of me.

"You boys Mormons too," Stanton inquired of Jamie and Jacob. Jamie quietly responded, and Jacob just smiled that smile of his and shook his head.

"Well, come on now, Will, lets you and I ride around your herd and see if we can come up with a dicker."

We were not fully around the herd before Stanton had bought my cattle. Not as cheap as he'd liked and not as expensive as I had hoped. I guess you could say, at a fair price.

Stanton sent the herd off with his men, while he accompanied us into Pueblo, where his banker made good on his price.

"I didn't know there were any Mormons in this country," I said as we stood in front of the bank.

"You're a convert, ain't you," Stanton said.

"Well, yes, but I still didn't know there were Mormon people here."

"Boy, we been here since before Brother Brigham made it into Utah. My Pappy was part of the Mormon Battalion. There's lots of saints here along the Arkansas River."

"Saints?" I heard Jacob say behind me.

Stanton looked sharply at Jacob, and repeated his statement, this time with a slight edge in his voice.

"It's all right, Jacob. I'll explain later," I said.

"How about you and your boys spending a couple of days at my spread?" Stanton offered. "Its only about five miles east of where we stopped your herd."

"I appreciate the offer sir, but in all honesty, we are pushing winter too hard already. I'd like to be back into the big valley before the snow gets too deep on the Green Horns."

"I understand, of course. But you remember now, you and yours are welcome at my place any time. My missus is going to be some disappointed. She has a sister in your group, a Hester Turner. She's married to a fellow by the name of Jess. Would you happen to know them?"

"Yeah, you could say that. Jess Turner baptized and confirmed me."

"You're married to Clatilda!" Stanton roared.

"Yes sir. Do you know my wife?"

"Never met her, but we feel we know both of you, what with Hester's letters. She wrote us your whole story. You know you stand pretty tall in Jess and Hester's eyes!"

"And they in ours."

"Well, that settles it. You and your crew have to come out to our place, at least to meet my missus. I don't bring you home, now that I know who you are, I might as well leave with you!"

"Brother Stanton, I have to tell you, nothing would please me more than to meet Hester Turner's sister, but we have to get all the way to Denver City then back home before the passes are closed, if they are not already."

"What you going to Denver City for?" Stanton asked, in his blunt manner.

I told him of the lists I carried, and mentioned several of the more important items I'd been charged to buy.

"Why, Will, I'll bet there's not one thing on those lists that is not available right here in Pueblo! Why don't we check? Why, man you could stay out to my place three or four days and still save time over what it would take you to get to Denver City, and back."

"Well, I don't know . . ." I began.

"Let's just take those lists over to Stodelmeyer's. I'll bet that what he doesn't have right on hand, he'll be able to tell us where it can be found, and right here in town."

We went to Stodelmeyer's Mercantile, and there found a pleasant little round man who checked my lists. After he'd looked over each list, carefully making notes as he did so, he turned to me.

"Mr. Jackson, you have about twelve or fourteen items here that I don't carry, but if you will allow me to sell you the other items, I will obtain those I don't carry and include them with your orders. Furthermore, I'll charge you no more than what the items cost me."

Stanton spoke up, "Will, I've dealt with this little Dutchman for years. I've never been able to get him to listen to me, when I try to teach him the gospel, but I've never found him to be anything, but one of the most honest men I've ever known."

Stodelmeyer smiled broadly, and it was obvious he was well pleased with Stanton's praise.

"Mr. Stodelmeyer, there is one other item not on the lists. Have you pack saddles that I may also buy, to pack all these goods?"

"My friend, I don't stock pack-saddles but Carl Mason, down at the saddle shop, has a whole back room full. He makes them during the winter when his business is slow."

"Well, I guess I'm all set. How soon can you have these orders ready? I'll need them separated, for loading, by lists. I don't want to get home and have to sort everything, maybe in the snow!"

"My clerks and I will have everything set out, according to the lists by late tomorrow afternoon, Mr. Jackson. When will you pay for the goods?"

Stanton guffawed at Stodelmeyer's statement. "I told you he was honest; I forgot to tell you he's right careful with a dollar!"

Stodelmeyer smiled, but his gaze never wandered from mine.

I pulled out ten double eagles and laid them on the counter. "There's two hundred dollars, Mr. Stodelmeyer. You tote up the cost of my order and I'll pay you the rest when I pick up my merchandise. Which, by the way, won't be until two days from now. I believe we have an invitation to meet Mrs. Stanton."

Stanton clapped me on the shoulder. "Well, now," he said, "lets get on with it then. We're going to be late for supper as it is."

We made quite a cavalcade as we swept into Stanton's door yard, just after sunset. Already, though, the house and yard were ablaze with lanterns and torches. I could see the Stanton house was quite substantial, indeed. It appeared to be of plastered adobe and had the red tile roof fancied in the south country.

Two hands came from the bunkhouse to help with the horses. By the time we had our mounts in the corrals, our gear stashed in the barn, and the top layer of trail dust washed from our faces and hands, it was dead dark.

Stanton had gone into the house immediately, giving over the care of his mount to one of his hands. As we approached the back door he came out and ushered us into a large open room which, obviously, served as both kitchen and dining area. The dining table appeared to be quite capable of seating twenty-five or thirty people. I thought, as I glanced around, that Clatilda would be in her glory in such a set-up.

I was last in, and as I cleared the doorway, I saw Stanton standing beside Hester Turner's double. I stopped short. I was that taken with the uncanny resemblance between the two women.

"Pearl," Stanton said, "like I told you, this here is Will Jackson, Clatilda's husband."

Without a word the woman stepped to me and threw her arms around me.

"So this is Hester's 'cowboy,'" she said stepping back to better see my face.

I was completely taken aback. I guess I looked it as I stood there with a silly grin.

"Oh, excuse me, Brother Jackson, it's just that we feel we know you, and your good wife. Hester has written so much, and so often about you and Clatilda. I'll swear if it wasn't for Jess and Clatilda, she'd set her cap for you herself."

"Yeah," spoke up Stanton, "Jess, and Clatilda, and thirty years or so she has on this man!"

They both laughed at this, then there followed a round of

introductions while they met all my men. Jacob surprised me with his manners. Underneath all those guns and knives, there appeared to live something of a gentleman.

Mrs. Stanton and a woman, whom she called Angie, began to bring food to the table. I thought they'd never quit. The food was a mixture of American and Mexican dishes. I never knew whether the latter was for my hands, or the Stanton's regular fare. No comment was ever made.

I mentioned, during the meal, the sharp resemblance between Hester Turner and Pearl Stanton.

"Not so strange," Mrs. Stanton answered, "when you consider Hester and I are twins!"

Later that evening Stanton and I were out on his veranda watching heavy clouds scud across the moon.

I turned to him, "Stanton, there's something I've got to ask you."

He nodded and turning to me said, "go ahead."

"Do you know Hester Turner very well?"

"Well, yes, as a matter of fact, I do. You see I married Pearl almost two years before Hester and Jess got together. Hester was at home all the time I was courting Pearl. Why do you ask?"

"Well, I don't want you to take offense, or anything like that, but I've got to ask. Is Pearl sort of forward, like Hester?"

Stanton just chuckled then turned to stare, fixedly, across the yard. It was a full two minutes before he spoke.

"You know, Will, Jess and I have had long talks about our wives. I think we both will go to our graves never having figured them out. But, why do you ask?"

"Clatilda is just like both of them."

Stanton paused, then standing, laid his hand on my shoulder.

"Will, you have my deepest sympathy and my hearty congratulations."

Without another word, he disappeared into the house and, I supposed, to his room.

We spent the next day loafing around, what I came to feel, was to be my plan for mine and Clatilda's ranch. I could find nothing I disliked about the place from the front gate to the corrals behind the barn. I even made a few sketches in my tally book.

The morning of the second day, we were at the Station's, dawned cold and blustery. The wind was right sharp, and out of the southwest.

"Weather wind," Pearl referred to it, at breakfast.

"Yes," Stanton said, "anytime we get this kind of wind in the fall you can just bet it's not going to be a lot of fun for a few days. Sometimes snow, sometimes just cold, but a wind like this blows up weather every time."

I became more uneasy as the morning passed, and the wind, if anything, grew more intense.

We were sitting in the kitchen just before noon when I made up my mind.

"Brother and Sister Stanton," I said rising from the table, "I'm afraid my boys and I will be leaving as soon as we can saddle up. I'm worried about the weather and we've a long way back."

"I thought as much," Pearl said, also standing. "I had Angie start making you some sandwiches for the trail, an hour ago."

I stood there a moment. "Sister Stanton, is it possible you, Hester and my Clatilda are somehow related?"

She just smiled and turned to the kitchen. I looked over at Stanton. He just shrugged his shoulders.

Chapter 6

We left the Stanton's place right at noon. The wind, by then, was blowing so hard that we each had our collars turned up, and our hats cinched down tight. The ride to Pueblo, with the wind quartering from the left, was not too bad, but by the time we reached Stodelmeyer's, it was late afternoon and the temperature must have dropped twenty degrees since we left the Stanton's.

Good as his word, Stodelmeyer's clerks had neatly stacked the merchandise with each stack's list carefully pinned to the top item.

We spent the rest of the afternoon, and into early evening, arranging the items for quick loading the following morning. Jamie and Al Medina checked each pack saddle. They both had experience with mule trains and were more familiar with pack saddles than the rest of my crew.

That evening I treated everyone to a steak supper and a good hotel bed. I had a hunch they'd need such a memory, in the days ahead.

The next morning I stepped out on the hotel porch to find a two or three inch blanket of snow had fallen during the night. The sky was clear, but the temperature must have been near zero.

We had a good meal in the hotel dining room and were standing on Stodelmeyer's dock, when he opened.

While at Stanton's, we had borrowed a couple of his pack saddles and tested our horses. We found a suitable number would tolerate a pack saddle. We didn't know, though, how they might act with more than just a few rocks in the panniers.

We were lucky. We had only one animal that kicked up when the canvas bags were tied on the saddle frame. But, he settled right down when Jamie stood by his head, and a little weight was added to better balance his saddle.

I was concerned about how to identify each pannier with the proper list.

"That's easy," said Jacob, "number each list, and paint that same number on the panniers containing the goods from that list."

That's what we did, and glad I was when we got home, for the simple solution.

It was almost noon by the time we got strung out, headed south out of Pueblo. It was warmer, but not much.

We were able to make much better time with our pack train, than we had been able with the cattle. Better even, than we would have done, in warmer weather. The horses didn't seem to mind as movement created heat and believe me, that day; any heat was welcome, to horses and men alike.

We camped that first night along a creek already partly iced over. The second night, we camped just outside Walsenburg. I'd been watching the mountains and it seemed the further south we rode, the whiter they were.

I was up early that next morning and rode into Walsenburg. I found the marshal in the town's only café. He chuckled, as he told me of Denton and his hands walking in after their boots and gear. I told him my reason for looking him up was to see what he might tell me about the trail west across La Veta toward Ft. Garland.

"I'm afraid all I can give you is bad news," he responded. "Young fellow came through here day before yesterday, headed for Aguilar. He said it had snowed hard on him all the way from Alamosa. He claimed he had to break four and five foot drifts above La Veta."

As I rode back to our camp I thought of what lay ahead. It was not that I had any choice. Of my entire bunch, Jacob was the only one who could actually opt not to make the trip across the mountains.

I told the crew, around the breakfast fire, what I'd learned.

"Senor Medina, you may have to leave your wagon along the way. I don't think we should kill animals trying to pull a wagon that can be easily retrieved next spring."

He agreed.

I turned to Jacob; "You are the only one who really has a choice. If you'd like, I can pay you off right here and you won't have to make, what probably is going to be a very rough trip."

"You letting me go?" He asked.

"No, I'm not saying that. I'm only giving you the choice not to make this trip."

"You ain't letting me go?"

"No," I answered.

"Well, then, I'll go with you. I signed on for the trip. Wasn't nobody said, 'unless there's snow'."

We finished eating, loaded the pack animals and turned west.

Chapter 7

We were twelve or fourteen miles west of Walsenburg that grey morning, when it started to spit snow. Not much, at first, just an occasional flake. Soon, however, it began to snow a little harder. I glanced up, just as Jamie rode up beside me. He was pointing out what I saw when I raised my head to look up the trail. I'd seen rain come like that, but never snow. It was a wall of snow. So much snow, you could actually hear it being whipped against the pine grove off to our left. The wall was not coming fast, but it was coming. I turned to Jamie and shouted for him to get back to the tail of our train, and push for that pine grove.

He whipped his horse around as I spurred my pony, and we went for those tall trees at a dead gallop. I believe the suddenness of our move saved us. When we were all in the grove we could, even then, barely make out each other's shape. We were able to gather the horses into a rough grouping among the trees. Jamie and I gathered saddle ropes and made a rope corral around the animals, while the rest kept them from spooking too badly, in the heavy snow. It was strange; there was little, or no, wind. Just the steady, impenetrable, snowfall.

Jacob came to me when Jamie and I were once again inside our rope corral.

"You ever seen it snow like this?" he asked.

"Never. I've also never seen snow come in a wall like that."

"I'll tell you, there was a minute or so there, that I surely regretted my big talk this morning."

"Yeah," I answered, "I've got to be honest with you, there was a minute or so that I wished we were somewhere else!"

It was nearly an hour before the snow let up. Then it stopped completely, as suddenly as it had begun. The sun even poked through in several places, among the clouds.

"Senor Jackson," Medina said, coming from his wagon, "I believe we've come to the place where I'd best leave my wagon."

"Do you think, now?" I asked, "It doesn't seem there is that much snow."

"I just saw a bull elk come out of those quakies over yonder," he said, pointing to an Aspen grove north of where we stood, "and he was up to his knees in snow. I'd rather leave my wagon here, where it can be sheltered and hidden, than on some rocky slope further on."

I walked out to the edge of the grove, and sure enough, the snow was at least eighteen inches deep, where before there had been only a skiff on the ground.

We spent better than an hour placing Medina's wagon and cutting branches to cover it. When we felt we'd done as much as we could, we loaded what supplies, from the wagon, we could carry on our pack train, and once again headed west.

The snow did not deepen much as we pushed on past La Veta, but the wind came up and riding was even more miserable, than the snowfall would have been.

We rode well into the night before we could find a place sufficiently protected to offer shelter to us, and our animals. What we found was a cave, of sorts. It was an area, almost a full half acre in size, back under a massive rock overhang sheltered in front by a dense growth of buck brush mixed in amongst a large grove of bull Aspen.

That was a miserable night, and we were all ready to be out of our cold blankets and back on the trail at daybreak. We had biscuits and jerky for breakfast and that was eaten in the saddle.

For the next three days, we plodded through that white hell. Every afternoon was spent looking for a sheltered area to spend the night. Twice we stopped in mid-afternoon finding what we felt to be the best possible shelter. The third day we rode far into the night before finding an area to our liking. During those three days there was not a moment any of us were warm, even to the slightest degree. About midday of the fourth day, after we had slept sheltered that last time, Jamie rode up beside me.

"Senor Jackson, I think I smell smoke. I've been smelling it for the last hour or so. I believe we should be near Fort Garland. What if I ride ahead, and see if I can locate it."

Within three hours we were in the trading post in Fort Garland, having stabled the horses in a long lean-to, and provided each with hay.

We spent that afternoon, and night at Fort Garland. The next morning, the sun was shining so brightly, you could hardly see. But, cold! It was so cold that as you breathed, it seemed your nose would freeze shut.

The horses were reluctant to leave their shelters, and more than one pack saddle had to be picked up and replaced on the frisky animals. It was almost mid morning before we got lined out. But we were back in the big valley. And cold and icy as it was, it was the last leg of our trip. No more drifts. No more white outs. No more fear of sliding down a mountainside. We all relaxed. There was even good-natured banter, among the crew.

We finally made it to Alamosa where I treated the bunch to a big feed, and a warm hotel bed.

We spent the next night on the trail, but no one seemed to mind. We were too close to home.

We reached the Medina place before noon, the second day out of Alamosa. Senora Medina was overjoyed to see her husband and sons. The rest of us busied ourselves with the horses, while they enjoyed their homecoming.

We spent the night at the Medina's. I decided the next morning that I'd not need the whole crew to make the last short leg of our trip, So I paid off the Arellano brothers, and the Lopez boys, leaving only Al and Jamie Medina to help Jacob and I go on in.

We pulled up to John Terry's store just after noon. Our welcome was that of returning heroes.

John told me that he'd been especially worried by the stories travelers brought of the snow in the mountains on the eastside of the San Luis.

"You've not let Clatilda hear any of those stories, have you?"

"No, Will. She and your children have been to church every week and into the store three or four times since you've been gone. I don't think she's heard anything."

We unloaded all of the packs except the ones for Clatilda and Anne Blalock's lists. We arranged the stacks of merchandise in the stores warehouse, as they had been at Stodelmeyer's,

"Each list has the cost written right on it. John, will you please collect from each family and give the money to Clatilda?"

John looked at me strangely, "Will, I can just as easily give you the money. I'll be seeing you at church."

"No, you just give it to Clatilda. That's the way I'd like it."

"Whatever you say, Will. You know I didn't think you'd be back for another two or three weeks. How did you get back so soon?"

I told him of the sale of my cattle and being able to get everything in Pueblo.

"My friend, you were surely blessed. Particularly with the weather shaping up like it is. We've already had two pretty bad snow storms and some of the coldest weather I've ever seen this early."

I paid off the Medina boys at Terry's store, and Jacob and I left them looking through John's stock of pistols.

"Be all right with you if I lay over for the night?" Jacob asked. "I'd like to rest Herbert before I head south."

"Stay as long as you need. We'll be happy to have you."

We rode most of the way to the ranch in silence. We were busy with the pack animals as well as the horses now freed of their packs. I'd left the extra pack saddles with Terry, with orders to sell for the best price he could get.

When we reached my south pasture, Jacob and I turned the horses loose there, and continued on with the few pack animals left. As we came around the barn and into the dooryard William had just stepped out of the barn with a full milk bucket. Behind him was Anna Laura with a smaller bucket.

When he saw me, William sat his bucket on the ground and ran toward us. Anna Laura was not so careful. She dropped hers and ran to the house yelling for her "mama" at the top of her lungs. Before she got there Clatilda stepped out of the cabin. Her hands went to her mouth, then in a run she hastened to me. I stepped down and enveloped her in my arms. She was crying and laughing at the same time.

"It's all right, I'm home safe," was the only thing I could say as I held her. I said it over and over.

Finally she stepped back, and as she did, I realized that William and Anna Laura were also entwined with Clatilda and my leg. I hugged them both and then turned to Jacob, still sitting on Herbert with the pack train lead rope in his hand.

"Jacob, I want you to know my family. This is my wife Clatilda, my son William and my little girl Anna Laura," I said turning William and Anna Laura to face the man.

Clatilda stepped over to Jacob's horse extending her hand.

Jacob had ripped off his hat when I had made the introductions. With Clatilda's outstretched hand, he was faced with a real problem. In one hand, he held the pack train lead rope and in the other he held his hat. Herbert's reins were draped over his saddle horn.

Seemingly, as natural as you please, he simply dropped his hat to the ground, on the off side of his pony and extended that hand down to grasp Clatilda's.

Clatilda took his hand saying, "I am very pleased to meet you Mr . . . er, Jacob," she stammered over the use of Jacob's given name as a surname.

"It's Jacob Webber, ma'am," Jacob said, "and it is definitely my pleasure. And, hello to you William and Miss Anna Laura."

From that moment, Anna Laura was Miss Anna Laura to Jacob and he was, to Anna Laura, her knight in shining armor. One had only, ever after, to watch her just glance at Jacob to see the sweetest, purest kind of love and hero worship.

"Jacob, let's get these horses in the barn and their packs off. I long to have my feet under Clatilda's table."

Clatilda gathered the children and milk buckets, and went into the house. Jacob and I made quick work of pack saddles, horses, and riding gear. It was only minutes before we stomped the snow from our boots and stepped into the cabin.

Home! It was more than just familiar surroundings. It was the smell of fresh baked bread, the lingering odor of meat cooked earlier in the day, and most of all, it was the clean, clean smell that was ever a part of Clatilda's home.

When Clatilda served us hot cocoa and cinnamon rolls, I thought Jacob would founder himself. I'll swear he ate three of those cinnamon rolls and each near the size of a dinner plate.

"Mrs. Jackson, I've not eaten home baked cinnamon rolls since I was a boy, no older than William. I hope you will excuse me for making such a pig of myself. But, in all honesty ma'am, if I wasn't afraid your husband would kick me outside, I'd probably eat two or three more!"

"Could you really eat more cinnamon rolls, Mr. Webber?" Anna Laura asked, her eyes large in wonder.

"Probably not, Miss Anna Laura, but your mama's rolls are so good, I'd surely be tempted to try."

"Mr. Webber, you may have as many rolls as you would like. As long as you pay such praise to my baking, I promise I'll not let Will kick you out!"

"Thank you ma'am, I surely appreciate the offer, but I have to help Will unload those panniers, and even now, I will have trouble bending over. Any more and I'd have to crawl to the barn."

Jacob Webber had already made a conquest of my daughter that afternoon. He did himself no harm with my wife, either.

Jacob and I spent the rest of the afternoon and early evening sorting out Clatilda's and the Blalock's packs. When we finished we carried Clatilda's into the house. Another hour was spent oohing and aahing over most of the items. When everything was properly stored, I sat at the kitchen table and called William to me. I unwrapped a small package and handed its contents to him. His face was a picture of disbelief, surprise and, at the same time, wonder. I had brought him a belt knife, complete with scabbard.

There was another package, much larger, on the table in front of me. I glanced, out of the corner of my eye, at Anna Laura. She could hardly sit still, but at the same time, she wasn't really sure the other package was to be hers.

"Anna Laura, would you do me a favor and open this package for me, please?" I said.

She approached the table much as a doe coming out of the woods into an open meadow. Eager to reach the prize but reluctant to hurry for fear of denial.

When she unwrapped the package, she exposed the bottom part of it's contents.

"Oh, mama!" she squealed, making short work of the balance of the wrapping. What she had seen, were the legs of the doll, contained in the package.

"Oh mama, it has real hair!" She said running to Clatilda's side holding the doll in front of her.

Anna Laura and her mother made much of the doll as they carefully examined every detail. Finally Clatilda gave the child a nudge.

"Don't you think you'd better thank your father?"

Anna Laura turned and ran to me, grabbing my neck with one arm while holding fast to her treasure with the other. She said little that had not already been eloquently expressed by her actions, and attitude toward the doll.

When she had settled down Clatilda served us our supper. When the dishes were cleared, and we were enjoying a gooseberry cobbler, still steaming from the oven, Jacob turned to me.

"Will, I don't know how this meal could be better, unless it was topped off with a hot cup of coffee!"

"You'll not find coffee here pard. There's none in this house."

"You folks don't like coffee?"

"Jacob, Mormon's don't drink coffee, as a matter of religious conviction."

Jacob sat for a moment, enjoying his cobbler. Soon, however, he put down his spoon and looked over at Clatilda.

"Ma'am, I am right sorry. After the kindness you have shown me, a stranger in your home, I feel right bad if in any way I've embarrassed you or Will, here."

"You are not to feel badly, Mr. Webber. There is no way you could have known. Our people hold beliefs, that some find strange. We don't drink coffee, any alcoholic beverages nor do we use tobacco."

Jacob sat for a moment then turning to me asked, "Why?"

"We believe those things to be harmful to your health, and unnecessary to happiness and contentment."

"Well, for a fact I don't remember ever being more content than I am right now, even without coffee." Jacob said as he scooped up the last of the cobbler.

After supper Clatilda and Anna Laura cleared the table, and Jacob pulled a stone from his pocket and began to show William how to sharpen his knife.

"Not too sharp, Mr. Webber!" Clatilda said, "I don't want him cutting himself."

"Ma'am, its always been my opinion that most people cut themselves with dull knives and shoot themselves with unloaded guns. Don't you agree, Will?"

"I'm afraid I do. I want my tools sharp, and my guns loaded. A dull tool, or an unloaded gun, are of little use."

"All the same, until William is a tad more sure of how to use his knife, I'd like it to be a little less of a razor," Clatilda said.

"Well, ma'am, it's not my right to say, but I'd imagine if William were told simply, that a knife's for cutting and if there's no cutting, to be done it should remain in it's scabbard. That might be all he should know about how to use a knife."

Clatilda turned to Jacob, and with that direct gaze pinned him to his chair.

"Mr. Webber, how long do you intend to visit with us?"

Jacob looked as one who had been hit with a big stick.

"Well, ma'am, as I told Will, I'd like to be able to spend the night before I head south."

"You have people south of here?" Clatilda asked.

"No ma'am. I have no people at all, at least none that I know of."

"You have a job to go to, south of here?"

Jacob looked at Clatilda for a long moment before he answered.

"No ma'am, I have no job, no lady friends, nor lost horses. It is just that this late in the season, I doubt I'll find work this far north. I'm hoping, that will not be the case, further south."

"Then the only reason you have for going south is to find work?" She asked.

"Yes, ma'am."

Clatilda turned to me, "Will, did you get near what you wanted for your cattle?"

"Well, yes, I got just about what I expected."

"Then it's settled," she said turning back to her dishwashing.

Jacob and I looked at each other. Each unsure we wanted to know what was "settled."

"What do you mean, Clatilda?" I asked.

"Why Mr. Webber can work for us, at least for the winter." This without even turning around.

"Doing what, Mrs. Jackson? Will tells me he sold all but a handful of his cattle. And, near about all I know how to do is cowboying."

"That's just fine Mr. Webber. I was all set to have one cowboy hanging around my kitchen all winter. Now, at least, maybe you two cowboys can find enough mischief to get into to keep both of you out of my way."

With that said, she turned to the children and ushered them, both protesting, to their beds.

Jacob turned to me, with questions in his eyes, and started to say something.

"Don't you say a thing Webber!" I said, "All I want from you is a simple yes or no."

He looked at me a moment longer, then simply said, "yes."

"Come on then, I'll show you where you'll be bunking. It's not a bad place and it has a good stove."

Chapter 8

As I returned from the barn, I noticed it had begun to snow. Not much and not large flakes, but the temperature must have been fifteen or twenty degrees colder than it had been at sunset.

I found Clatilda seated at the kitchen table when I returned. There was a large metal box on the table in front of her.

"Will, we must talk."

"I'll say we do. Clatilda, I don't appreciate the way you offered Jacob a job."

"Had you not intended to do the same?"

"Maybe, but I would have liked to have given the matter more thought."

"Are you satisfied that he now works for us?"

"Yes, I am. But, please, don't ever do anything like that, again."

"Like what, Will?"

"Run our ranch, that's what. We've had an agreement for years, Clatilda. Up to now it has been, at least to me, a good way."

Clatilda sat, for several moments, looking down at her hands folded on the table.

"Will, you're right! I apologize. I guess I just got carried away with my conversation with Mr. Webber. He seems so down to earth, and wise."

"You're right, of course, and, in all truth, I had such a thing in the back of my mind. But, now Jacob might have some questions in his mind about who he works for, you or me!"

"I'll settle that at breakfast. That will be easy."

"No, I'll take care of it. You've done enough to poor old Jacob. When I left him a while ago, I think he was still wondering what had bit him."

"Will you forgive me?"

"Of course. Have I got something to show you!" I said, stripping the money belt from beneath my shirt.

Laying the belt on the table, it made a solid chunk sound.

"There, madam, is over thirteen thousand dollars, in gold. We haven't cattle any longer, but I don't believe we'll starve!"

"Oh, Will, I'm so proud of you. There have been those who have been saying you were on a 'fool's errand,' making the drive this late in the year."

"Well, the truth be known, there were times in the past few weeks I'd not have argued with them."

"But the drive is over. We got a good price for our cattle and we are all safely together again. What's more, I have two surprises for you. The first is this!" I said, removing a small package from my vest.

I handed the package to her and she opened it like a child, eager, her eyes shining.

The cameo broach lay upon the table, while she just stared at it.

"Oh, Will, how could you have done this?" she almost sobbed.

"What? What have I done? I've planned this for months. I thought you'd be pleased."

"Oh, I am. But, Will, how could you have known. This is exactly like the one my mother left me, which I sold. Sold to get money to come west, those years ago."

"Then you're pleased?" I asked, still dumbfounded by her response.

"Oh, my dear sweet, Will! I could not, in my wildest dreams have wished for more!"

I breathed a long sigh of relief, as Clatilda rose and came around the table to plant a big kiss on my cheek as she hugged me.

Clatilda returned to her chair, where she picked up the broach and holding it in her hands, looked down upon it as if it was solid gold. I don't remember her releasing it before we retired.

I then told her of my second surprise.

"Now, ma'am, I've got something else for you," I said pulling out my tally book.

"I don't have all the dimensions worked out yet. I thought you could help with that, but basically, this is what I'm talking about," I said, opening the small book to the final drawing I had worked out on the way home from Pueblo.

"This is the home I intend to build for you, come next spring. I can build this, I believe, and still have plenty of money left to buy stock, to start another herd and also have a nice nest egg. What do you think? Would you like to have a better home than this cabin?"

Clatilda sat quietly looking at me, for long enough that I began to be uncomfortable.

"What don't you like about it? We can change anything you'd like. It's just that when I saw this house, I thought it would be perfect for you."

I then told her of meeting the Stantons. About Pearl Stanton being Hester Turner's sister. When I'd completed the story, Clatilda broke into a grand smile and reached over to cover my hands with hers.

"Will," she began, "have you any idea what is in this box?" she said, nodding at the metal box.

I shook my head, then she unlocked and opened the box.

"There is part of my share of the stores profits for the last eight years. I know you've never ever acknowledged my share in the store, but do you know why I got it out this evening?"

"Not really," I responded.

"Will, I had intended to try and convince you to build us a new home!"

We both sat for a moment, then laughed like children.

That evening, the Jackson's planned their new home. I learned that much of the yard goods Clatilda had included in her list were for her, hoped for, new home. Many of the other items from her list had also a place in that new home.

We planned far into the night, and by the time we went to bed, we had a new drawing of our home, complete with dimensions, and a couple of changes Clatilda wanted. I also added one of my own, an inside water well.

That next morning, we were awakened by William.

"Mama," he said, standing at the door of our room. "You and pa better come see what happened last night."

His seriousness prompted us to quickly get dressed and come out into the kitchen. William and Anna Laura were both standing in front of the window. The kitchen was warm, but the window was completely frosted over except for two small open holes scratched by the children. I stepped to the door and opened it to find the snow packed tightly, and better than knee deep. I looked toward the barn, but I could see nothing but a white wall. There seemed to be no wind, and the flakes were drifting straight down; but so densely that it seemed that if I extended my arm outside the door, I'd not be able to see my hand.

"Mr. Webber!" Clatilda, standing behind me. "How can he get to the house. He won't even be able to see it!"

As I turned to answer her, I caught something out of the corner of my eye. I turned to see Jacob step up to the door, a rope's end in one hand, and a full milk bucket in the other.

"How's about trading you a bucket of fresh milk for some meat and eggs?" Just like that. It might have been the middle of July and ninety degrees in the shade.

"Get in here," I said reaching out for the bucket.

"How in the world did you find the house in this storm?" Clatilda asked.

"Used an old blizzard trick, ma'am, I just tied a couple of ropes together, then tied one end to the barn door and started walking. I figured if I reached the end of my rope before I found the house, I'd just go back and get more rope. As it was, I had just enough," he said holding up the rope end before tying it to a nail beside the door.

"Well, get in here!" I said. "It looks like you and I both will earn our money before this days over."

"How's that?" he asked stomping his boots clean before stepping into the cabin.

"Like I told you, I only have about two dozen head, but I can't leave them alone in this mess. We'll have to get hay to them."

"That won't be a problem, Pa," William said. "Mama had me bring them into the barn corral two weeks ago when it snowed last."

"You mean the cattle are all up here and not down by the stack-yard?"

"Yes sir," William said, all smiles.

"Well, young man, I'd say you've more than earned that belt knife. You keep this up and I'll have to talk to your ma about putting you on the payroll."

There stood before me one proud, pleased little boy.

"Then that only leaves the horses," I said to Jacob.

"Pa, where did you put your horses?" William asked.

"We turned them into the south pasture son, why?"

"Well, when I brought the cows in, I left all the gates open between here and the south pasture, in case I had to take the cows back to the stack-yard. Do you suppose the horses might have come up by the barn?"

"I'll tell you what, my boy, I'll just bet you that new single-shot .22, Brother Terry has in his front window, that's exactly where they are!"

It would have been hard to tell, at that moment, who was more proud, me or my son.

Clatilda cooked a big breakfast, and afterward Jacob, William and I bundled up and went out to check on the stock. The cattle, we found huddled against the barn wall, and every single one of the horses was standing against the corral fence. It was quick, easy work to get them into the corral. I was glad of the barn loft bounty of hay. Within two hours, all of our stock was sheltered, fed and the water trough filled.

We sat around the stove in Jacob's room, warming ourselves after our chores, when I asked William about the weather since I'd been gone.

"Well, Pa, we had a big wet snow the first Sunday after you left. It melted in a couple of days. Then about a week later we had another snow. Not much, just two or three inches, but then it got real cold. That was when mama had me bring the cows in. She said she thought we might have an early winter. Look's like she was right."

"Ain't no question about that!" Jacob said. "About how much snow you usually get in these mountains?"

"That's the strange part of this country," I said. "Sometimes we won't get but sixteen or eighteen inches, all winter. And that, three or four inches at a time. But I've seen three years in a row that we got over a hundred inches each winter. I once measured thirty inches right outside the cabin door. But, that was in February."

"If this keeps up," Jacob said, standing to look out the window, "we're going to get that much and it's not November yet."

"I'll tell you, Jacob, you can't believe how glad I am not to have that herd to look after, in this storm."

"You know, I was looking your place over as we rode up, yesterday. You ain't leaving this country are you?"

"No, as a matter of fact we're talking about building a bigger house."

"Figured as much when I seen you doing all that drawing when we were at the Stanton place. But, then, why did you sell off all your stock?"

"That's hard to explain. Just say I had a hunch."

"Mama said the Spirit was directing Pa!" William said.

"The Spirit!" Jacob said.

"Yeah, well it's a long story, Jacob. Sometime when we've got nothing to do and a lot of time to do it in, I'll explain it all to you."

"That's a story I'll look forward to hearing," Jacob said.

"Well, now, we'd better see about the firewood situation before those two women get after us."

We spent the rest of the morning stacking as much stove wood, as there was room in the kitchen. We split and stacked near half a cord in Jacob's room, and after dinner, we went at it again, and by the time Clatilda rang the bell for supper, we had better than two cords, split, and stacked in the barn.

We also had almost three feet of snow on the ground.

At the supper table I asked Clatilda what she'd seen of the Blalocks. She said Seth had been by the day before I'd got back just to see how she and the children were doing. He'd said both of the boys had colds, but were doing fine. He'd been to town to settle up with John Terry for the years potato crop. He'd said it had been a good year.

"You raise spuds in this country?" Jacob asked. "I'd have thought it to be too high."

"Our friend Seth Blalock has been farming potatoes for several years, just up from the barn. He's done real well except for one year," I said.

"I think, come morning, I'll saddle a horse and go up and see that they're all right," I said.

After Jacob and the children had gone to bed Clatilda and I stayed up, planning more about our new house.

"Will, there's not much you can do until spring, is there?" Clatilda asked.

"Yes, I believe there is. I was thinking Jacob and I could go up in that black timber behind where the folks are buried. I don't believe the snow will be so deep there. Maybe we can drop and limb out enough logs to build the house, and possibly even enough for a new barn."

"Oh! You are planning a new barn also?"

"I am. I figured that by the time Jacob and I got the foundation stones set for the barn, and the house, most of the brethren will have their crops in and I can get enough help to set the logs and raise the roof rafters. If we can get enough help to get that done, I believe Jacob and I can get you in your new home before next winter. At least those are my plans."

"That will be grand, Will. I think I've never looked forward to many things as I do our new house."

Chapter 9

The morning dawned clear and very cold. The blizzard had left better than three feet of powdery snow on the ground. After breakfast, Jacob, William and I shoveled paths to the barn and the wood pile. I left Jacob and William to care for the stock while I saddled a tall roan and headed for the Blalocks. The first thing I noticed, as I rounded the barn, was the absence of smoke from the Blalock chimney. I would have urged my pony into a trot but, even as long legged as he was, he was having trouble breaking trail, at a walk.

The closer I got, the more troubled I became, for I could see no sign of life at the Blalock place.

I stepped down from my horse, right beside their door. I had to kick the snow away even to be able to knock.

My knock went unanswered, even when I banged on the door.

I thought a long moment before my next action. Even then, I looked around the yard. I saw no evidence of any activity.

I kicked the door open. It was only slightly warmer inside the house than it had been outside.

I quickly went to Seth and Anne's bedroom. They were both in bed, and at first I feared both to be dead. I went to Seth's side of their bed and when I touched his forehead it was very hot. Anne was the same. I then went to the children's bedrooms and found them to be in the same condition.

My horse must have thought me crazy for I forced him almost to gallop through the deep snow all the way home.

I burst into the cabin to find Clatilda and Anna Laura at the table making bread.

"Where are Jacob and William!" I demanded.

Clatilda stood suddenly, "They're taking care of the stock. Will, what's wrong?"

I quickly explained the situation. I then told Anna Laura to get her coat and fetch Jacob and William immediately.

While Anna Laura went to the barn I further explained what I'd found at the Blalock's.

"As I see it, we have three things to do, and right now! You and Anna Laura have to go up there and see what you can do for them. I'll have William and Jacob get up there with wood, for a fire. I saw no wood in their house, and I must get help from the settlement. If nothing else, at least John or the Bishop, to assist me in ministering a blessing to the Blalocks."

Clatilda went quickly about gathering what she felt would be needed.

When William and Jacob came in from the barn, I sent them to hitch our draft team to a sled I made years before for hauling hay in the snow. I told them to load it, with as much split firewood as it would hold. While they did this, I helped Clatilda gather blankets and food.

When all was loaded on the sled I turned to Jacob.

"Jacob, I am sorry to do this to you, but I have to ask you to represent me in this trouble. It is absolutely necessary I go to the settlement for help. Clatilda will tell you and William what she needs done. Please help her."

"No problem, pardner, but that ride to town is really going to be a killer. Are you sure you have to go?"

"Yes, Jacob, but you and William should be able to take care of everything here."

I got back on the leggy roan and started my trip. Jacob was right. It took me three hours to reach John Terry's store. Luckily he was open.

When I told John of the problem, he said he would go back with me as Bishop Terry and his family were also down with lung fever.

It was near dark by the time John and I approached the Blalock's house. This time there were two healthy plumes of smoke coming from the Blalock's chimneys.

We stepped into the house, which by now was comfortably warm. Jacob and William had more wood in the kitchen than they could have carried in one sled load. Clatilda said they had brought two sled loads up and were now working on Seth's woodpile over behind Seth's barn.

Seth's fever had broken, as had Daniel's, but Anne and Aaron were still asleep and their fevers were quite high.

"Will, can you, Jacob, and the children take care of yourselves? I believe I am more needed here." Clatilda said.

"Jacob and the children can care for themselves, and I will stay here with you."

Turning to Jacob, who came through the door with, yet, another armload of wood, I said, "Jacob, will you be all right with that?"

"You never mind us, partner, we'll be fine. I might even teach the kids how to make camp biscuits. I think we have enough wood to take you through the night. William and I will make sure you have enough water to last. Is there anything else we can do before we go back down to your place?"

I turned to John. "I think you should spend the night here, or at our place, John. I don't think the ride back to your store is something you should attempt this late."

John agreed, and after helping bring water into the house, he, Jacob and the kids returned to our house.

There was little we could do beyond the blessings John and I had given to all of the Blalocks. We kept the house warm and Clatilda made soup for Seth and Daniel. We kept cold wet rags on the foreheads of Anne and Aaron and kept the house warm.

It was almost daylight when Clatilda came into the kitchen.

"Will, Anne is awake, and her fever seems to have broken. She's already asking me if I shouldn't be going home to take care of my family!"

"Sounds like she is better! Can I do anything?"

"No, just keep the house warm, and I'll make some corn meal mush. I think some warm food is what's now indicated."

I went into the children's bedroom to check on the boys, and found them tossing a small pillow back and forth at each other.

"Looks like you boys are feeling better. Do you feel like you could eat something now?"

Their response left little doubt that they were on the mend.

When I got back to the kitchen, Clatilda was working at the stove.

"Will, I'm worried about Anne. When I went back to the bedroom she was sleeping, and I'm afraid her temperature is going up again."

"What can I do?"

"Do you think you should get John, and the two of you give her another blessing?"

"No, I think that should be Seth's decision. Is he awake enough to talk about it?"

"You go talk to him, and I'll finish getting this mush ready."

I went in and spoke to Seth, and he agreed that he and I should, once again minister to Anne. I stepped over and closed the door. Later, when I came back into the kitchen Clatilda was still working at the stove.

"I would have thought that would have been ready by now," I said stepping to her side.

"This is new. I fed the other to the boys, and I wanted fresh for Anne and Seth. How is she?"

"I don't rightly know. She's still sleeping. But, at least she doesn't seem to have a high fever."

"Well, I won't wake her to feed her but I will see that Seth eats, then I'll watch Anne. What will you do?"

"Not much, Jacob and William can care for the stock, and I'm sure Anna Laura is well along the way to having your kitchen under her control. So, I'll stick around here and help you, at least until the boys are up and about."

So it went for the next couple of weeks. There were short periods when Clatilda would go to our house to help Anna Laura, but mostly we lived with the Blalocks. The only problem was once when Anne tried to tell Clatilda that she was all right, and that Clatilda and I should go home. Clatilda just smiled and in two or three sentences reminded Anne of when she had taken care of Clatilda, under similar circumstances, before Clatilda and I were married. Clatilda finished by telling Anne she would do well just to be quiet, for nothing she could say would have any effect on what Clatilda would do.

Anne sputtered and grumped, but it was easy to see the affection between the two women.

It was during this period that the two Blalock boys began referring to us as, "Aunt Clatilda and Uncle Will." The interesting part was they were encouraged to do so by Seth. I wondered at how far we had come in the past few years. All the way from a near gunfight between Seth and me to his encouraging his sons to treat me as family. Somehow, even so, it felt right.

By late November, we had suffered two more blizzards, though neither as bad as the three feet of snow just after my return from selling the cattle.

Clatilda and I went home on the first day of December, and on the next day, bundled so they could hardly see, we took the Blalocks to the first church service any of us had attended in almost seven weeks.

We were saddened by what we learned. Eight people, in the valley, had succumbed to illness, and a Brother Hawkins, who had taught me most of what I knew about irrigation, had been found frozen trying to tend his small cattle herd.

Nine people gone, and what was probably the worst of a bad winter, yet to come.

It was not a happy service, but Bishop Terry reminded us of our many blessings.

We took the Blalocks home with us, and the ladies cooked a grand meal. When we had finished, Jacob rose to leave the cabin.

"Jacob, won't you stay and visit?" Clatilda asked.

"I don't want to be in the way, ma'am, I thought to go out to my room."

"Is it more comfortable there, Jacob?" Clatilda asked.

"Well, no ma'am . . ." Jacob began.

"Well, sit yourself, Jacob, and I'll get you another cup of cocoa."

Jacob looked over at me, with a somewhat quizzical expression.

"Get used to it, Jacob. If you live here for whatever reason, you are considered by Clatilda, as her responsibility. And, believe me partner, there are worse things.

Chapter 10

Storm followed merciless storm that winter. There was seldom a day that I was not grateful I did not have, four or five hundred head of cattle to care for. Because there was little or no game around, we had to butcher several of my small herd that winter. I took a side of each beef Jacob and I butchered, to the Blalock's. Seth joked that if I kept it up, he, as a potato farmer, would wind up with more cattle than his rancher neighbor. He, Anne and the boys continued to improve, but it would be spring planting time before the family was good and strong once again.

Jacob and I began falling trees right after Christmas. During the January "thaw," we fell and limbed enough trees to build the house, barn and two sheds I had added to my plans. Even so, I was sure we would need more.

We found two huge cedar snags, dead, without bark and almost completely limbed by the elements. We dropped both and after having bucked each into three-foot lengths, we loaded the butts on the sled. Then after hauling them to the barn, Jacob and I began splitting shingles. We spent nearly the entire month of February in the barn, splitting shingles. Jacob and I would split, and William would bundle. As we diminished the hay in the barn loft, we used the space to store bundles of shingles. It was during this time that Jacob began calling William

"Bud." He used the name as specific to William, and not just an off-hand general reference. At first Clatilda didn't like it, but within days Anna Laura and I picked up on this nickname, and soon William was addressed or referred to in no other way. He seemed happy with his new nickname, and I believe, even somewhat flattered.

Chapter 11

The first day of March dawned clear, and warmer than it had been in over four months. Jacob and I began to make plans to skid the logs down to the new house site. Late that afternoon clouds began to build to the west, and by dusk the clouds had thickened so that it seemed we went from daylight to full dark in about twenty minutes.

We were sitting at the supper table when we heard the wind begin to come up. Clatilda noted, in passing, that after supper I should probably step outside and close the shutters. I thought little of it until as she was clearing the dishes Jacob stood and announced he would get the shutters. As he unlatched the door it was flung open, by the wind, almost knocking him down. A solid wall of snow swept into the cabin, driven by the wind. Closing the door was a task requiring both Jacob and I.

After we got the door closed, and secured, Jacob turned to me.

"Partner, sometime soon, you've got to tell me again about those mild winters you have here!"

I stepped to the window, but could see nothing. My first thought was of the woodpile. I glanced over to see that Bud had done his job well. The stacked wood extended well above the height of the stove.

"Looks like I'll have to rig another 'life line' to get to the barn this night!" Jacob said.

"Not this night!" Clatilda said. "We had a spring storm like this the very first winter I was in this valley. No one will be going outside the house tonight. If that wind catches you just right, it could knock down a grown man. You may have Anna Laura's bed and she can sleep on the trundle in our room."

Jacob looked over at Anna Laura.

"You be mad at me, Miss Anna Laura, if I borrow your bed for one night?"

"Oh no, Mr. Webber, like mama said, you shouldn't go out on a night like this!"

I glanced at the look on her face. If there had been only a heavy dew, she would have welcomed the opportunity to provide for her beloved, "Mr. Webber."

I was awakened frequently that night, by wind gusts that would rattle the cabin like a paper box.

Just before daylight the wind quieted and I dozed off to be shaken awake by Clatilda, sometime just after dawn.

"Will, come, you have to see this!"

I went into the kitchen in my stocking feet to see the window, a white spot in the wall. When I went to the door, I had a premonition what I would find.

I opened the door to another white wall. The snow was solid from doorsill to lintel. I pushed my fist and arm into the snow clear to my shoulder. When I withdrew my arm, there was no daylight in the tunnel my arm had created. Just more snow.

Over my shoulder, Jacob said, "partner I sure hope that's a drift, and not the snow depth."

"So do I, because I left the scoop shovel just outside the door. I think we'll have to dig out with the scuttle Clatilda uses to clean the ashes from her cook stove."

While Clatilda prepared breakfast, Jacob and I worked at the snow. It was difficult as we had no place to put the snow we dug from the doorway. Anna Laura solved that problem by suggesting we put a wash tub on the stove to melt the snow which we would carry from the doorway to the stove in milk buckets. We soon were simply scooping the snow with the buckets, and carrying them to the stove. It took only a short while to dig through the drift at the door, and before Clatilda had breakfast ready, we had broken through to daylight.

I was astounded by the drifts. We'd not only had terrific winds, it appeared we'd had at least two feet of snow. It was hard to gauge, for there seemed nowhere that the snow was not drifted or, at least, layered by the wind. After we had located the scoop shovel, we quickly cleared the doorway. After breakfast, Jacob and I worked our way to the barn. My main concern was the safety of the few head of cattle I had left, and the horses.

What we found at the corrals was a sad sight, indeed. One bull, two heifers and three horses were all that survived. The rest had been pushed against the barn by the wind, and when covered by the drifts, had suffocated.

I was relieved we had not asked William to accompany us. The sight of the dead animals was not one I wanted him to see.

Jacob and I got the six animals into the barn and after caring for them, and the milk cows and two goats already in their stalls, we returned to the house with our bad news.

Clatilda and the children were much saddened by the news. Clatilda turned to me, placing her hand on my arm.

"Will, can you imagine this morning if you had not sold our herd?"

"I thought of little else as Jacob and I were digging out those poor dumb beasts, against the barn!"

"Partner, whatever that 'Spirit' is that got you to sell your cows last fall, I want to know more about it. You sure did the right thing!" Jacob said.

Chapter 12

Seth Blalock lost his entire herd except for two cows he was milking and had in the barn. Two teams of draft horses were stabled safe in the barn, but he lost four saddle horses, in that terrible spring storm.

When we were once again able to get to town, we found that few had lost their milking stock, but everyone had lost other animals. Saddle horses, beef cattle and sheep were all hit. Animals that had been outside on that horrible March night had been laid wilted as so much scythed wheat.

The problems were the core of much discussion; both in and out of church.

While sitting at the dinner table one evening late in March, Jacob made a suggestion that was to effect many lives.

"Partner, why don't we take a little trip down into the panhandle country? We could pick up all the cattle and horses needed, and probably at a fair price; we could get them Medina boys and their pals. We ought to be able to restock this valley in six weeks or so."

We discussed it that evening and the more I thought of it, the better it sounded. The only question was the finances. I wasn't sure the people in the lower valley could afford such a venture.

Everywhere was a sea of mud as we drove to church that Sunday morning in April. By the time we got to town the horses were covered half way up to their withers, and the mud was splattered clear over the dashboard of our buggy.

I brought up Jacob's plan during priesthood and it was given a mixed reception. Some were immediately for the idea, but the rest, most, held back.

As we went home that evening, Clatilda and I discussed the problem.

"But Will, it's clear," she said, "some can afford to restock and some cannot. It would seem obvious that all would like to restock their farms, but many, it would seem, simply have not the money to do so."

I thought of the problem all evening. I even dreamed of it that night. A solution presented itself in the pre-dawn darkness.

While Clatilda was getting breakfast, I sent the children to help Jacob with the morning chores.

"How would you like to be married to a banker?" I asked.

"From what I have seen of bankers, cowboy, the idea doesn't please me."

"Then you may not like my idea of how to solve the livestock problem in our valley. I'm going to propose that Jacob and I buy all the livestock necessary for replacement. We would sell, at an agreed profit to those who could afford to pay and give the remainder five years to repay, with interest. They could either pay in livestock or cash. In the meantime, I could also buy enough seed stock to begin rebuilding our herd. Even if some were only able to pay off their entire debt with stock, we wouldn't lose, and the valley would, again, be productive farm and ranching country."

Clatilda sat for a few moments, pensively staring at the stove, while awaiting the browning of biscuits, therein.

"What you propose would work, of course, but I wonder how it will be received."

"Only one way to find out," I said. "I'll put the plan before the brethren at priesthood next Sunday."

And so it was that a panhandle cowboy became a banker. There were few dissenters to my plan, and even those who at first held back came to join before Jacob and I left for the Panhandle country.

By the time Jacob and I were ready to leave, we had orders for almost as many cattle as I had sold the previous fall, and better than twice as many horses as we had in the cavvy, including the drovers animals.

When we picked up the Medina brothers and two Lopez boys, there were six of us, headed out on a stock-buying trip.

Chapter 13

It was still cold when we crossed over Eagles Nest and started down toward Las Vegas, in New Mexico. I had no wish to tarry there for the town was still rough. Laying along the Santa Fe Trail as it did, I had no wish to spend any time there, considering the contents of my saddle bags and money belt. Clatilda and I had combined some of our money in order to take all gold. It was my feeling I would be in a better bargaining position if I was able to cover my bargaining with gold coins.

We turned southeast along the Canadian River, knowing the bigger ranches would not be far from a dependable water supply.

We were northeast of Las Vegas, about two day's ride, when we began to see more and more cattle. Most looked less than well. They seemed to be good stock, but were leaner than they should have been, even this early in the season. They all carried the same brand. We had been riding for half a day, seeing that brand, when three riders topped a rise south of us, then began loping purposefully toward our group.

We pulled up and waited as the men came on.

When they reached us, I noticed they were mounted on some of the best looking horses I'd seen in a long while.

"You fellows just passing through, or you have something else in mind," demanded one of the riders.

I pulled my pony around to face the speaker. As I did, I was aware Jacob nudged his horse up beside me.

"Mister, I don't know that our purpose, or destination, is any of your concern. Why do you ask?"

"I've got two or three reasons for asking," the man said. "One is that you've been on Half-Moon land for the last twenty miles, and you won't be off for another ten, if you keep heading east. So, I'll ask you one more time. What are you doing here!"

"Given the fact you've no fences, markers or signs, it's sort of easy to see we didn't know we were on anyone's land. So, what's your problem, friend?" I asked.

"My 'problem' is we've lost all the cattle we figure to, for any reason. We'll just see you fellows get off 'Half-Moon' land the same way you came on."

As he said this all three men placed their hands on their holstered pistols. As they did, I was startled to hear the sound of pistols being cocked, First on my left, then on my right.

"Partner, I ain't been in this palaver up to now," Jacob said, "but when a man puts his hand to his sidearm, I have to believe the talking is over. Now, if you're a mind to do anything but talk, just have at it. Before you do, though you might want to think about that empty chair at the supper table tonight. The one you used to sit in."

The two riders, on each side of the rider who'd been talking, suddenly got real busy adjusting their hats. The talker looked real uncomfortable, but went no further than the saddle horn with his gun hand.

"Friend," I said, "this thing got out of hand, right sudden. Let's slow down for a minute. You're awful fast to let your mouth overload your hardware. We're not looking to steal anything, least of all your cattle.

Just the opposite. We're in this country on a stock-buying trip. You know of anyone selling?"

"Mister, I guess you're right! My name is Ray Hollister. I'm the Half-Moon Segundo. We've lost too many cattle, for several reasons, this last year. We're all riding, looking over our shoulders."

"I'm Will Jackson, these two gunslingers, beside me, are Jacob Webber and Jamie Medina. What's happened to your herd; rustlers?"

"That and everything else. We've not had rain around here for seventeen months now, not a drop. We think there has been some rustling, but about that, we ain't real sure. It's just we're that weary of finding cattle lying dead beside dried up water holes."

"Mr. Hollister, you suppose your boss would be interested in selling cattle?"

"Just about as interested as a blind man would be, to be able to see."

"Well, then, let's go talk to him instead of jumping around each other, like roosters in a barnyard."

Hollister looked at me a moment, then nodding his head turned and lined out in a long lope over the rise where he and his hands had first appeared.

I was surprised to find it less than a ten minute ride to the Half-Moon headquarters. The first I saw was a grove of huge cottonwoods. Inside this shady forest was an assortment of adobe buildings presided over by the biggest barn I had ever seen. It would probably had held at least sixty or eighty head of livestock and it's loft was of a size to accommodate at least eighty tons of hay.

As we rode into the dooryard, a man stepped off the porch of the main house. At least, at first, I thought it to be a man. As we came to the hitch rails I saw that what I'd thought to be a man, was a very tall, angular woman, of an indeterminate age.

Hollister took off his hat, and addressing the woman, said, "Mrs. Buckman, these hombre's say they are looking to buy cattle. I brought them in to talk to you."

I stepped forward, removing my hat. "Mrs. Buckman, I'm Will Jackson. Mr. Hollister says you're in the middle of quite a drought. He said you might be willing to let go of a few head."

"Come in Mr. Jackson. Let's have a drink of cool water and talk about it."

As amazed as I had been to see the woman, I was even more astounded by her soft voice. It was difficult to reconcile the voice with her appearance. I introduced Jacob and Jamie. They went with me into the house.

The inside of that house impressed me; everything was open. The parlor blended in with a dining area, which was next to the kitchen. There were no walls. Just massive furniture and terrazzo floors and a coolness hard to imagine from the heat outside.

Mrs. Buckman went into the kitchen area and drew a large pitcher of water and brought it and several glasses out to the dining table, where she had directed us to have a seat.

Sitting, she turned to me, "Well, Mr. Jackson, so you're buying cattle? Just how many?"

"Ma'am, we're buying cattle and horses. We're looking for about three to five hundred head and maybe as many as fifty horses. We'd like to pickup about twenty head of saddle stock, and if we can find them, about thirty head of draft animals."

"I have that many, and more, to sell. But, Mr. Jackson, do you think to get bargain prices, just because we are in the middle of a drought? If so, sir, you'd be mistaken. We may sell some of our stock, but before I'll give them away, I'll have my hands shoot them and leave their carcasses as vulture and coyote bait."

I sat and looked at her for a moment, then reaching for my hat, I stood. Jacob and Jamie stood also.

"Mrs. Buckman, we surely thank you for the cool water and the shade, but it would seem you have a wrong impression of our intent. I think we might have difficulty dealing with one another. We'll be going now. It was nice to have met you ma'am."

I turned, and we left the woman seated at her table.

It took a few minutes to round up my crew and get mounted. As I turned away from the hitch rail, I saw the woman come out of the house.

"Mr. Jackson," she said, hailing me with her hat, "will you wait a minute?"

"Ma'am?" I said turning my horse to face her.

"We have kept about seven hundred head near here, and have been watering them from two wells that haven't yet gone dry. They are still in reasonably good shape. Perhaps you'd like to take a look at them and see if any are to your liking."

It was interesting that her attitude had changed completely. Also, she seemed to have no question we could now, at least, try to do business.

The cattle, she and Hollister showed me, were quite different from what we had seen on the range. They were not in tip-top shape, but they weren't bad. Interestingly, they were a good mix; steers, heifers, bulls and grown mother cows, some with calves at their side.

"If we were to come to a price, could I leave them here while we rode east to buy horses?"

"No, Mr. Jackson. There are two reasons I won't let you do that. First, if I sell any of these cattle it will be, primarily, to be immediately able to bring more in off the range to have water for them. Secondly, I suspect I have more horses than you could possibly need; both riding and draft."

"You have draft horses?" I asked.

"Yes, when we have enough rain, we cut our own hay. It appears that will not be a problem for a while. Therefore, I could probably let you have up to forty or fifty good animals."

Two days later, we headed west with a few over four hundred head of cattle, thirty of the best looking saddle horses I'd seen in years and forty-six draft horses fit for any farm in the country, along with a signed and witnessed bill of sale.

We also left Jacob talking to the widow Buckman. He told us to go on ahead. He said he'd catch up in a couple of hours. Frankly I was surprised to see him ride up about noon.

"Jacob," I said as he pulled up beside me, "I gotta tell you, I'm surprised to see you."

"It took all the strength I had, partner!" That was all he ever said.

The drive back across the mountains was really uneventful. The Medina's and Lopez's were hard workers and good hands, and the animals were quick to settle into a mood fit for the road.

We bedded our herd on a Mesa north of Rancho de Taos, and Jacob and I rode in to the plaza to replenish our supplies. We had not the luxury of Senor Medina's chuck wagon and meals were pretty much of a grab and run situation. We thought to pick up some extras to give us all a treat.

We were standing in the store while a clerk filled our order when Jacob took my left elbow.

"Partner, don't turn around, but Cecil Denton just walked through that side door."

"You mean the Three Star Denton?" I asked.

"One and the same. And it looks as if he's got two of his gunsels with him!"

"You don't have to get involved, Jacob. I expect it's me he'll be wanting to see."

"You firing me?"

"No, I just wouldn't like to see you hurt, in my fight."

"Been a long time since you rode for a brand, ain't it?"

I glanced at him and I guess my dumb look said it all.

"Enough said!" Jacob muttered. "You parlay with Denton or make your play, whichever suits you. I'll watch out for the other two."

I knew there was no use attempting to ignore Denton so I turned to face the man, as he strode toward me. He walked in the manner of one who brooked no interference from any man. But, when he saw me, he stopped, as if he'd run into a wall.

"Well, mister, I see you're without your pistoleros, What are you doing in this country?"

"Again, Denton, you and I are having the same problem. You're always asking things that are none of your business!"

I was sure not all of those standing around spoke English, but it was not hard to tell by our tone and stance that this was not a meeting of friends. Denton, his men, Jacob and I quickly had a large part of the store to ourselves.

"Don't get smart, mister," Denton said. "You don't have a crew to back your play today."

"Nope," I said, "just me and Jacob, that's all."

I believe he had been concentrating so heavily on me he had not even noticed Jacob. His head jerked around.

"I wondered where you'd run off to, Webber. I figured you was just yellow."

"No, I'm not yellow, Cecil. Just fed up with your ways. I see, even today, you're still afraid to go anywhere without your wet-nurses!"

"Now, you hold on!" One of Denton's hands said, taking a step forward.

"You hold on, Landon," Jacob answered, "you know me. You say another word and somebody's going to be riding in your saddle!"

The man stopped. Both his movement and his talking. Suddenly.

"What will it be, Denton?" I demanded, facing the man squarely.

Ever so slightly his whole demeanor changed.

"Nothing from you, mister! Just stay out of my way. I'm in no mood to fool around with your kind."

With that, he abruptly turned and went into another part of the store.

Jacob and I finished our business and returned to the herd. I was prompted to move the cattle further from town, but they were settled in on the mesa and as it was late in the day, I decided against the move.

After we'd had the best meal we'd enjoyed for a while, Jacob and I were standing by the fire as the Medina boys went out for the first shift with the cattle.

"Partner, you know you should have killed Denton back there in Taos. He'll do the same to you if he can. You've backed him down twice now and a man with his ego can't stand that."

"Jacob, I'd not like to kill anyone. I've had enough of that in my life."

"Knew you hadn't always been a Mormon farmer. Where are you from?"

"I grew up just about two days ride from the Half-Moon. After that I drifted all over the panhandle country."

"You ever been to Cimarron?"

"Quite a few times."

"You know an old boy over in that country by the name of Buck Harris?"

"I expect I do. He was my uncle. My mother's brother."

"What you mean, 'was'?"

"I heard he got stomped by his horse about eight or nine years ago."

"If he did, he had a great recovery. He sobered me up and let me earn a road stake, to get up to Colorado country, not a year before I met you down by the Three Star!"

I thought for a moment about that. It was nice to know that somewhere I did have some blood kin, in addition to Anna Laura. It was not that I was likely to ever see Uncle Buck again, but his very existence was somehow comforting.

"What you intend to do about Denton?" Demanded Jacob.

"Nothing, Jacob. I'd be just as good if I never saw him again."

"Be nice, partner, but don't count on it."

Chapter 14

We swung the herd slightly east of north to come into the San Luis Valley by way of Fort Garland. When we turned west, just north of the Fort, I was reminded of that white hell of less than a year before. It was right pleasant driving the herd there, now. It was getting warm as only the high country can, but the cattle were moving at their own pace and I'll swear they were gaining weight on the trail. Several of them had dropped calves and as I intended to keep them for myself, I took quite a ribbing from Jacob and the hands about my baby herd.

When we reached Alamosa, we swung the herd north of town to stay away from the farms springing up south of there. I decided to give the animals a couple of days rest and allow the crew, in rotation, a day in town. I felt I need not worry for there was not a drinker in the crowd. I wondered about Jacob but he told me that since my Uncle Buck had helped him sober up down in Cimarron, he'd not had a drink nor any intention of ever doing so. Jamie Medina and his brother, Al, were first into town along with Carlos Lopez. The Medina brothers were back by noon but without Lopez. The story they told caused Jacob and I both to be riding hard for Alamosa in less than five minutes.

Denton and his two friends had followed us all the way from Taos and had cornered the Medinas and Lopez in a café in town.

Denton had remembered Jamie from Walsenburg. He had pulled down on Jamie and Al while his two men had beaten Lopez almost to death.

We found Lopez in the doctor's office.

The doctor told us Carlos would live but he would be blind in his left eye, and it would be some time before he could sit a horse. Probably at least a month.

I made sure the doctor was paid to care for Carlos until one of the Medina boys, or his brother would return to take him home, a month hence. I then had Jamie and Al return to our camp. I sent them there for two reasons. One, to help hold the herd and also to make sure the other Lopez boy didn't try anything foolish. I intended Jacob and I to take care of that part.

Jacob and I went hunting. We went first to the town Marshal's office. I hoped to find Jamie Nava, but that was not to be. The new Marshal made it crystal clear he had little interest in fights among strangers. Particularly as long as no property damage or physical injury involved "his town or its people." He told us he would be quick to come after anyone who might cause problems for "his town or its people."

We went, next, to three of the towns saloons and both hotels. No trace of Denton or his men. We then started at the east end of town and checked every commercial building and, not a few, private homes. We were just leaving a livery barn, on the west end of town, when the town Marshal rode up.

"I told you fellows once, I wouldn't tolerate you causing trouble. Now, I'll be telling you to get out of my town or I'm going to have to run you in. I'll let you spend a couple of nights in my jail. Maybe that will settle you down and prove to you I mean what I say!"

"Mr. Marshal," Jacob said, nudging his horse up close in front of the man's mount. "You've made it clear you're too scared or lazy to help us find those that beat our hand. Now let me make something clear to you. You get in my way one more time and I'm going to pull you off that sorry animal you're riding, and I'm just gonna naturally make you wish you'd never been born. Now you scat on back to your nice chair and coffee pot. Should I see you coming again, alone or with friends, I'm going to just naturally expect you to come shooting, for I will."

Jacob then reached over with his quirt and slapped the Marshal's horse. The last we saw of the man he was headed back toward town, trying to regain control of his mount.

"Jacob," I said as he turned back to me, "I've seen politicians get elected, saying less than you just did."

He grinned, sheepishly. "In all honesty, partner, I was really trying to talk myself out of cleaning his plow, right then and there."

"That's not going to help us find Denton or his men."

"We're not going to find them here anyway. By now, if I know anything at all about Denton, he's long gone."

"I think you're right. Let's go back to that doctor's house and make sure Carlos is all right. Then we'd best be moving our stock. We've still got more than a week's work before we get them home."

We rode, with care, the next few days but nothing else happened except that the Medina boys were very quiet and withdrawn, and Tony Lopez said not a word for the rest of the trip.

Chapter 15

The morning we headed up the river toward our settlement, I was filled with a sense of foreboding. I could not understand for I thought I should be happy, ending our trip with such success.

We had agreed, before we left, that we would turn the stock in on Bishop Terry's farm. He was centrally located to most of the valley residents. It was there I paid off the Medinas and Tony Lopez. I gave Jamie Medina seven twenty dollar gold pieces, and instructions that he was to go for the Lopez boy in three weeks. I told him he was to keep forty dollars for his trouble and give the other one hundred dollars to Carlos.

He protested about the forty dollars but I just turned away telling him to be careful and not be late getting Carlos home. I cautioned him not to take Tony Lopez with him. I did not want him running afoul of that stupid Marshal. I told him I did not want Tony to make the trip. I was concerned about what he might do.

As Jacob and I were cutting out mine and Seth Blalock's stock, John Terry came riding into the pasture.

"Will," he said as he rode up, "you'd best get on out to your place. There's been bad trouble."

"What!" I demanded., "Are Clatilda and the kids all right?"

"Clatilda and Anna Laura are all right, but William's in pretty bad shape."

I said nothing. It seemed before I even realized it, I had my horse in a hard gallop.

It seemed that ride took forever, those few miles home. I swept into my dooryard at a dead run on a horse I'd almost killed on the ride.

Clatilda opened the door just as I stepped down.

"Oh, Will! I thought you'd never get here."

"Are you all right?" I said, as she rushed into my arms.

"Yes, now that you're here, but Bud is hurt bad."

"What in the world happened?"

"Three men came here last Friday. They said they were looking for Will Jackson's place. When I told them I was your wife they forced me back into the house where Bud and Anna Laura were still at the breakfast table. When they shoved me into the kitchen Bud jumped up and gabbed a poker. He tried to attack the one doing all the talking. Oh, Will! They beat him terribly."

"Where is he?"

"He's in our room. Anne and I have been taking care of him. Seth has been out every day trying to find their trail, but no luck."

I went into the bedroom and what I saw there broke my heart.

Bud was bandaged from head to toe. He had both arms in splints and one foot was heavily bound. His face was a mass of bruises and cuts.

I turned to Clatilda, "Grown men did this?"

"Yes, Will," Clatilda answered. "Two of them held Anna Laura and me while the leader beat and kicked William. Then that beast deliberately broke both of the boy's arms on the edge of the table."

"We'll take him to Alamosa," I said, "there is a real doctor there."

"I don't think we need to, Will. Seth and I set and splinted his arms and we bound his foot tightly. Everything else looks worse than it is except for where that man stomped on his foot and broke his arms. Most of the rest came from slaps and the back of the man's hand."

"What did they look like?" I demanded.

"The two that held me and Anna Laura were just cowboys but the other had on a black vest with fringe on the front."

"Denton!" I'd not heard Jacob come in. But, when he practically shouted Denton's name, both Clatilda and I turned to face him.

"Are you and Miss Anna Laura all right?" He demanded of Clatilda.

"We're all right, Mr. Webber, but not so with William."

Jacob stepped around Clatilda to better see Bud on our bed.

"A growed man done that?" He demanded.

"I'm afraid so, Mr. Webber," Clatilda answered.

"Well, now, we'll just have to take care of this. Do you know which way they went, Will?"

"No, and this is not yet the time to be chasing off after them."

"Then, when?"

"Soon, Jacob, soon. But for now, let's be sure my family is settled and on the mend."

Jacob said not another word. He turned and left the yard in a long lope. I wasn't quite sure until later that afternoon if I would see him again.

I heard cattle and stepped out the door to see Jacob and Aaron Blalock, driving our stock into the barn corral.

"You tell your Pa he's to come get his stock anytime he pleases." Jacob said to Aaron as the boy turned his horse homeward.

"Didn't figure you needed stock to worry about," Jacob said stepping down from his pony.

I followed him into the barn as he put away his saddle and tack.

"Jacob, I'm worried about Bud. I talked to him this afternoon and the fear in his eyes is bad to see."

"When do we leave to find Denton?"

"I don't know, Jacob. I just don't know."

"You scared?" Jacob asked.

"No, I'm not scared of Denton and his crowd. I am afraid of what I might do."

"Why should you be afraid of what you'd do. This man beat your kid. Anything short of killing him would be too easy."

"I've killed a man, Jacob. I don't look forward to doing it again."

"The only past you need worry about is what was done to Bud. Seems to me everything else kind of pales upside that!"

"I know Jacob. I have two people to talk to before I make up my mind what I will do, and when I'll do it. I'll have my mind made up by this time tomorrow."

"That's fine partner. Denton already has enough of a start. We couldn't catch him this side of his home place anyway. So another day won't matter."

Supper that night was tense. Clatilda and I fed Bud and he seemed in better spirits than he had been earlier in the afternoon. Once when he was resting between bites he turned to me.

"Why did that Denton man do this to me, Pa?"

"He wanted to hurt me, Bud. And you were small enough that he had nothing to fear from you or your Ma or Anna Laura. He figured to get at me through you."

"Did he, Pa?"

"Did he what, Bud?"

"Did he get at you?"

"Oh, yes! He got at me in a big way! Now it's time to figure out how he is to be punished for what he did to you."

"We'll talk about that later William, your father and I. You just finish your supper," Clatilda said, handing him more food.

After Jacob and Anna Laura had gone to bed, I was seated at the table while Clatilda put away the dishes.

"Just what do you intend to do, Will?" Clatilda said turning to face me.

"I don't know, ma'am. I have been struggling with that all day. My first thought was to hunt Denton down and kill him like the cur dog he is."

"What was your second thought?"

"You might not even want to know. But then I began thinking what the saints went through, back east, and how they handled their mistreatment. Can our problem be any worse than their's?"

"I have never understood the strength and faith they must have had," Clatilda said, sitting down at the table, "I have always prayed I would have their courage if anything like what they went through ever happened to me or mine. I am afraid I am failing, miserably. My thoughts of what I'd like to see done to that beast are anything but saintly. And, Will, I'm ashamed of myself."

"Clatilda, how would you feel if it had been Anna Laura instead of Bud?" I asked.

She turned and looked at me strangely for a moment.

"I've had those thoughts, myself. In fact I studied on that some, Will. I can honestly say, I would feel no differently."

"Yeah, well that's the same conclusion I came to right before supper. I guess it just don't matter who gives your child life, as long as you love him as your own."

Clatilda's face wreathed in a smile. She reached over and placed her hand on my arm. "You know, cowboy, I've heard you say it a hundred times; 'I guess you'll do to ride the river with'!"

"Now," she said, "let's turn in and you sleep on your problem. I'm sure what you decide to do will be right."

At breakfast the next morning, I told Clatilda I was going over to see Jess Turner and I'd be back before noon.

I found Jess and Hester having a late breakfast.

"Come in here, Will Jackson!" Hester said when I knocked at their kitchen door.

"I've some fresh baked cinnamon rolls and if you don't eat some that old man will stuff himself with every last one!"

"Take a breath, woman and let the boy set down," Jess said, rising and pulling a chair from the wall to the table.

I sat, ate a cinnamon roll, and discussed my stock-buying trip for a bit.

"Will, how's that sweet little boy?" Hester asked. "We went over as soon as we heard. That was before you returned. Clatilda and little

Anna Laura had their hands full, but they insisted they could care for him without help. Jess and I are planning another visit this afternoon."

"He's well as can be expected, I guess. You must know he's a pretty scared little boy."

"Have you learned anything about who it might have been that did this thing?" This from Jess.

"Oh, yes, I know exactly who it was!" I said, then I told Jess and Hester all of the events which led up to William's beating.

"You say that poor boy in Alamosa lost the sight in one eye!" Hester said.

"Yes, and he won't even be able to come home for another week or two."

"Well, I'd like to get my hands on this Denton. I'd take a buggy whip to him til he couldn't stand either." Hester said, her eyes flashing like two bolts of lightening.

"What will you do, Will?" Jess quietly asked.

"I don't rightly know, Jess. That's why I came over this morning. I thought, if you have time, I'd like to talk it over with you."

Hester stood, picking up the dirty dishes and stacking them by the sink.

"I'll let you men alone to do your talking," she said.

"Hester, would you set, and talk with us about this?" I asked.

She turned to her chair, placing her hand on my shoulder as she passed.

"Thank you, Will, I'd be blessed to be in the conversation."

"All right, then, woman, but let's wait a while before we get out the tar and feathers," Jess said.

Hester said nothing, just sat and placed one hand over mine and her other hand over one of Jess'.

"Jess could we pray before we start?" she asked.

After the prayer Jess asked me again what I planned to do.

"I'll tell you, Jess. My first impulse was to saddle up and find Denton and to shoot him on sight. I had the thought, at the same time, that it might be wrong"

"What will you do if this Denton came back, Will?" Hester asked.

I looked at her, then at Jess, who was obviously awaiting my answer.

"I will defend my family and home with every skill I have!"

"Even to the point of killing the man?" Asked Jess.

"Absolutely!"

"You will kill to protect, but not to punish. Is that it, Will?" Jess asked.

"I guess that's what it boils down to, Jess."

"Well, then, Will. May I ask you another question?" Hester said.

"Of course."

"If you will kill to protect and question the same act in retribution, what is the probability this Denton man will again try to harm you or your family?"

"Well, he knows where we are. He seems to hold a pretty big grudge. I suppose I'd have to say he will probably try something again."

"Then, one last question, Will," Hester continued, "just how far will you go to prevent another incident."

I sat for a moment, then my course of action was clear.

"Just as far as necessary, Hester. And I guess that settles the matter. I don't know what kind of man this makes me, Jess, but I cannot allow an animal like this to be a constant threat to me and my family. I know of no law enforcement agency that I can call on so, I guess I will take care of the matter myself."

"Talk it over with Clatilda, Will, then do what your heart tells you must do," Hester said.

I left the Turner's feeling better than I had in two days.

Jess and Hester stood at the door watching Will ride off.

"Woman I hope you've not started something bad," Jess mumbled.

Chapter 16

When I got home Clatilda, Jacob and Anna Laura were just sitting down to dinner.

"How's Bud?" I asked as I hung up my coat and hat.

"Much better," Clatilda said. "He's asking for you, and he had a big dinner."

I stepped to the door and spoke to Bud. He asked me to come in.

"Pa, do you think that man will ever come back?"

"No, Bud. I will make sure he doesn't. I'm going to find him and convince him of how bad an idea that would be."

I heard the cabin door close as I stepped back into the kitchen. A quick glance showed me Jacob was gone. His full plate still on the table.

"Where's Jacob?" I asked.

"He heard what you told Bud and left immediately," Clatilda despaired.

"You and Anna Laura finish your dinner, then after that, you and I will take a walk."

I turned and went to the barn. I found Jacob in his room with enough firearms laid out on his bed to start a small war. Maybe even a good sized one, I thought, as I took a second look at the array of weapons. I wondered if he had been carrying them all as he had at Walsenburg or if he had kept them in his bed roll.

"When we leaving?" Was his greeting.

"I think probably tomorrow morning, but that's not settled. I have yet to talk to Clatilda."

Jacob stopped checking his weapons and turned to face me.

"Partner, I've got something to say and I don't know any other way to say it, but to just say it. When I saw you back down Denton and his crowd, that time when he tried to cut your herd and then again in Las Vegas, I figured you were a pretty salty old boy. But, these last few days, I've begun to wonder. If that was my boy laying in there in that bed, Cecil Denton would be dead by now. And, what's more, he would have been glad that I'd finally put him out of the misery I'd brought upon him. I just don't savvy this stumbling around act you've been going through."

He stopped and leaned against the wall, his arms crossed and his eyes boring into mine.

"Well, Jacob, I guess it's time you and I had a talk. First off, I'm afraid of no man I've ever seen. My Uncle Bunk backed me up a couple of times when I was a kid, but no man has since those times. It's not that I'm afraid to go after Denton; it's not even that, now, I'm afraid to leave Clatilda and the kids alone. All I have to do is ride into town and when I come back, I could have up to ten men guarding this place night and day. It's something else entirely, Jacob. I could tell you tales about what Mormon people have endured over the years that would shame anyone who thinks they want to 'get even' with someone for what they have done. It's been tough for me to try to live my religion. You were right when you said I'd not always been a 'Mormon farmer!' No, Jacob, I've been over the hill and seen the elephant, but the past few years I've spent with Clatilda and these people have been the best of my life."

"What I'm trying to do is put together my rage against Cecil Denton, for the thing he did to my family, and what I understand of the gospel of my church. You thought you were ready to go after Denton when you saw Bud? I was ready to kill the man and anyone that got in my way when I did so. But, Jacob, I've made a vest for myself that is, right now, just a little tight. I must talk to Clatilda but this I promise you. I will find Denton, and one way or another, I will convince him of the error of his ways."

I stopped and looked at the man who had remained standing still during my long speech.

"Are you saying the only reason you haven't gone after Denton before now is you wanted your woman's permission?" Jacob said as he remained standing at the foot of his bunk, his arms still crossed.

Somehow, this question was the last straw. I felt myself losing control as I took a step toward the man.

"I'm going to tell you one more time, Jacob Webber, and only once more. I've had trouble putting together my anger and my religion. I have found a way, to act in defensive protection of my family, that will not betray what I believe or the trust my friends and neighbors have placed in me. I ask permission from no one to do what I think is right, but I will welcome all thoughts and conversation that help me come to my decision. If you don't like the way I come to a problem, just cut that rope that has you tied to this place and drift on down whatever trail suits you. But, friend, don't you ever look me in the eye and say, in any way, that I'm a coward. For that Jacob, I'll kill you where you stand. I'm Mormon, but before I even heard of Mormons, I was a man. I still am. If that don't suit you, then take your best shot, and do it now."

"Well, like an old boy said to me one time;" Jacob said, uncrossing his arms and putting both his hands in his pockets, "he'd seen politicians get elected saying less than that!"

I looked at him for a moment, as a sly grin spread across his face.

"First I met Clatilda, then Hester Turner, now you!" I said.

"What's that supposed to mean?"

"I spend all that time working up a good mad then you just turn that silly grin on me!"

"Ain't nobody ever told me this life was gonna be easy. You get some other kind of promise?" Jacob said, still with that grin on his face.

"You just be ready to leave tomorrow morning at sun-up. And, unless you intend to wear out a good horse by noon, you might leave some of that hardware here."

I left the barn, still about half mad. When I saw Clatilda stepping off the cabin steps, wrapping a shawl around her shoulders, my anger left.

"You said you wanted to take a walk," was her greeting. "Where would you like to go?"

"I thought we'd go up to Sarah's grave. I've not been there since I got back."

We walked comfortably up the hill. Before we reached the little graveyard, Clatilda slid her arm through mine.

"When will you be leaving?" She asked.

"I thought to go at daybreak tomorrow."

"Be careful, Will."

I stopped and turned to face her.

"That's all; 'be careful'?" I asked.

"Yes, you've decided what you will do. What else would you

expect me to say?"

"I sort of expected some kind of argument."

"Will, had it not been necessary for me to care for Bud and Anna Laura, I believe I would have gone after than man, myself."

"What happened to 'turn the other cheek'?"

"Don't tease me, Will Jackson!"

"I'm not, ma'am. It's just you've always been the calm one and I the one to fly off the handle."

"Will, if there was a lawman within a week's ride from here I thought would bring this man to justice, I would argue for that course. But, Will, I'm afraid that crazy man will come back. I can't live with that."

"That's what I finally came to."

"Did you talk about it with Jess?"

"Yes, with him and Hester."

"She sat in on your discussion?"

"Yes, and even insisted on prayer first."

"She would! Did you stop and talk with Bishop Terry?"

"No, by the time I left the Turner's, I had made up my mind."

"Do you have any idea how long you will be gone?"

"I would hope no longer than ten or fifteen days. I'll bet Denton headed right for his ranch from here. That's somewhere south of Walsenburg. Jacob will know where."

"Will what will you do when you find him?"

"I don't believe that will be my choice, Clatilda. I'd guess he will dictate that."

"Cowboy, I don't think I could go on without you."

"I don't intend to see that happen, ma'am. I figure to be eating your pies and cobblers for a long time to come."

"Would you be wanting a little cream on top?"

"Always!"

I folded my Clatilda in my arms while we stood there on that windswept hill and basked in the love we had for one another.

Chapter 17

It was already warm, the morning Jacob and I rode out of my dooryard, on a mission I did not cherish.

Neither of us had much to say as we rode through the village toward the river, seeing no one. As we headed down the river the sun began to beat down in earnest.

"I didn't think it would get this hot in the mountains." Jacob said.

"The temperature doesn't have to get too high for it to be miserable," I said. "I think it's because the air is so thin."

We both came out of our vests before mid-morning.

It seemed no conversation was possible that day. One or the other of us would make a comment or ask a question and invariably the response was a grunt or a short answer or comment, at best.

We reached Saguache that afternoon and decided to spend the night at the stage station.

The owner and his wife looked to be copies of each other. Neither were tall and both were round and smooth. Senora Maestas was the only one of the two who spoke English, but even so, she was pleased to find both Jacob and I to be comfortable in her language. She seemed to immediately take a shine to Jacob. She obviously served him the best and largest plate. Even gave him a folded napkin. To me, she gave a piece of cloth of indeterminate origin.

"It seems you have a way with older women," I said.

"I guess it's just my sweet disposition."

This from a man who at any given time could reduce his weight by a quarter, simply by disarming himself.

Supper was good, and the bunks we were given, satisfactory.

Before dawn the next morning, I was up, and at the well. I scrubbed the sleep from my face.

While I was so engaged, Senora Maestas came out to fill a water bucket.

"Senor," she said, "do you and your friend have wives?"

I turned to see she was serious.

"I have, Senora. He has not. Why do you ask?"

"I have two unmarried sisters."

"Would you like me to speak to my friend?" I asked.

"Si, Senor," she said, "but carefully. These matters must be handled with care."

As I looked at her I realized she was completely serious.

At that moment, Jacob came out of the building.

"Remember, Senor! Carefully." Senora Maestas said as she scurried away with her bucket of water.

"What was that all about?" Jacob asked as he came up, rolling his sleeves.

"Not much. It seems Senora Maestas has a couple of unmarried sisters. It would appear you can take your choice."

Jacob stopped in mid-stride, and seemed, momentarily, to hang, as a puppet on a string.

"I ain't much hungry this morning," were the first words from his mouth. "What say we just mosey on down the trail."

Sun-up found us on the flats above Monte Vista with Jacob setting a brisk pace.

There was more conversation that morning, albeit one-sided. I wanted to discuss Jacob's love life. He seemed disinclined.

We spent the next night in Alamosa and I was tempted to look up the Marshal but we agreed, it was probably a waste of time.

The third morning out from home, I began to think what I would do when, once again, I confronted Denton. I knew he would probably dictate the action and there would be little, if any, chance to talk. I thought long and hard that day about the errand upon which I found myself. I questioned my testimony of my beliefs, but when I did, Bud's beaten face would come to my mind. I kept trying to convince myself that a grown man had done this to a child. It seemed unreal.

Finally, as we were approaching Fort Garland, I rode up beside Jacob.

"Jacob," I said coming alongside his mount, "is there anything you know about Cecil Denton that would make him do what he did to Bud?"

"You know, partner, I been studying on that for awhile. I've known some pretty mean old boys in my time, but I can't say I ever saw a man I thought capable of doing what was done to Bud."

"Oh, I've known some that might do that to another grown man. But, to a kid? I just can't figure it. Unless Denton went plumb off his rocker, I can't explain it."

"You know I have only one thought on this trip. I intend to see

Denton never does such a thing again. I'd like to be able to do that some way short of killing the man."

"Partner, I think you're spitting into the wind if you think there's any other way. Had it a-been me, I'd have shot him in Taos. It was clear then he would do something to hurt you. He was only waiting for the right time."

It was a troubling ride we made across La Veta and down onto the plain, west of Walsenburg. When we reached the area where Denton first confronted me, I asked directions from Jacob.

"It's only three or four miles south of here," Jacob said. "But we can expect to see Three Star cows anytime now, and we 're just as apt to see Three Star hands."

Jacob and I rode easy in our saddles, not really knowing what to expect, but sure we could be confronted at anytime.

We had ridden only a couple of miles when we came up out of an arroyo and for miles around we seemed alone on the prairie.

Jacob stopped and sat back in his saddle.

"Partner, I don't understand this. We should have seen a lot of Three Star stock by now and if you'll look over there by that stand of spruce, you can see the tin roof of Denton's place. It looks deserted."

I had brought my field glasses and taking them and I scanned the house, out buildings and the area between us and the ranch buildings.

"Jacob, I don't see anyone around. You suppose Denton's forted up, waiting for us to get closer?"

"Wouldn't put it past him, but what would he do with his stock? Are there no horses in the barn corrals?"

"I don't see anyone or anything, live, around the whole place."

"Well, let's go on in, but take it right easy, partner. And, sit right light in that saddle."

We rode on toward the ranch, swinging around to put the spruce grove more between us and the man's house.

We rode within less than a hundred yards of the place when Jacob jerked his pony to a stop and stood up in the stirrups.

"Well, I'll be . . ." He said.

"What is it Jacob?"

"Put those glasses on the front door of that place and tell me what you see."

I scanned the front of the building carefully.

"There's no one there," I said.

"Isn't that door wide open, and it looks like the big window is either wide-open or busted out."

"The front door is not just open. It appears to be laying on the porch and every window in the front and near side is either broken out or wide open."

"Let's ease around behind the barn and come up behind the house," Jacob said, gigging his pony into a walk.

We circled the barn and came up behind, what was obviously a deserted place.

We each went to separate corners of the rear of the house and dismounted. I went toward the front of the house and Jacob into the back door. We met at the opening where the front door had once hung.

"Boy, that place is a mess!" Jacob said, holstering his pistol. "Every drawer is turned inside out and every window opened wide or broken out. Looks like someone went through the place and took everything that could be carried."

"Let's check the barn," I said.

After returning to our horses, Jacob and I rode into the barn's main alley. There was nothing there. In fact, the only worthwhile things we saw, except for the structure and a small amount of hay in the loft, was an old horse collar and a pitchfork with a broken handle.

"You know, partner," Jacob said, looking all around, "it looks like someone has purposefully taken everything of value from the whole setup"

We rode around the house, barn, and all of it's smaller buildings. Even the mattresses had been taken out of the bunkhouse. After almost an hour of scouting and finding nothing, Jacob said maybe we should ride into Walsenburg.

"Denton used to be right friendly with an old boy who runs a small saloon there. Maybe he knows what happened here."

We were both quiet as we rode the few miles back to town. It was almost spooky the way the Three Star outfit had been stripped.

We rode up to a shack on the southeast end of town. No windows, one door, and a crudely lettered sign hanging askew above the door that read, simply, "whiskey."

Both Jacob and I had to bow our heads to enter the door. Inside, the room was dimly lit by two lamps, one at each end of a bar made of two planks supported by a keg at each end.

There was one person in the place. He stood behind the bar wearing a filthy apron, reading a paper that he had spread out on the planks.

"Hey, George!" Jacob greeted the man. "Where's everybody?"

"Too early for anyone 'cept for the likes of you, Webber." George said, not even looking up from his paper.

"George, what happened to Cecil Denton? We were just out to his place and there's not a soul out there. Not even a stray cow."

"Surprise's me the buildings are still there," George answered.

"What happened?" Jacob persisted.

"Ain't you heard? Denton finally pushed someone too far. It seems a couple of Mexicans named Medina did him and one of his hands in, up in the San Luis. Shot the second boy up pretty bad, fellow by the name of Landon. He's over to widow Barnes boarding house. Folks don't know which will run out first, his blood or his money. Either way, that old woman will throw him or his body out into the alley, whichever runs out first."

"When did this happen?" I demanded.

"Who's your friend, Webber?"

"I work for him, George. Answer his question!"

"Don't rightly know, except Landon rode into town about a four days ago, half-dead and mumbling about how one of those Mexicans had held a gun on him and Charlie Weston while the other Mexican had beat Denton 'til he could hardly stand. Then had given him his gun back and made him draw. Landon said that the Mexican kid shot Denton four times before Denton hit the ground. Old Landon was still scared while Bill Grant was digging the two slugs out of his shoulder. Scared that Mexican kid was still coming after him. But, we ain't seen hide nor hair of any strangers 'til you and your friend rode in."

"What's happened to all the Three Star stock?" Jacob asked.

"Hand's split up the herd and took off. Some down Purgatory way, and some toward Pueblo."

"What about all the stuff in the house and barn."

"When folks around here heard Denton was dead and his hands had all run off they just naturally went out and helped themselves."

"So all that's left of Denton is the house and barn?" Jacob said.

"Yeah, that, and I reckon them Mexicans treated him to a grave. I ain't sure about that though."

Jacob and I left Walsenburg in the late afternoon. We could have stayed at the hotel there, but somehow, that night I wanted the clean mountain air and stars I could see.

Chapter 18

Jacob and I rode into the Medina's dooryard the afternoon of the third day after leaving Walsenburg. I hailed the house and Pedro Medina stepped out of his door, holding a rifle in one hand.

"Que paso?" He asked, holding his hand to shade his eyes.

"It's me, Senor Medina, Will Jackson and I've got Jacob Webber with me!"

"Step down and come into my house," Pedro responded, his face now wreathed in a smile. "I did not know who you were at first," he said sitting the rifle back inside the door.

Jacob and I tied our horses and followed Medina into his house. His wife recognized us immediately and after greeting us both, she began to set food on the table.

"What's wrong, Senor Medina? I've not seen you answer your door with rifle in hand, before."

"Bad business, Senor Jackson. I'm afraid my Jamie has killed two, maybe three men."

"Where are Jamie and Al now?" I asked.

"They have gone to Alamosa to return Carlos Lopez, as you instructed."

"When did they leave?" I asked.

"This is the fifth day they've been gone. Unless they've run into trouble, they should be back anytime. Surely no later than tonight."

"Senor, do you mind if we wait for them here? I would like to talk to Jamie."

"Of course not, Senor Jackson. Jamie is not in trouble with you is he?"

"Absolutely not, and when I tell you the whole story, I think you will understand he's probably not in trouble with anyone."

We spent the rest of the afternoon telling the Medinas the whole story of what had led to Jamie's confrontation with Denton.

The only interruption was when I told them of what Denton had done to Bud. Senora Medina stifled a sob. Or, at least she tried to do so. When I had finished, Medina told us he knew some of what I had told him, but not all.

"As you can see, sir," I said, "there is no way anyone can, or will, fault Jamie or Alfonso for what they have done. What's more Carlos Lopez stands as mute testimony of what this Denton was capable of. No, sir, do not worry about your sons."

While we had been talking, about sunset, Senora Medina excused herself and disappeared into the rear of the house. She soon returned with both Jamie and Alfonso in tow. It seemed she had heard them ride up. We had not.

After the greetings were over Jamie told me that Carlos was much better and was able to distinguish light, and even large objects, with the eye so mistreated by Denton. He said Carlos had been grateful for the money I had sent, particularly as the Marshal in Alamosa had impounded his horse and saddle for fifty dollars. The Marshal claimed Carlos owed a fine for fighting in town. Jamie said there had been nothing he could do as the Marshal and his deputy had threatened to put all three of them in jail if the fine wasn't paid.

When Jamie had finished, I turned to Jacob and asked him how tired he was.

"I'm not so tired that a little moonlight ride toward Alamosa wouldn't make me feel a lot better!" Jacob answered.

I asked Jamie if he would mind riding over to my place the next day and telling Clatilda I'd be an extra day or two. I offered to pay him for the errand, but the whole Medina clan answered me that even the offer was an insult.

Jacob and I left for Alamosa shortly after moon rise.

Chapter 19

Jacob and I camped on the flats between Monte Vista and Alamosa just before dawn. We had decided to rest both ourselves and our horses for a bit before riding on into Alamosa.

I was more tired than I had thought, for the noontime sun awoke me. Jacob had been smarter than I for he had bedded down under a big sage and was shielded from even the noon time glare of the sun. I kicked him awake, and we rode on to Alamosa and the good smells from a cantina on the west side of town.

At first, we were regarded with a sullen attitude by the cantina's patron. But, when we requested our food in Spanish, the atmosphere warmed somewhat.

I asked the bartender if he knew the Marshal. After casting serious doubt upon the Marshal's genealogy, he said that he knew the man only too well.

"Why do you ask me, Senor? He is a gringo, such as you and your companion. Why not talk to those who hired him?"

"Because, Senor, I have only one question and I want a truthful answer," I told him.

Our host smiled and wiped away an imaginary spot on the clean bar. "What can I tell you, sir?" He asked.

"How many deputies does your Marshal have?"

He looked directly at me for a moment before he responded.

"He has one, my friend, only one. His worthless brother-in-law."

I tossed a coin on the bar. "That should cover our food and a little more for your hospitality."

"Muchas Gracias, Senor, and hasta la vista," the man said sweeping the gold coin off the bar.

As we were mounting outside the cantina, Jacob asked me my plans.

"Not much, Jacob, I'm just going in and get Carlos' money back."

"Just like that?"

"Yep, or would you rather I check with my woman first."

Jacob's head snapped around toward me but I only smiled back to his consternation.

"Well, partner, let's go get the kid's money. Do we ask for some interest for the use of that fifty dollars?"

"No, I think we'll be well enough paid by the look on that tin-horn's face."

We found the Marshal and his deputy taking an early afternoon siesta in the Marshal's office.

When we walked into the office the deputy awakened suddenly and slammed his feet out to the floor from where they had been propped on the Marshal's desk.

"What you need fellows?" The deputy said as the Marshal, now also awake, pushed his hat back to better see.

"Fifty dollars, and I would prefer it in gold coin," I said

"You trying to rob us?" The deputy said, lurching to his feet.

"Don't be foolish enough to touch that pistol, friend!" Jacob said.

I turned to the Marshal who, now, was also standing.

"Remember me friend?" I asked. "I'm the one who asked your help in finding those who had beaten my cowhand."

"Oh, yes, I remember you. I told you then and I'll tell you again. Start trouble in my town and I'll lock you up."

Jacob laughed aloud, "Maybe you forget. I'm the one who sent you galloping for your 'mama' the last time you pulled that on us."

"Marshal, you fined that same cowhand of mine fifty dollars for fighting. I came for that fifty dollars and if you're real nice and prompt, I won't charge you another fifty for the use of the money."

"I don't have the fifty. I turned it over to the City Magistrate. You'll play hob getting that money back from him. He'll eat you two for lunch and won't even need a toothpick after."

The deputy chuckled, slyly, at this.

"Who is your magistrate?" I asked.

"He's our ex-sheriff and a tougher man you've never seen!" the deputy said.

"What's his name?" I asked.

"Jamie Nava!" Answered the Marshal.

"All, right you pair of tin horns, let's go see your Magistrate," I said.

The deputy grabbed his hat and led the way, chortling to himself all the way down to the court house.

Jamie Nava's office was as spotlessly clean as it had been the last time I'd been there. His daughter still served as his clerk and her dislike of the Marshal and his deputy was plain on her face. She looked at me for only a moment before turning back to the Marshal.

"What can I do for you Marshal Snyder?" She asked.

"We come to see the Judge. This here cowboy seems to think the city owes him some money!"

The girl said nothing. She stood and went back into Nava's office which now had blinds on the windows and the door painted to block the view from the outside.

The girl was back immediately.

"He says come on in," she said returning to her desk.

We trooped in, with Jacob and I bringing up the rear.

I don't believe Nava recognized me at first, but before the Marshal was done with his taunting tirade, a look of remembrance crossed his face. When the Marshal had finished Nava turned to me.

"And what is your side of the story, Mr. Jackson?"

I would liked to have been able to preserve the look on that deputy's face. It was priceless.

I told the whole story, beginning with Denton's unsuccessful try at cutting my herd. I made it as brief as possible. When I had finished, Nava turned to the Marshal.

"Sounds to me as if you owe this man fifty dollars, Snyder."

"I ain't got fifty dollars. I turned it in to you yesterday."

"Well then, I guess the city will just have to cover your debt. Of course we will take it out of your's and your deputy's pay."

"You can't do that!" the deputy almost shouted.

"Who says I can't, Kelly?" Nava said turning his gaze at the deputy already frightened by his own outburst.

"It ain't right," Kelly whined, "I ain't the one who collected the fine."

"Well, you share in Snyder's part of the fine don't you?"

"Well, yeah . . ."

"Then you will share in it's repayment."

"How do you want your money, Mr. Jackson; gold coin?"

"That'll be fine," I answered.

Nava wrote out a draft and handed it to me.

"Just take this over to the bank and they'll give you your money. Oh, and by the way, I never had the opportunity to thank you for the Stetson. I still wear it."

"It was my pleasure, Judge. And, I thank you for straightening out this matter."

Jacob and I walked across to the bank leaving the Marshal and his deputy to the gentle mercies of Jamie Nava.

"How did you come to know that Judge?" Jacob asked.

"He helped me straighten out a little land title matter when he was sheriff."

"I'd sure have hated to get on the wrong side of him when he toted a badge! I don't know that I've ever seen a man that big."

In less than an hour after arriving in Alamosa, we were on our way back to the Medina's.

We spent a short night in a pine grove four or five miles south of the Medina place. When we rode into their dooryard the next morning, Pedro Medina and Jamie came out to greet us. Jamie was very pleased to take the fifty dollars to Carlos Lopez while Pedro, Jacob and I whiled away a pleasant hour over a late breakfast served up by Senora Medina.

Chapter 20

It was dark when Jacob and I rode into my dooryard. Jacob took my horse and I went on into the cabin. My homecoming, this time, was much better than the last. Bud was at the table playing a game with his sister while Clatilda sat by the stove, sewing.

All three came to greet me. Bud was surprisingly agile on his still heavily bandaged foot.

When the welcoming was over, they all insisted upon hearing the whole story of my trip.

After the children were sent to bed, Clatilda set out a piece of pie and a big glass of milk.

"Will, I am glad this whole mess turned out as it did. I was concerned you might be more involved with Denton than you were."

"Well, I'm glad too. I meant to see he never harmed any of you again. Frankly, Clatilda, I could see no other way than to kill the man."

Clatilda sat with her head bowed for a moment.

"Will, I have news. I don't know how you are going to take it. I hate to burden you with it at this time, but you must know."

I was concerned by her tone and leaned forward not to miss a word.

"I'm afraid I'm going to have another child," she said, looking down at the table.

"That's great news! Why would you think that to be a burden?"

"We've had such bad luck the last two times. First Robert, then little Sarah. I dread the thought of bringing another baby into this world only to lose it."

"Well, we'll just have to see we don't lose this one. Clatilda, I will be glad for more children."

She looked up and reaching across she clasped my hand in both of hers.

"I was so afraid you wouldn't want more children."

That night began one of the most troubling time of our lives.

Clatilda was morose and withdrawn almost the entire period of her pregnancy. Anne Blalock spent much time at our home, and that mainly alone with Clatilda. When Jacob and I started the new house, I expected Clatilda to show some interest but she seemed not to care. We worked long hours raising the log walls of both the house and the barn. When we had some of the men from the church help us raise the roofs on both the house and barn, she and Anne prepared food and kept cool water available. Clatilda did so almost mechanically, and seemingly with no joy or even much interest.

Jacob commented several times about Clatilda's demeanor and how he missed her teasing. To this I had no answer.

The children also were wary of their mother and when Bud's splints were removed, he spent every day with Jacob and me.

The house went up quickly. When we had completed the exterior, including shingling the roof, Jacob went to Santa Fe and brought back terrazzo tile to finish the floors. We finished the house and the barn by the time the Aspen leaves began to turn. That summer had been one of grinding, steady, hard labor. Jacob and I, in addition to putting up the house and barn had, with help of course, brought in a good hay crop, branded our cattle and with Seth's help, we'd also managed to lay in a good supply of firewood for both families. More, than was usual, with the past winter fresh in our memory.

One evening after supper, Jacob and I were sitting on our new porch watching the evening shadows creep into our valley.

"Partner, you suppose you'd miss me too much if I took a little trip for a week or so?"

"Of course not, Jacob. When would you like to go?"

"I thought about in the morning, first thing."

"You coming back?"

"Yeah, I expect so. I've got me this hankering to have another chat with the Widow Buckman."

"You'd better be careful, Jacob, that lady could use a good hand like you."

"I don't know, Will, life gets lonely and I won't go back to what I was when I met you, just to put a little spark in my days."

"Well, Jacob, you go on, and take as much time as you please. We'll be here when, you get back, and so will your job."

Jacob left the next morning and Anna Laura cried for an hour after he'd gone. She kept saying she'd never, ever, see her Mr. Webber again.

There was not much to do around the place. Jacob was a good hand and between the two of us, we had prepared well for the winter. What work I had was mainly in the new house and barn. That fall Clatilda spent much time at the little graveyard, and Anna Laura and William along with Aaron and Daniel Blalock rode into the village each day to school. Ruth Terry, the Bishop's wife had started a school a few years before, and now there were three women teaching the valley children.

I tried several times to talk to Clatilda about her moodiness, but with no real success. She was briefly happier when I moved her into the new house. I had John Terry send away for a new kitchen stove and when it came, it was the talk of everyone who saw it in the store. Clatilda was pleased and made over it some, but it did not seem to really raise her spirits.

In the early fall, I went up and had a long talk with Anne Blalock. She told me she would offer me no real insight, but she said I must be patient for this was something Clatilda would have to work out.

Winter was late in coming that year. We had no snow before the first of December. It was lonely, for Clatilda kept more and more to herself. Jacob had sent word that he'd probably be back by Christmas. But, frankly, I never expected to see him again, short of visiting the Buckman ranch.

I found myself wanting to go somewhere, anywhere. I was restless, lonely and finding myself spending more and more time riding around the ranch and the surrounding mountains. That fall I must have carefully examined every head of livestock on the ranch, at least a half dozen times. I'll swear I was to the point of naming each one. I supplied several families with wild game that fall. I spent more time hunting than I had ever, in my life.

One afternoon, the third week in December, I came in from a hunt to find Clatilda in bed, and in much pain. She sent me for Anne Blalock and by the time I got Anne back to the house Clatilda was well along in childbirth.

Anne sent me to the kitchen, more to be out of the way than for any real chore. Oh, I boiled water and fetched sheets, but I mostly stayed out of the way. Seth and his kids brought supper down, after which, we all sat around waiting.

It was almost nine that evening when Anne came out and

announced that we had a son. When I asked when I could see Clatilda, Anne informed me not yet, that Clatilda still had work to do. She offered no further explanation. Seth and I were both at a loss to understand. The children were, by now, asleep. The Blalock boys doubled up in a spare bedroom.

It was almost eleven when Anne came out and asked me if I'd care to see my new babies.

"Babies!" I said. "More than one?"

"Yes, Will Jackson. You and your sweet wife now have a set of twins. One boy and one girl. Both as pretty as pictures!"

I went quietly into the bedroom not knowing quite what to expect.

"Well, cowboy, it seems I doubled up on you. Do you mind?"

She lay there with her hair spread out over the pillow and two squirming bundles beside her, one in each arm.

"Are you all right, ma'am?" I asked.

"Yes, Will. Are you? Do you mind that we have two more children?"

"Sweet lady, I couldn't be more pleased!" I said, kneeling by the bed. "I'm only worried about you."

"Oh, Will, I'm so sorry I've been such a fool. Anne and I have guessed all fall that I was carrying twins. I was so afraid something would happen. But, Will, they are perfect. A little small, but perfect in every way!"

From that moment, to the day I lost her, Clatilda never again shut me away from her thoughts. And outside of those times, when she would get upset with "her men," as she called us, she was a happy, pleasant woman to the day she went back to her Heavenly Father.

Chapter 21

Shortly after the twins were born I asked Clatilda if she had thought of names for the babies.

"Yes," she answered, "and I hope you approve."

"What are they?"

"I want to name the boy, Jacob and the girl, Jessica."

"I know a couple of old boys that will please!"

"Do you mind?"

"No. As a matter of fact I couldn't be happier."

So Jacob and Jessica it was, and before any time at all, it became Jake and Jessie.

Christmas came and went with no sign of Jacob.

Clatilda asked me, one morning at the breakfast table, if I thought we'd ever see Jacob again.

"I don't know. I about half expected to hear he'd married that Buckman woman. But, I thought if he had, we'd have heard by now. I guess it's possible we've seen the last of Anna Laura's Mr. Webber."

"Don't say anything in front of her or we'll have another crying spell."

After Clatilda was up and around we took the babies to church to bless them. Of course Jess Turner stood in the circle and frankly, although he said nothing, I think he was a little miffed that he was not asked to bless Jessica. He made up for it, however by carrying the little girl around for the rest of the day, never missing the opportunity to call attention to the fact that the child had been named for him. This to everyone he met, to some, twice and, even three times.

Winter began in earnest that second week in January. It snowed for almost a week. First, light and powdery, then heavy, big flakes. By the time it was through, we had almost two feet on the ground. This year was not like the last. I had plenty of live stock to keep both Bud and me going from early 'til late. Ruth Terry sent word that there would be no school in January due to some of the kids' inability to get to town. Bud was happy and so was Anna Laura. Bud had time to be a cowboy and Anna Laura was able to play with the twins to her hearts content.

It turned unseasonably warm the last week in January, and it was just as well. It seemed to Bud and me that every cow we owned took the opportunity to calf. We spent long hours seeing after our ever-increasing herd.

Winter was long that year but in the spring it seemed we went from cold blustery winds and icy rain to green shoots and soft breezes, overnight.

When Bud got out of school, I got him to help me with the branding.

I think he had more fun than at Christmas time. The work went well, and fast.

Clatilda had her hands full that summer. The twins were at an age to demand much attention. Clatilda was only then beginning to become involved with her new house. It seemed every time we went to town, we had some new item arriving at the store and something new to order.

John Terry and I had gone in together to open a small bank in one end of his store. We hired John's nephew, who came over from Salt Lake City, to run it for us. It was an unusual set-up. I believe it to have been the only bank I ever saw to name a corral as one of its assets. We had to have it to accommodate those who were still paying off their livestock loans with new born animals.

I took most of these, however the bank was able to sell some, and at a respectable profit, I might add.

We finally had to buy a safe for the bank. It had gotten to be too much of a hassle using John's store safe. Moving that monster into the bank required several men as well as both teamsters who had brought the safe from Denver.

When we had our first audit meeting in August, that summer, I was astounded, and I must admit, more than a little ashamed at the amount of profit we'd made from the venture.

I argued long and hard and was, finally, able to convince John and Abraham, John's nephew, to lower the interest rates we charged. Abraham felt the old customers would resent new loans being made at a lower rate than they were paying. The solution to that was obvious, we lowered rates straight across the board; old loans and new, alike. At this, Abraham was shocked. He said he'd never heard of such a thing. I asked him if he was happy with his salary and working conditions. He admitted he was quite satisfied. I just looked at him while he squirmed, and John chuckled.

When Clatilda and I were on the way home that evening, I told her what we had done.

She moved over closer to me and linked her arm through mine.

"Cowboy, I guess you'll just never be a real banker, and that suits me right down to the ground."

Supper that night was topped off with a generous slab of fresh apple pie with about half gallon of fresh cream on top.

Chapter 22

Haying that summer had been easy, and with the smaller herd, I didn't cut as much. I turned the herd in on the pastures I wasn't cutting and by the middle of September the whole herd was rolling fat and in great shape to go into, even a bad, winter.

Bud and I were moving the cattle from one pasture to another one late July afternoon when I looked down toward the river and saw a rider coming across the field.

I knew immediately who it was. No one I knew, but Jacob Webber, rode such a sorry looking animal as that pot-bellied grulla. I pointed him out to Bud and we both spun our horses to ride out and meet our old friend.

When we rode up to him, I was shocked. No other word described the Jacob Webber I saw that afternoon. Mean. He looked hard and drawn into himself.

"Hi, Mr. Webber," Bud was the first to speak.

"Hello, Bud. Well, Will, I'm back. Didn't quite get here when I said. Did Clatilda break my plate, or do you suppose I could beg a meal?"

"Anytime, old friend. You look tired."

"I've seen some hard country in the last year. Most I'd like not to see again."

"Come on, let's go on up to the house. We've got a couple of surprises for you."

"Yeah!" Bud said, "A pair of them."

We said little beyond Jacob's comment on the cattle and range conditions on the way to the home.

Clatilda was standing on the ramada when we rode up. After the initial greetings, she said she had been where she could see out the kitchen window and had recognized Jacob immediately.

We went to the kitchen where Clatilda served us cold milk and fresh baked cookies. After setting the milk and cookies on the table, she disappeared into the back of the house.

Before we'd finished our snack, Clatilda and Anna Laura emerged from the bedroom with two bundles. Anna Laura walked straight up to Jacob and turning so that Jacob could see into the bundle. "Mr. Webber, I'd like you to meet Jacob Jackson!"

I'll swear, I thought Jacob was going to break down and bawl. He looked at little Jake every way he could but did not touch the baby or even it's blanket.

"Here, Mr. Webber, don't you want to hold your name sake?" Anna Laura said reaching out with the baby.

"I wouldn't know how," Jacob said, physically drawing away from the child.

"Here, I'll show you," Anna Laura said stepping around to Jacob's side.

Looking at Jacob, I couldn't help laughing. I believe if he could have, he would have run.

Between Bud and Anna Laura, they finally got little Jake into Jacob's arms. Jacob didn't move, he hardly even breathed. He just sat looking down in the baby's face.

Clatilda brought little Jessie in and showed her to Jacob. He was nice enough but he wasn't much interested in anything but the young man in his arms.

At first, I thought he held the baby because he didn't know how to turn loose of it. But, as the afternoon wore on it became clear he didn't want to release Jake. Two or three times Clatilda offered to take Jake from him but each time Jacob refused. At first tentatively and then firmly. It was clear he wanted to hold the boy.

Finally Clatilda took the babies back into the bedroom to feed them and put them down for naps.

Several times before supper, I questioned Jacob about the past year. But, he would only say he'd tell me later.

After the supper dishes were cleared Clatilda practically had to drive Bud and Anna Laura to bed, but then that was finally over.

We were still at the table, Clatilda, Jacob and me, dawdling over pie and milk when Jacob sat back in his chair.

"Partner, I owe you an explanation as to why I broke my promise to be here last Christmas."

"No, you don't. I'm sure you had your reasons."

"Yeah. But let me say this, because I'd like never to talk of it again."

"What ever you want," I said.

"Well, as you know, I went down to see the Widow Buckman when I left here. We got along pretty well. Did you know her name was

Cecila? Same as my mother's. Anyway, I was kind of working around, helping her crew. They finally got rain and things were looking real good. The stock was fattening up and everything was greening up right well. You know, partner, I don't know how I ever got up the nerve, but one Sunday afternoon, we went for a ride, Cecilia and me. And, I just right out asked her to marry me. Scared myself half to death. But surprised as I was at myself, I was even more shocked when she said yes. I was right happy. We figured to get married Christmas Eve and take a trip up here so she could meet Clatilda. You would have really liked her ma'am."

I looked at Clatilda and watched as one big tear ran down over her cheek.

"Well, things just didn't work out like we'd planned. Right after the first of December Cecilia got real sick. At first, she said she didn't feel like getting out of bed. She didn't have a fever or anything, but she said she just felt weak. One of her hands was married and had a cabin south east of the main house. So, one afternoon I rode over and got his wife to come and see Cecilia. While she was there, she got Cecilia into her robe and we tried to get her up out of bed. She couldn't stand and by noon the next day, she was completely paralyzed. She got worse and right quick. I sent one of the hands to Las Vegas to see if there was a doctor there. But, before he got back, we lost Cecilia. She seemed to smother. She couldn't get her breath. I stayed for the funeral then I drifted. I was all over that country for several months. I worked a while for an old boy down south. Then, I got a hankering to see your Uncle Buck. Don't know why, but I did. So I lit out for the Cimarron country. I ran into a mess. When I got there, I found your Uncle Buck and Aunt Gladys living in a little old tar paper shack out east of town. I went first out to his ranch, but a couple of hard looking old boys told me, in short order, that he didn't live there anymore. When I found Buck, he was in pretty bad shape. He'd been shot twice and was having a hard time getting better. They didn't even have money to buy bandages. Your Aunt Gladys had been cutting up her petticoats and sheets to make bandages.

All I could get out of Buck was that his place had been taken away from him by some folks that claimed they held his marker for a gambling debt. Well, now you know, as well as I, that Buck Harris wouldn't even bet on the sun setting to the west. I talked to the sheriff and even to a magistrate and they claimed to have seen the marker, and there was nothing they could do. I tried to tell them Buck never gambled. But, neither one would listen, You know how Buck always stuck to himself. In the couple of years I knew him, I don't think he was off that ranch half a dozen times. I asked the sheriff about Buck's wounds, and he said Buck had confronted the new owner and his foreman and had been shot in the gunfight that followed. Now, you know the only firearm Buck Harris ever used was a saddle gun, and that old twelve gauge he'd hunt prairie chickens with. So, I went out to see this Glen Martin that now has Buck's place. The first time they run me off. There was four of them, Martin, and his Segundo, a big fellow name of Perea, and a couple of hands. I waited and caught Martin and Perea in town, by themselves. I did for Perea, but Martin got me down low in my side. When I came to, I was in jail. The sheriff kept me there until I was able to ride, then he ordered me out of town. I'm sure I got lead into Martin, but the sheriff wouldn't talk to me. He just brought my horse to the front of the jail and gave me five minutes to get out of town. I came here."

Jacob then seemed to relax as if a heavy burden had been removed from his back.

"How are you now, Jacob? Should we see about your wound?" Clatilda asked.

"Oh, no ma'am! I kind of loafed along on the way up here. It's just a couple of pink scars now. One in front and one in back."

"Jacob, what about Uncle Buck and Aunt Gladys?"

"I don't rightly know, partner. While I was there, I saw to it they had what they needed and I'd given Gladys forty dollars the morning I had the trouble with Perea and Martin. But, that's been almost five or six weeks now. I just don't know."

"Will, can you leave in the morning or do you need time to arrange things here?" Clatilda asked.

I looked over at this woman. I knew I would never quite understand her. Every person I'd ever known, to whom so many things were absolutely black or white, had such a narrow and unbending view of everything. But, not my Clatilda. To her some things were just to be done. This, it would seem, was to be one of them.

I went to the Blalock's that evening and arranged for Aaron to help Bud while I was gone. Seth and Anne promised to look in on Clatilda and the kids.

Clatilda and I talked that evening about how I was always sky-tooting around the country, leaving her alone.

"Cowboy, there's just two things I want you to promise me."

"Anything!"

"Be careful, my husband. You don't know what I ask."

"If there is anything I can give you, you know you have only to ask."

"All right. First, I want you to bring your Aunt and Uncle back with you. It sounds like he will need more time to recuperate from his wounds. And, even if they want to go back to their ranch, it will make a nice visit."

"Whoa, wait a minute. Who says they will have a ranch."

"You and Jacob said your Uncle never gambled."

"That's right."

"Well then, if that's the case then he couldn't have lost it, and you'll straighten things out and get his ranch back."

"I'll try, but I don't know everything I'll be getting into."

"Well, anyway, you'll get his ranch back, then you all can come back up here. Your Uncle Buck and Aunt Gladys can stay here with us or if they want, they can have the cabin."

"All right, miss fix-it, and what's your second promise?"

"I want to ride the steam cars next summer. I want to go to Denver City then ride the cars to Salt Lake City. Then I want to go to the Temple there and then we'll come home overland. As I remember, the country is beautiful. I'd like the children to all see it."

I looked at this woman and thought of all she had been through and all she had been to me.

"I'll make the second promise on one condition."

"What's that?"

"That you will always be mine."

"Cowboy, that's why I want to get you to the Temple, in Salt Lake City. I intend to tie you up for longer than always!"

"Longer than always!" I thought. "With my Clatilda! Not a bad deal."

Chapter 23

Jacob and I did not get away as early as I'd planned. It was mid-morning before we left.

Jacob had said his goodbyes to all but, had lingered longest with Anna Laura and little Jake. I thought, as we rode off, that I'd best watch myself or Jacob would have two of my children as his own. Not by capture, but simply sweet surrender.

It was a pleasant day, that fall day as we rode east. We passed a nice hour in the Medina home. Jamie told us that Carlos Lopez had regained most, if not all, the sight in his injured eye. That was the best news of all.

We, once again, camped just east of Saguache. I couldn't talk Jacob into the stage stop. The second night we made it to Fort Garland, then on to Eagles Nest. Then, finally, on a dusty evening we rode into Cimarron.

I couldn't believe the condition of my Uncle Buck and Aunt Gladys. They were starving to death. There was half a loaf of stale bread on the table, and barely, a cup of beans in a pot on back of a cold stove. Not another morsel in the house and not a penny with which to buy anything. I thought then of the people in that town and area that I knew my Uncle Buck had helped over the years.

Jacob went out immediately and brought back two tow-sacks full of groceries. Neither of the old folks could tolerate much besides some scrambled eggs and fresh bread Jacob had gotten at a café.

When we checked Uncle Buck's wounds, we found they had healed nicely and the old man would probably be fine with a couple of weeks of good food and worry-free rest.

Jacob and I camped right outside the folk's back door. When I came in the next morning I found Uncle Buck sitting at the table eating a piece of bread.

Jacob fetched wood and we fixed a breakfast fit for a king. Aunt Gladys ate sparingly, but with relish. I thought Uncle Buck would eat right through the bottom of his plate and into the table. He even had a glow on his cheeks when he finished.

Aunt Gladys excused herself right after breakfast. I assumed she was going to lie down.

I asked Uncle Buck if he felt like talking to me about his situation. He said he felt better than he had in a while and would like, very much, to tell me what had happened.

What he told me fairly well matched Jacob's story except for a few additional points.

He told me that Martin had tried, very publicly, he added, for two months to buy the Spur Quarter Circle before coming up with the phony marker.

"How did he get you in a gun fight, Uncle Buck?" I asked. "I never knew you to carry a pistol"

"Never did. Always thought to do so was just asking for trouble. But, a couple of weeks before the shoot-out, someone took a shot at me three separate times. Since then I've been thinking about it. Those three shots missed me by such a wide margin I don't believe they were trying to hit me. I think they were only trying to scare me into carrying a pistol. It worked!"

"Let me ask you something, Uncle Buck," I began. "If we were able to get your place back, would you and Aunt Gladys move back out there?"

"No, son, I'm afraid my days running a ranch are over. These wounds have just taken too much out of me, and even your Aunt Gladys. Besides if I could get title back to my place, John Hennessey of the Ladder Y was talking to me about buying it to add to his spread, just the day before I got shot. Said he was going to see Jim Baker over at the bank that same day."

"What about livestock and equipment, Buck?" Jacob asked.

"Oh, they were smart! That marker was real detailed. It covered everything; lock, stock and barrel, even the little cash I had on deposit at the bank!"

"Who has that marker now?" I asked.

"The last I heard, Judge Wagner said he would keep it on file for a year or so, 'to avoid any complications;' as he put it."

"What about your sheriff?" I asked.

"You mean Hoffman? That short horned idiot don't have enough sense to pour sand out of a boot, even if you was to write the directions on the bottom of the heel! He'll do whatever Wagner tells him to do."

"How well do you know this Wagner?" I said.

"Not well, he just moved down here from Colorado as a lawyer about five years ago. Then, when old Judge Simpson died, he was the natural choice. Jim Baker, from over to the bank, made a sort of half-hearted attempt to get the job, but even he admitted he probably didn't know enough about the law so he stepped aside for Wagner. I never really had any dealings with Wagner before this marker thing."

"Was there any kind of hearing or such?"

"Oh yeah, I couldn't go. Gladys went and she said there wasn't much to it. She told them I never gambled, but Martin had four 'witnesses.' No matter, three of them worked for him. But, the fourth witness was that idiot Hoffman. Anyone that knows me would tell you that even if I did decide to do some dumb thing like get into a poker game with the likes of Martin and Perea, I wouldn't allow Hoffman in the same room."

"When were you supposed to have got into this card game?"

"The night before I was shot. Martin claimed he was trying to bargain with me or collect, but I got mad and went for my gun. Truth of the matter I was on my way over to Hennessey's to fetch your Aunt Gladys from a quilting bee Faye Hennessey had given for her new daughter-in-law. He jumped me on the road. Right on my own place!"

"Uncle Buck, Jacob and I are going over and talk to Sheriff Hoffman and Judge Wagner. Will you be all right 'til we get back?"

"Be all right, if your back by dinner. I don't aim to wait much after noon to eat again. I'll tell you boy, I really enjoyed that breakfast and am already looking forward to dinner."

Jacob and I both laughed with the old man and went to the front room to leave. We found Aunt Gladys putting the finishing touches on cleaning the room. We could see into the bedroom to the freshly made bed.

"Never been so ashamed of my house in my life, as these past few weeks. I'll swear I didn't even feel like sweeping the floor."

"You be careful, Aunt Gladys," I said. "There's plenty of time after you get your strength back."

"Boy, having you and Jacob here is all the rest I need. I heard what you said to Buck. You be careful now, you hear?"

We assured her we would and left to saddle our horses.

"Partner, you really think I ought to go with you?" Jacob asked as we were working with our mounts.

"Why, because Hoffman ordered you out of town?"

"Well, yeah, that's a good place to start."

"Here," I said handing Jacob several gold coins. "Call this a loan or advance on your pay, or whatever. About the only way Hoffman could order you out, and make it stick, is if he could prove you a bum. With that money in your pocket, he might find that tough to prove."

Jacob reluctantly took the money, then put it in an empty leather sack he took from his pocket.

We rode into town to the sheriff's office. He was sitting on the walk, out front, with his chair leaned back against the building. At first, as we rode up to the hitch rail he seemed not to recognize Jacob. But, as we dismounted, I heard the front legs of his chair slam down on the planks of the boardwalk.

"I thought I ordered you out of this town, drifter!" The man fairly shouted.

"Just a minute, sheriff. We'd like to just talk to you for a minute," I said.

"Who are you?" He demanded.

"Name's Will Jackson. I'm from Colorado and I'm Buck Harris' nephew."

"What's that old man doing, importing gun hand's for his revenge?"

"Nope. I'm just here to see if we can't straighten this matter out peaceably."

"Ain't nothing to straighten out. That old man lost his spread in a fair poker game and then tried to shoot his way out. He was lucky he wasn't killed."

"I understand you were in the game," I said.

"No, I was just watching. But I sure saw that old man lose and more money than he had. That's why he had to give Glen Martin his marker."

"Did you see him sign the marker?"

"I sure did. I was standing right at the table when he wrote it out and signed it."

"Do you suppose I could see that Marker?" I asked.

"I reckon so. Judge Wagner has it over to the courthouse. Won't do any good, but go on over. I 'spect he'll let you see it, you being kin, and all. But your Pistolero is going to have to leave."

"Why?" I asked.

"Why, the last time he was here he killed Martin's foreman and shot Martin in the leg. I'd have held him for trial but some solid folks said Perea drew first and Martin also joined in. But, that don't change nothing. He's still a drifter, and I'll not have such loafing around my town."

"How do you define a drifter, sheriff?" I asked.

"Like everyone else. A broke down, out of work cowboy, feeding off his betters on the grub line."

"Mr. Webber is my ranch foreman and I believe he has sufficient money for his needs. Would you be kind enough to show the gentleman, Jacob?"

Jacob took out the leather pouch and emptied its contents in his hand which he then reached toward Hoffman.

Hoffman's eyes narrowed at the sight of the gold coins.

"Don't matter. He's a danger to the town so he must leave."

"Has Mr. Martin been given such an order?" I asked.

"Well, no . . ." Hoffman said.

"Let's go over to the courthouse, maybe the Judge can settle this. In the meantime you can come with us and make sure we don't cause any trouble."

It was a grumbling sheriff who accompanied Jacob and me to the courthouse.

We were able to see Judge Wagner immediately.

When he asked my business, I explained my relationship to Uncle Buck and asked only to be allowed to examine the marker.

Judge Wagner willingly produced the document. Written on cheap paper and in pencil, it was still quite legible.

"Let me ask you again, sheriff, you say you saw Buck Harris write and sign this paper?"

"Yes siree, if you look down in the right-hand corner, you'll see my initials and Perea's. Course, Perea's dead now, thanks to your pistolero, but I'm not, and those are my initials. Put there to witness your uncle's signature."

"Well, I've got just one thing to say;" I began, stepping away from the desk upon which lay the document,"you, sir, are a liar!"

"Judge's chambers, or not, don't you ever call me a liar! I won't stand for it!"

"I don't care what you'll not stand for. If you say you saw Buck Harris write and sign that document, you are a liar!"

"Just a minute, Mr. Jackson," the Judge said, stepping around from behind his desk, "that's a pretty bold accusation. How do you intend to prove it?"

"It's really pretty simple, Judge Wagner, if anyone claims they witnessed Buck Harris write and sign that document they are, on the face of it, a bold-faced liar, and for one simple reason. Buck Harris can neither read or write!"

"Are you sure of this?" The Judge asked, reaching around and picking up the document. "His signature seems clear."

"That's just it, judge. When Buck Harris signs anything, he uses his 'Mark'."

"What is this 'Mark'?" The Judge asked.

"Simple, he uses his brand. A spur and a quarter circle."

"Have you any way of proving this?" Judge Wagner demanded.

"He may not, but I sure have!" Jacob said.

"When I was here four years ago, Buck bought those shorthorns he was so proud of. He borrowed part of the money from the bank. I came to town with him and Gladys. They met John Hennessey and Buck and Hennessey went over to the bank together. I'll bet Hennessey and that banker can both straighten this out."

"That's easy," the Judge said, "let's all take a walk over to the bank."

We made quite a parade as we headed across the street to the town's bank.

Jim Baker, the banker, was pleased to see the Judge. Maybe not so pleased to see the rest of us.

"Jim," the Judge began, "this is Buck Harris's nephew. He has questioned the signature on the marker Harris gave to Glen Martin on Harris' ranch.

"Let's see the marker," Baker said. "I know Buck Harris' signature as well as my own."

The Judge handed over the marker.

"I've heard you witnessed this," Baker said to Hoffman, who by now was noticeably nervous.

"You bet I did," Hoffman answered, "and this baloney about Harris not being able to read or write is just that, baloney. I seen what I seen."

"Well, Mr. Hoffman, I'm afraid you might have some explaining to do," the banker said, turning back to the Judge. "I can settle this right now."

He went to a cabinet on the wall of his office. Extracting a paper from one of the drawers, he turned and spread the document on his desk.

"This was a note Buck Harris signed four years ago when he borrowed the money to buy those shorthorns he was so proud of. As you can see, it is witnessed by John Hennessey and there, gentlemen is Buck's mark. The Spur Quarter Circle. Same as his brand. Buck Harris has never learned to read or write. He always brought his friend Hennessey to make sure of what he might be signing."

He pushed the note around so we could all see the document, which incidentally, was marked "Paid" in big letters across the face of the note.

Judge Wagner turned to Hoffman.

"Mr. Hoffman, your badge, please."

"You can't take my badge! I was elected!" Hoffman sputtered.

"Sir, I can not only take your badge, but I am placing you under arrest. And, as soon as I can find a suitable person to take your place, I intend to see Glen Martin in a cell next to yours."

Jacob and I stood to one side as the play unfolded in front of us. He and I both touched our pistols when it looked, for a moment, that Hoffman might resist the Judge. But Mr. Hoffman ran true to Uncle Buck's description. He quietly handed his badge to the Judge.

We went back to Uncle Buck's to give him the news while Wagner and Baker, the banker, went about jailing Hoffman and rounding up a crew to send out to bring Martin in.

Judge Wagner, after inquiring if Uncle Buck would be able, had told me to have him at the courthouse the next morning.

Uncle Buck just closed his eyes and sat right still for a couple of minutes after I'd told him the news.

"Webber," Uncle Buck said, "I need you to do me a favor. I want you to go out to John Hennessey's place and tell him I need him to be at that hearing tomorrow morning. Can you do that for me?"

"You bet, Buck! I'll be back for supper, Gladys. Make this worthless nephew of yours bring in some more stove wood. I plan to be hungry."

Nine o'clock the next morning was quite a show. This fellow, Martin, and Hoffman were brought into court by a big burley fellow now wearing Hoffman's badge. Hoffman and Martin were both in chains.

The banker, John Hennessey, and I told our stories about Uncle Buck's inability to read or write. The Judge then turned to Uncle Buck.

"Is this true, Mr. Harris. Do you neither read or write?"

"It don't give me no pleasure to admit it judge, but that's a fact. I can cipher pretty good. I have to know numbers to take care of my ranch and herd, but as for letters, I can neither read or write words," Uncle Buck said, his head slightly lowered.

Aunt Gladys had her hand on Uncle buck's arm as he admitted his illiteracy; I could see the slight pressure as she squeezed his arm, in gentle affection and encouragement.

"Mr. Martin," the Judge began, turning his attention to the two men in chains, "would you or Mr. Hoffman care to tell me again how Mr. Harris wrote and signed this marker you used to steal his ranch and livestock?"

Everyone in the room, including Martin and Hoffman heard the Judge use the word "steal." At that point we all knew it was all over, save for the shouting!

Hoffman and Martin both tried to bluff and bluster their way out of the hole in which they found themselves. But, Wagner was having none of it. He turned to the big fellow wearing Hoffman's badge.

"Mr. Haney, will you please take Mr. Hoffman and Mr. Martin back to their cells. The first of next month, I will see they are tried for rustling, grand theft and attempted murder. And, oh yes," he said looking out over the crowd until he located Jacob, "Mr. Webber would you be interested in filing charges against Mr. Martin? I understand he and his late foreman tried to cause you harm."

Jacob stood up and looked at Martin for a moment. "No, Sir, Judge, I'd say you've got everything pretty well roped and tied!"

A ripple went through the crowd, and Mr. Baker laughed out loud. Even the Judge grinned.

"Very well, Mr. Haney you may take your prisoners away. Now, Mr. Harris," he said turning his attention to Uncle Buck, "I don't know what kind of deed you had to your ranch, but I'm sure some sort of certificate of ownership can be found. If you and your wife will come back at two this afternoon, I will have the distinct pleasure, and I must admit to, some shame, in seeing that your property and livestock, and all other property of your's covered by that phony document, are officially and legally returned to your control and ownership. Now, I will close this session for I want to see that the document I present you this afternoon, Mr. Harris, is properly drawn up and duly signed with every stamp and seal I can find in this courthouse."

A subdued but strong ripple of approval went through the crowd. As we left the courtroom, several men came to shake Uncle Buck's hand and congratulate him.

Uncle Buck turned to John Hennessey."John, you still want my place?"

"Yeah, but don't you and Gladys want to stay there 'til you get back on your feet?" Hennessey answered.

"Nope. I've done my ranching. I'm afraid this little fandango has taken too much out of Gladys and me both."

"Well, sure, Buck, I still want your place. How do you want to take care of the sale?"

"Can you afford the price we talked about?" Uncle Buck asked.

"Well, most of it and Jim Baker agreed, when you and I first talked about it, to take a mortgage on your place for the difference. I expect we could close the deal about anytime you choose."

"How does ten tomorrow morning suit you?"

"Right down to the ground, friend. I'll see you at the bank tomorrow morning."

The court hearing that afternoon was pretty simple. Judge Wagner presented Uncle Buck with a court order which verified his ownership of his ranch and all livestock carrying the Spur Quarter Circle brand as well as all tools and equipment to be found, as of that date, on the ranch, plus all monies found on the ranch and on deposit at the bank, in Martin's name. Uncle Buck asked the Judge if the order could be used to transfer ownership of the ranch.

"Yes, Mr. Harris, you may use this order as you would a deed or bill of sale."

It was a happy crew that sat down to supper at Aunt Gladys' table that evening.

After supper, as we sat around the table, I asked Uncle Buck what he intended to do after tomorrow when he would once again be homeless.

"I figured to see Jack Horton about building Gladys and me a home here in town. He's been letting me use the shack for free, and he's a pretty good carpenter. I may still be homeless, but I'll tell you something, boy. After I sell that place tomorrow, I ain't ever going to be hungry again!"

"How would you like to see Colorado?" I asked.

"Is it as pretty as everyone says?" Aunt Gladys asked.

"Yes, ma'am, I'd say it's right pretty country."

"Is it as cold as everyone says?" demanded Uncle Buck.

"You've forgotten what it's like to be rounding up strays and get hit by one of those blue northers, out on your own place?" I asked.

"Yeah, but I hear the only weather you get up there is ten months of winter and two months late in the fall."

Jacob laughed and said, "Get him to tell you about the light snows they get up there!"

"Uncle Buck, we have pretty hard winters sometimes, but we have the nicest spring, summer and fall seasons you could ask for."

"Well, I don't know. Maybe Gladys and I'll get up there next year or the year after that."

"Well, Uncle Buck, that kind of puts me in a corner."

"How's that, Will?" Aunt Gladys asked.

"Well, my wife Clatilda is, right now, getting ready the cabin we lived in before I built our new home. She told me to bring you and Uncle Buck back with me and you are to live with us in our house, or if you prefer, you can have the cabin."

"Will, you never told me you were married!" Uncle Buck said.

"There's a whole lot of things he ain't told you!" Jacob said.

"Such as," Uncle Buck said.

"Well, he goes to church right regular and he's got four of the best looking younguns you've ever seen. He even named one of them Jake, after me!"

"Is that a fact, Will?" Aunt Gladys asked.

"Yes, ma'am, although it was Clatilda that stuck our poor baby boy with that awful name."

Jacob sat right up in his chair.

"Will Jackson, you may be my boss, but you say anything like that again about little Jake and I'm going right to Clatilda when we get home."

We all sat for a moment before we all broke out in laughter.

"Now, now," said Aunt Gladys, "if you school girls don't straighten up, I'll send you both to your room."

We talked well into the night. First about my family. Then I really got Uncle Buck's attention when Jacob and I told him about my ranch.

We all went to bed without any real agreement on anything.

The next morning, after breakfast, Jacob and I took Uncle Buck and Aunt Gladys to the bank. The sale of Uncle Buck's ranch took less time to close than it does to tell about. Uncle Buck was pleasantly surprised to find Martin had, on deposit at the bank, more than three times the amount in Buck's name when he had been shot and stripped of his ranch. Aunt Gladys did make a request that, at the time, seemed strange. She had Uncle Buck keep a team of draft animals and his big hay wagon in addition to a Jersey milk cow. The milk cow I understood, but the hay wagon and team kind of threw me.

As we were leaving the bank, I had two questions for Uncle Buck. First why did he require payment for his ranch to be in gold when he was just going to leave the money in the bank's safe? Second what in the world did Aunt Gladys want with a hay wagon?

"Well, boy, your Aunt Gladys intends that you and Jacob put sides on that hay wagon so she can get all her stuff in it when we go to Colorado. And, I wanted gold so when we leave, I don't have to fool around with any of that paper junk. I lost almost five thousand dollars on that Confederate specie. Don't like paper money."

Just like that it was decided. Jacob and I spent the better part of three days preparing the wagon to Aunt Gladys' satisfaction, and loading her furniture; even a small organ.

The morning we pulled out, Jacob and I on the wagon, and Uncle Buck and Aunt Gladys in a buggy. Uncle Buck laughed and said he felt like a kid again, off on an adventure.

We stopped by the bank and picked up Uncle Buck's gold coin. This we stored in a heavy metal box Uncle Buck already owned. He had us place in a compartment we'd built in the floor of the wagon.

We made pretty good time. I'd guess we made twenty, maybe twenty-five miles that first day out of Cimarron. But, of course, we had a road, of sorts. The rest of the trip to Taos took longer than we'd hoped. When we could, we kept to any trail or road we found. But, in that country and at that time, wagon roads were chancy at best. When we finally got to Fort Garland and I told Uncle Buck that we would have a pretty good road, at best to Monte Vista, Jacob and I had trouble keeping up with his buggy.

I had hoped we would reach home in the daylight, but the sun was going down as we went past John Terry's store and I knew we would be close to midnight. I knew Uncle Buck and Aunt Gladys both had to be worn plumb out. But, when I offered to find a place to stay in town Uncle Buck refused.

"Didn't you tell me it was only six or seven miles on out to your spread?" He asked.

When I said it was, Aunt Gladys said if Jacob and I were up to driving the wagon, they were surely up to a "nice little ride in a comfortable buggy."

We went on home.

As we pulled around our house and to the barn, Clatilda and the two oldest children came out with lanterns.

After the introductions and hugging was over, the children and ladies went on into the house while Uncle Buck, Jacob, and I saw to putting the wagon and buggy inside the barn, and turned the horses into the barn pasture.

When we got inside, Clatilda, bless her heart, had hot stew, fresh bread and about enough apple cobbler to fill a number two washtub.

"How did you know when we would get here?" I asked as Clatilda served the cobbler.

"Mama's made a pie or cobbler every night for the last week!" Anna Laura said. "It's been real nice. She was going to make gooseberry pie tomorrow night. That's my favorite. I sure wished you'd waited another day!"

Everyone laughed and Aunt Gladys who was sitting next to Anna Laura reached over and hugged her.

"Maybe tomorrow your Aunt Gladys can make you a gooseberry pie. Would you like that?"

Anna Laura looked at Clatilda, "Would that be all right, Mama?"

"Of course, baby. That'll be just fine if your Aunt Gladys feels like it.

After the late supper, Clatilda took Uncle Buck and Aunt Gladys into one of the spare rooms which now held a new bedroom set I'd never seen.

"I hope this will be all right," Clatilda said. "We can fix it up as you like or, as Will probably told you, there is a cabin if you'd prefer."

I could tell Clatilda was nervous and as soon as everyone went to bed, I sat her down in the kitchen.

"Are you concerned about the folks being here?" I asked.

"Well, yes and no. I just want them to be comfortable."

"They are. And, tell me, where did that new furniture come from?"

"From the store, where else? Do you mind?"

"No, not really. But, it was a surprise. How did you and Bud get that big old chifforobe out here?"

"Oh, that was no problem. Seth and Bud brought it out. Are you sure you don't mind?"

"Wouldn't matter if I did, would it?"

She looked at me sharply, then seeing the grin on my face, relaxed.

"Not much, but if you really minded, I'd make you take it back by yourself. I wouldn't even let Bud help you!"

"Oh, I know how hard you can be, lady. I'm still waiting, after all these years, for that raise you promised, even before we were married."

"Will Jackson, I never promised you a raise, and anyhow, didn't I buy you a new saddle just last year?"

"Huh! That's because you wanted to make sure I'd have no excuse not to ride night herd on your cows."

"Don't push it cowboy, remember, you're talking to a propertied woman!"

It was so good to be home again.

Chapter 24

I was lying awake, watching the room lighten with the rising sun, when Clatilda came into the room.

"You'd better get up, Will, your Uncle Buck is sitting out on the front porch. He has his spurs in one hand and his gloves in the other. It's just a guess, but I think he's waiting for you to show him the ranch."

After I'd dressed, I went out to find Uncle Buck patiently sitting on the front porch, as Clatilda had said.

"Thought you were going to sleep all day!" Was his greeting.

"When did you get up, or did you ever go to bed?"

"Got up with the sun! Always have. 'Cept for a time there when I was getting over being shot. Always got up and did my house chores before breakfast. Don't guess you people got any house chores. Don't even see no chickens."

"Oh, yes, we have chickens. The house is down behind the old barn. We have so many fox in this country, we have to put them up at night."

"Say, I was noticing that you have two barns. Running a dairy?"

"Nope," I said, sitting down on the porch rail. "Just decided to build a new barn when I built the house."

"Nice place. How many kids you say you have?"

"We have four."

"I must have counted at least ten rooms when I got up. You running a hotel?"

"Uncle Buck, why don't you and I go pick out a couple of saddle horses and I'll show you around the place, then when we get back, we'll have breakfast."

"Be sure and tell your wife when we'll be back. I like my coffee hot. Ain't had a good hot cup of coffee since we left Cimarron!"

"Sorry, Uncle Buck, we don't have any coffee."

"That's all right. Gladys has some in her wagon. She can get it."

"No, Uncle Buck," I began, turning to face him, "I mean we don't drink or serve coffee in our house."

He looked steadily at me for a moment.

"Ever?"

"Never."

"Well, now, ain't that something. I guess, then, I'll have to have some sweet milk. You do allow sweet milk in your house?"

"Oh, yes sir. We have an uncommon amount of sweet milk!"

"Sweet milk, you hear. Won't drink that buttermilk, the ladies favor."

"We have plenty of sweet milk, Uncle Buck."

"Good then, let's you and I go see this place of yours."

I went in and told Clatilda when I thought we'd be back for breakfast, and we went out to the barn to get Uncle Buck's saddle out of his wagon. We found Jacob throwing down hay for the animals.

"How much hay you got room for?" Uncle Buck asked.

"We probably keep close to fifty or sixty tons in the loft," I answered.

"Boy, where do you get stanchions to support that?" He asked.

I walked him over to show him the tree trunks we had bracing up the loft.

"How come you got iron bands around the stanchions?"

"We put them up when the logs are still green. The band's keep the logs from splitting as they dry."

"Well, this is a whole different country than I've ever seen. I guess I'll be asking questions like a kid. Hope you won't mind."

"That would be pretty bad if I did. Especially seeing as how you come to be the one who taught me most of what I know about ranching in the first place."

We covered the ranch fairly quickly that morning. I did no more than touch the high spots. When we got back to the house, I headed for the barn.

"Ain't you got a hitch rail at your house?" Uncle Buck asked.

"Sure, but I thought we'd put the horses up before breakfast."

"I'd rather see the rest of your place after breakfast. That is unless you have work to do."

"Nothing that won't still be there tomorrow," I said turning toward the house.

Clatilda and Aunt Gladys had a feast prepared for breakfast. I saw Jacob actually lick his lips.

After breakfast was over Uncle Buck sat back and was drinking the last of his milk.

"Ain't bad milk, boy. Not as good as coffee, but ain't bad, at all."

"Buck, you just be quiet about coffee. Clatilda told me they don't drink coffee, so we won't either."

"I know that already. Will laid the law down to me before we went for our ride."

At this, Clatilda looked sharply at me.

"Uncle Buck, I didn't 'lay down any law,' I just said we don't keep or drink coffee!"

"That's what I said. You told me you don't have coffee. That's your law, and it suits me just fine."

"Sir, it's not a 'law' we 'lay down,'" Clatilda said, "it's just our belief, not meant to insult our guests."

"A belief should be a law to those who believe. Ain't nothing wrong with that. Besides, Will told us we were family. Not true?"

"Of course, it's true. It's just I didn't want you to feel uncomfortable."

"Young woman, I'm almost seventy and my woman's only a few years younger. There ain't much, anymore, that doesn't make us just a little bit uncomfortable. But, I'll warrant you, there ain't nothing my family can do, or wants me to do, that will cause me much discomfort. As long as you and Gladys get along, me and the boy here will try to stay out of you ladies way."

Clatilda looked at him for a moment; then stepped over to the stove and placing a piece of ham in a biscuit she brought it to Uncle Buck, handing it to him, she reached down and kissed the old man on the cheek. "This is in case you get hungry later."

"Get away from me, young woman, I'm a married man!"

Clatilda slapped him playfully on the shoulder and went into the kitchen with Aunt Gladys.

Uncle Buck and I went out and once again I began showing him the ranch, but this time we made a more detailed inspection.

By mid-afternoon, Uncle Buck had eaten his biscuit and ham, and had seen the entire spread.

We went back to the barn where we found Bud and Jacob cleaning stalls.

"Well, Buck what do you think of this layout?" Jacob asked.

"Nothing need's fixing as near as I can tell." Uncle Buck said, "Except maybe, I'd run a few more head of stock."

"Would you believe that up to a couple of years ago, Will was running about five hundred head?"

"That'd be about right. What happened, boy, bad winter?"

"Well, yes, but not until after he'd sold his herd," Jacob answered. "Would you believe this guy drove his entire herd to Pueblo and sold them not thirty days before the beginning of the worst winter I'd ever heard of, let alone seen!"

"What made you do that, son?"

"It seemed like the thing to do at the time," I responded.

"Yeah, well Bud says the 'spirit prompted' him to do it."

"You know, that's not so hard to believe. About eight or ten years ago, I got a feeling about combing my bunch out of the arroyos and draws down on the east end of my place. You two recollect where I mean. Well, I got the urge to get them cattle out of there and right then. I got my crew together and we put in a couple of the hardest days I've ever seen; but, the next morning after we'd driven the cattle up on that mesa north of the main house, it came a cloud burst like you never seen.

Why some of those arroyos were spilling over their banks and them twenty to thirty feet deep. It rained 'til afternoon like I've never seen. Then all of a sudden it quit. But, it was three, four days before you could ride plumb across that country and some of those cuts had mud holes for better than a month. Oh, you bet, I've heard that 'whispering' in my ear!"

Jacob stared at the old man then looked at me.

"How come you two get these feelings and I've never had such a thing."

"Clean living, Jacob, and hard work. Some day maybe you'll put those two together." Uncle Buck teased.

"This from an old geezer whilst leaning against the wall and I'm cleaning stalls," Jacob humphed, and went back to his work.

When we went into the house to try to find a snack, we found the women and babies gone. Anna Laura was busy with her dolls in the living room.

"Where's your mama?" I asked.

"She and Aunt Gladys took the twins and went up to the Blalocks. Said they would be stopping back by the cabin."

Uncle Buck and I found some milk and leftover biscuits and honey. We were so engaged when Clatilda and Aunt Gladys came back. Both talking and laughing like a couple of school girls.

When they walked in the door, Clatilda put the twins down on the floor and turned to me.

"Will, I'm afraid Aunt Gladys and I have come up with another project for you men."

"Only when and if they find time," Aunt Gladys said quickly.

"Don't give them that out, Aunt Gladys, or they'll never get it done!"

"What's this project, woman?" Uncle Buck demanded.

"Uncle Buck, Aunt Gladys and I just came from the cabin and she loves the place. And, Will if you and Jacob can drill a well on the south side of the house, you can then close it in, like we have. That way Aunt Gladys can have an inside well in a new kitchen!"

"When do you want us to start this 'project'?"

"Well, it's still pretty, so if you started tomorrow morning, I'll bet you could get the whole thing done before the snow flies!"

"If we do that we'll have to postpone your trip."

"That's all right. Aunt Gladys and I are going to be too busy this summer anyway."

"What trip?" Aunt Gladys ask,

"Oh, just some foolishness of mine. It'll be better next year anyway."

"You sure?" I ask.

"Absolutely!" Clatilda said, ending the matter.

We didn't get done before the snow flew. We finished chinking the walls and building a new porch in between the first two storms of the season.

That was all right. We spent the time during the second storm installing Aunt Gladys' new stove. After she saw Clatilda's, there was nothing to do but Uncle Buck had to order her a similar one. She made him a bargain. She said if he would get her the new stove she would always have cinnamon rolls for him. Uncle Buck had a real sweet tooth for cinnamon rolls. From the time he and Aunt Gladys moved into the old cabin, it always smelled slightly of cinnamon and scorched sugar. In addition to that lingering pleasant odor, you could generally find Bud and Dan or Aaron Blalock hanging around Aunt Gladys' kitchen between chores. They too, liked cinnamon rolls . . . a lot.

That first winter Uncle Buck and Aunt Gladys lived in the cabin was quite an initiation for them. It wasn't as bad as some had been, but we did not see the bare ground from mid-November until Easter.

I know Uncle Buck grew weary of the snow, but he said he just kept reminding himself of the Indian Summer we had enjoyed. He said he'd never seen prettier weather in his life.

Spring came, as it often does in the high country, over night.

I came out one morning to find Uncle Buck sitting on the cabin porch, holding a glass of milk and a cinnamon roll big as a plate.

"Little cool to be sitting on the porch?" I asked as, a greeting.

"Maybe, but a real good morning to ride around the countryside!" He responded.

"Well, let's do it!" I said. "I was going down to see how our new calf crop is doing, if you want to come along."

He jumped up and went into the cabin to return immediately, without the milk and roll.

We were shortly, in the saddle, headed toward the south pasture.

"I've never been so fed up, staying inside, in my life. Next winter you're going to have to set up a few chores for me. Either that or I'm going to take up knitting!"

"Uncle Buck, I was thinking about that the other day. If you want, why don't you pick up a few head of stock. You can put your own brand on them and run them in with mine."

"We'll see," was his terse response.

I thought no more about it until later in the morning when we stopped to water our horses.

"How many you figure your outfit could stand?" Uncle Buck asked.

"How many what?" I asked, having forgotten my earlier comment.

"Spur Quarter cattle!" He answered.

"Well," I answered, "I've run as high as over five hundred head plus my horse herd. I'm running less than a hundred now, and about half the horses I used to run."

"Think you'd have any problem with a couple of dozen, or so?"

"Absolutely not! The only thing is, I don't know where, short of way east of here, a hundred miles or so, you'll find that many for sale."

"I do."

"Where?"

"Right back there about a half a mile."

"I have no stock for sale."

"You gonna keep all them calves?"

"I'd not thought of that. Why, sure, I could sell you fifteen or twenty calves. Mixed stuff, even."

"Good. How much you asking?"

"What did you sell your last bunch for, down in Cimarron?"

"Last weaned calves I sold, I got six dollars apiece."

"I'll tell you what, you help us with the branding next month and I'll let you have your pick. Twenty head for a hundred even."

"Done, and done!" Uncle buck said.

When we rode up to the house for dinner, Aunt Gladys was just going to our place. So Uncle Buck came in with me after we'd cared for our mounts.

"Well, old woman," Uncle Buck said as we walked into the kitchen, "we're in the ranching business again!"

"Ooh?" Aunt Gladys said.

"Yep! Will just sold me twenty head of his new calves. It'll be a few years before we'll be ready to sell anything, but we won't go hungry. With a spud farmer on one side and rich relatives on the other, we're gonna be all right!"

Even Jacob chuckled.

Chapter 25

We finished the branding early that year. Mainly because Uncle Buck was anxious to get his calves branded with the Spur Quarter Circle.

We stood around the fire after we had worked the last of the calves.

"Best looking cattle in the country!" Uncle Buck said.

"Well, we have a nice herd but as for being the best looking in the country, I don't know about that."

"Ain't talking about the herd. I'm talking about them Spur Quarter Circle calves."

"Yeah, they'll be all right if they survive the branding. Where in the world did you get that iron. I almost got stoop shouldered just carrying it back and forth to the fire," Jacob joked.

"Ain't nothing wrong with that iron. Made it myself."

"Out of what, a railroad rail?"

"Beats that cinch ring I caught you with the first time I ever laid eyes on your sorry self!" Uncle Buck said.

"What's that?" I asked.

"Oh, it's nothing," Uncle Buck said glancing at Jacob. "Just a little joke between Jake and me."

"You might as well tell him, Buck, cat's out of the bag now."

"Oh it ain't nothing, Will, you know Jake had a drinking problem once, don't you?"

"He's mentioned it."

"Well, he and a couple of his saloon buddies got drunk once and I caught them with a hot cinch ring trying to change a Spur Quarter brand. Wasn't nothing. I put him to work and run off his worthless partners. Wasn't a big thing. Just some fellows out on a toot."

Jacob had nothing to say the rest of the day as we herded the cattle into new pastures.

We were washing up for supper when I saw Jacob leading that pot-bellied grulla out of the barn. His bed roll and sack of possibles were tied behind the saddle. I walked out on the porch as he tied his pony to the hitch rail.

"Going on a trip?" I said.

"Yeah, I figured to draw my time and slope off down the road."

"Why?"

"Oh, I figured after what Buck told you today, you might not want to have a thief around the place."

"You still have those gold pieces I gave you in Cimarron?"

"Yeah, never quite figured they were mine," he said pulling the little leather sack from his pocked. "You want them back?"

"No, I was just wondering why you'd think I'd let a thief keep over a hundred dollars this long?"

Jacob looked sort of sheepish and stared down at the ground.

"Jacob, I won't stand in your way if you want to leave, but Clatilda's going to be madder than an old wet hen at you."

"Why?"

"Well, she's been after me to take her to Denver so she can ride the steam cars. I figured to leave you to run the place 'til we get back. Figured to be gone most of the summer. But if you're leaving, that will change everything."

"You mean you'd let me run this place after you knowing I'd tried to steal cattle from your uncle."

"Tried, but you wasn't crooked enough to get it done. Just drunk enough to try!" This from Uncle Buck who'd stepped out on the porch behind me.

"Now, I'll tell you what, Jake. Me and Will are going to take a stroll down by the barn. Clatilda and Gladys are in that kitchen right now making plans for that trip on the steam cars. It seems she's invited Gladys and me to come along. Partner, I purely don't want to be around them women when they're told their dream is going up in smoke. So, while Will and I go down to the barn, you go tell them ladies that as a result of your quitting, they won't get to take their trip."

With that Uncle Buck and I started to step off the porch.

"Now, hold on. I'm not going in there and upset Clatilda, or Gladys either!"

"Ain't but one way it can be helped," Uncle Buck said.

"You mean you'd leave this whole ranch for me to take care of?"

"Why not?" I asked.

"Knowing what Buck told you?"

"Jacob, you forget you told me over a year ago that Buck Harris had sobered you up and road-staked you."

"Yeah, but I didn't tell you about trying to steal his cows."

"No, he told me that today. And frankly, Jacob, I'd give a hundred dollars to have seen you, half drunk, with a hot ring in your hand trying to change a Spur Quarter brand. Tell me, friend, just what in the world were you trying to change that brand to?"

Jacob stood there for a moment then mumbled something.

"What did you say, Jake. I didn't hear you?" Uncle Buck said.

"Bar-Sunburst Circle," Jacob said only slightly louder than a whisper .

"Bar-Sunburst Circle?" Uncle Buck said.

He looked at me for a moment and we both laughed.

"Who'd you figure to sell your cows to, Jake. Some dude with a liking for sunflowers?"

Jake lowered his head further still.

"Oh, Jake, stop this foolishness. Take that poor excuse for a horse back to the barn and get ready for supper. With your imagination for brands, I don't think I have any worries. If you rustled any of my stock, you'd probably try to sell them to Seth Blalock."

"He buying stock?" Jacob asked as he led his pony to the barn.

Uncle Buck couldn't resist the temptation. He told the whole story, including Jacob's brand at the supper table.

"Shame on you, Jacob Webber!" Clatilda said, when Uncle Buck had finished his story.

"Ma'am, I was drunk. I was plumb out of my head. I was stone lucky Buck Harris didn't shoot me on the spot."

"Oh, Jacob, I'm not talking about that foolishness. I'm talking about you're almost spoiling our trip to Denver!"

"Ma'am, I'm real sorry. If I'd known, I'd never have thought about leaving."

"Mr. Webber, Anna Laura spoke up, "Will you, for sure be here when we get back?"

"Yes he will, baby," Clatilda said. "And for a long long time after. Isn't that right Jacob?"

At that moment Clatilda could have asked Jacob for his hand and I'm sure he would have found a way to give it to her.

"Yes'm I 'spect that to be so. If you'll have me."

"Oh, we'll have you, Jacob, and with pleasure and trust," I said.

Chapter 26

It took a buggy and a surrey to get our crowd to Denver. I hired Jamie and Al Medina to go with us, and they were to bring the horses, buggy and surrey back to our place. I think they would have been happy just to go along for the ride, what with our staying and eating in hotels most of the way. That is except for the two days and nights we spent with the Stanton's. Clatilda had seen Hester Turner in the store and when she told Hester of our impending trip, Hester made her promise to stop by her sister's. She had even given Clatilda a letter to take to Pearl Stanton. I believe more to assure we would stop by the Stanton's than to communicate any important information. When we arrived at the Stanton's, the Medina boys and I could just as well dropped off the ends of the earth. Pearl Stanton and Clatilda immediately became fast friends, and Aunt Gladys fell in, as with a pack of thieves. Uncle Buck and Earl Stanton hit it right off, also. They got busy right away, and had no time for anyone else. Fact was, Jamie, Al and I felt pretty alone for awhile. Oh, we were fed well, and regular, but there seemed to be little we could add to what had become fast friendships. I continued to be amazed at how closely Clatilda and Pearl Stanton resembled each other; not physically but in just about every other way. When we left the parting was not happy. Both women seemed really sorry to be separating.

We could have caught the train in Pueblo, but we would have had to wait three days and we were too excited to hang around that long.

When we got to Denver, I couldn't believe what I saw. There were more people, houses and buildings than I'd ever imagined. Why they even had two buildings over three stories tall. They were working on a new railroad station. But it wasn't done then.

It didn't matter, we all boarded the train anyway. After we were aboard it didn't matter whether we'd come out of a fancy depot or off a wooden platform.

As we rolled out of Denver I couldn't understand, as we seemed to be going backwards.

I stopped the conductor and asked him about it. He said we'd back up into Cheyenne then go straight out from there.

"But, sir," Clatilda said, "we're not going to Cheyenne. We're going to Salt Lake City."

"That's right, ma'am. We go first to Cheyenne, then to Ogden, Utah. There you take the shuttle down to Salt Lake."

He then went on about his business, while Uncle Buck and I watched the prairie roll by. The women were busy trying to settle down the children. Bud had refused to sit with the "kids" and sat beside Uncle Buck.

Nighttime settled as our train pulled out of Cheyenne behind three of the biggest machines I'd ever seen. Uncle Buck and I watched as they switched the mountain engines onto our train. They were monsters.

Shortly after we left Cheyenne, the twins started complaining their heads ached. We were at a loss until a porter came by and told Clatilda to hold their noses and then pat them sort of hard between their shoulder blades. He claimed it was the change in elevation that was stopping up their ears. It worked. Of course, then Anna Laura had to have the same treatment. This had to be done twice more before we reached Rawlins.

We all got off at Rawlins for a midnight supper. The food was good but Uncle Buck and I noted that we'd never seen as many rough looking men. It seemed everywhere you turned was another wearing two, sometimes three guns in plain sight.

"Wouldn't be the sort of place a fellow would want to complain about much of anything, would it?" Uncle Buck commented.

We were both a tad uneasy until a cowboy, who clearly had a drink too many, lurched against Aunt Gladys' chair causing her to drop a fork full of food, already half way to her mouth.

Before Uncle Buck or I could even get up, two of those hard looking hombres stepped over from the counter. One on each side of the cowboy, they physically lifted him until his feet cleared the floor.

One of the men took off his hat and bowing slightly to Aunt Gladys, said quietly, "ma'am I sure hope you'll excuse this cowboy. We'll see he don't cause you no more trouble!"

With that, they carried the hapless young man to the door. From the sound, I'd guess he bounced twice, maybe three times, when he hit the boardwalk.

When the two came back to the counter, the one that had been on the off side of the cowboy, nodded and tipped his hat to Aunt Gladys. His quiet, "sorry ma'am" was hardly hearable.

"Now, aren't those two real nice young men," Aunt Gladys said.

Uncle Buck and I looked again at these two hard-eyed gents well enough armed to start a war with just about anyone. Somehow, "nice young men" seemed not to fit.

But, in all honesty, Uncle Buck and I both sat a little easier after that incident. The rest of the night was long and jolting. Just before noon the next day, we pulled into Ogden freight yards as the conductor came by.

"Folks, there are going to be a lot of people come up to you and offer to carry you to Salt Lake City. Stay away from most. They will charge too much. Take one of the regular stages, or you can wait until late this afternoon, about five, and take the shuttle."

"Which way will give us the best view of the Salt Lake?" Clatilda asked.

"Why ma'am, I believe that would be any one of the stages."

I'd never seen so much water all together like that. Clatilda said it was too salty to drink and if you tried to drink it, you would get real sick.

As we rode past the temple that first time, I just couldn't believe my eyes. I'll swear it was just about the prettiest thing I'd ever seen, and far and away the biggest man-made structure. I've seen the sun come up over the mountains in the winter in just such a way to turn a snow covered peak bright pink, but that temple was the grandest sight I've ever seen. We luckily found right nice rooms just up the street from the Temple.

After we were settled in our rooms and were taking a short rest before supper, Uncle Buck knocked on our door. When I opened it, he and Aunt Gladys stood there.

"Will, we have something to ask you," Aunt Gladys said.

They came in and Uncle Buck stuttered and stammered around for a moment then came right out with his problem.

"Will, I ain't seen anybody in this whole town carrying a weapon. Even the teamsters we saw didn't seem to be armed. Will, I've carried some sort of firearm all my life. Before the trouble with Martin it was mostly a long gun but your Aunt Gladys has carried a derringer in her purse for years. You suppose maybe we shouldn't?"

"I don't really know, Uncle Buck, but from what I've seen and from what Clatilda's told me, I don't think it will be necessary. At least I've already stowed mine in my valise. You do what you're a mind to, but I really don't think you'll need them."

It was, by then, late enough that we gathered up the children to go out and find a place to eat. We went no further than the parlor of the home where we were staying. The lady of the house met us and said she was in the habit of providing meals for her lodgers, and would be happy to do so for us. We were well pleased not to have to go to the trouble of finding a café. At the end of the meal, we were not only happy, but well fed, also. We gladly took all our meals with Sister Mitchell while we were there.

The next morning, Clatilda the children, and I went down to the temple. We went inside and Clatilda talked to a lady there.

We found the letter Bishop Terry had given us was quite good enough to allow us the privilege of the temple.

When Clatilda and I got back to Sister Mitchell's that afternoon, I was a little stunned and Clatilda shown like a spring sunrise.

"Well, come on, now," Uncle Buck said when we were seated at the supper table. "Tell us about your experience in the temple."

"Well, I really can't tell you everything that went on, except to say it was quite an experience and one I won't soon forget," I answered. I did explain the process of sealing the wife to the husband and the children to the parents.

We spent another week in Salt Lake City. The kids and ladies had a big time, but Uncle Buck and I were some restless.

I talked to some of the teamsters I came upon and they strongly advised against a cross-country trip back to our valley. They said that due to the heavy snows this past winter and much spring rain, all the rivers were running bank full and many of the available ferries were not even working.

It was decided we would ride the steam cars back to Denver and the ladies could pick up what they'd been planning to buy, there. The sight seeing would have to wait for another time.

By the time the ladies had completed their shopping in Denver, I had to buy a wagon and a team to carry all they bought. It took better than a week to get home from Denver. I think there are few sights that have ever pleased me so much as the sight of our home.

The cattle looked good, the graze appeared to be in fine shape and Jacob had already put up one cutting of hay. I thought, as we drove by the stack-yard, that I would have liked to have been in the priesthood meeting when Jacob Webber arranged for help with the haying. Bishop Terry had promised to send someone to the ranch to tell Jacob when the meeting to schedule the help was to be held.

Jacob met us at the barn and helped with unloading the wagon.

The women and children went on to the house and to bed for it was almost dark, and we all looked forward to a night in our own beds.

The next morning Uncle Buck, Jacob and I took a ride to look at the cattle. Everything looked to be in top shape, and I told Jacob he had done well.

"Just one thing, Will, some guy by the name of Emil Glaston came out one morning. He said he was a good friend of you and Clatilda. He wanted I should let him have two head. He said he was having a shindig over to his place and wanted them for his big feed. I told him I couldn't sell any stock without your say so. He insisted I give him the two head, and he'd settle up with you when you got back."

"Did you give him the cows?" I asked.

"Well, no, I didn't, and he left here hopping mad. He said he'd have my job the minute you got back."

"He couldn't handle your job! Don't worry about it. I doubt he'll ever say anything to me. But, if he does, I'll tell him you acted just as I would have."

"Well, that's a load off my mind. There was only two problems while you were gone. That's one and the other was having to go to that meeting to get help for the haying. Wasn't so bad after I got there, but I was scared to death before."

"That's how I felt the first one I ever went too," I said.

"Man, I'll tell you something, there were twelve of those old boys came out to help with the haying. They darn near worked me to death. There was one old boy; he must be seventy years old, if he's a day. That old man swung a scythe like a machine. I'll swear he kept a sulky-rake busy, all by himself!"

"Jess Turner?" I asked.

"Yeah, I think that's what he said his name was. When we got through the first day, he asked if it would be all right if he did a little fishing in your creek before he left. Said he would like a mess of fish and didn't have time to go all the way over by his place. Darned if he didn't sit out there for almost an hour before he'd caught all he wanted. Only then did he head for home. Toughest old man I believe I ever saw!"

"That was Jess. You're right, he's about as tough as they come."

Chapter 27

We had a late fall that year, and again Uncle Buck commented on the beautiful weather. Many evenings, after supper, he'd hitch up a buggy and he and Aunt Gladys would take a long ride. Often it would be after dark before I'd hear the trace chains rattling as they drove back into their door yard. About a week before Christmas, Jacob and I were in the barn when Uncle Buck came running.

"Where's Clatilda?" He shouted.

"She's up at the Blalock's. What's wrong?" I asked.

"Something's wrong with Gladys. I can't wake her."

I grabbed a pair of bridles and the two horses we had in the barn. I went out in a gallop. It took less than fifteen minutes to have Clatilda back to the cabin. We left her buggy and the twins at the Blalock's.

Clatilda went directly into the bedroom. She came out in only a few minutes. She walked over and put her hand on Uncle Buck's shoulder.

"I'm sorry, sir. She's gone."

Uncle Buck stared at her for a moment, then went into the bedroom, closing the door behind him.

"Let's let them be for awhile, Will. Why don't you go up and get the twins and the buggy. Tell Anne what has happened and ask her if she can come down and help me."

I brought Anne and the twins back to our house where I found Clatilda preparing dinner.

"Has Uncle Buck come out yet?" I asked.

"No, and I think you might want to go see about him," Clatilda said as she continued at the stove.

I found Uncle Buck sitting at their kitchen table. I asked how he was doing and he just shook his head.

"Is there anything I can do for you, sir?"

"No, son. Oh, I don't know, I seem not to be able to think what to do. I just don't know where to turn."

"Uncle Buck, I never heard you or Aunt Gladys mention it and I never thought to ask, but, did you have any children?"

"We had two. Both are buried on the old place down to Cimarron. Lost both at birth."

"Uncle Buck, would you let Clatilda and I take care of everything?"

"Yes, son. I was going to ask you if we could put Gladys in your little graveyard. I know it's only for your family, but I'd be right grateful."

"Of course we'll put her there. She's family. Where else? Besides Seth and Anne Blalock buried their daughter there when they lost her four years ago. There are many we consider family. Surely you and Aunt Gladys, above all."

I built Aunt Gladys' coffin, and we had Bishop Terry take care of the services. Clatilda and I had not expected much of a crowd. We were wrong. We held the service in our house. There was no room left.

After we had buried Aunt Gladys, most people left quickly, but, there were some who lingered for an hour or so. Finally, after all were gone, we found ourselves seated around the table.

Clatilda turned to Uncle Buck.

"Uncle Buck, would you like to move over here? You can have the big room at the back of the house. It has it's own outside door and it should be real nice for you."

"Clatilda, I hope you don't mind, but I'll stay in the cabin, if it's all right."

"Of course, sir, but you can take your meals with us. About that, I'll not argue."

"I would appreciate that. The thing is, Gladys and I slept in the same bed for over forty years. I think there's still something of her in that room."

Uncle Buck worked harder that winter than he should, but no one said anything to him. We understood his need and while we said nothing to him, one of us tried to find ourselves near him all the time.

By the time school was out that spring, Bud and Uncle Buck had developed quite a friendship. Saturdays had become their day and often they would be gone from before daylight until after dark. Sometimes they would tell us where they had been, but often not.

Late in May, Uncle Buck and Bud came up to the barn, in a rush.

"Pa, Pa!" Bud yelled as he came running into the barn.

"Slow down, Bud," I said.

"Pa, we got rustlers!"

Uncle Buck came in behind Bud.

"He's right, Will. We found their tracks up the mountain over east of the Blalock's. Then me and Bud went down to the stack-yard. Near as I can tell, they got away with about twenty or thirty head of your stock and all of my yearlings."

"You mean someone's got away with almost fifty head!" I said.

"That's what it looks like. Bud and I didn't go back on the mountain. We came straight here from the stack-yard."

I sent Bud for Jacob, who was over by the west creek. After saddling my pony, I went into the house. I briefly explained the situation to Clatilda.

"Be careful, Will. I remember the last time we had this problem."

Jacob, Uncle Buck and I rode out, after sending Bud, who wanted to go, to the house.

We went, first to the stack-yard where I confirmed Uncle Buck's estimate of our losses. I had Jacob and Uncle Buck stand still while I circled the area. I picked up the tracks east of the river. We were able to follow them at a long lope. Soon we started up over the mountain, east of the ranch. I wondered how we could not have heard the animals or have not seen them. The trail we followed was fully visible to the ranch for almost two miles. The only conclusion I came to was the theft had occurred at night. There had been no attempt to cover the trail. But, then, how do you cover the trail of forty or fifty cows.

The trail dropped off the eastern side of the mountain then north into a long, narrow valley. We had ridden three or four miles when I stopped. I turned to Jacob.

"Jacob, you ride on east 'til you hit that ridge then head north. Go along the west side of the ridge for an hour. I'll wait here 'til you reach the ridge. Uncle Buck, you go back into those trees where we came from, then you go north, for an hour."

"If either of you spot our cattle, come right back here. I'll go right up this valley. We'll all meet back right here in two hours. If we haven't seen anything, we'll all go on up the middle of this valley together."

Two hours later, we were all back where we started. I was the only one who had seen anything. I'd followed the tracks of the herd right up the center of the valley.

We all continued, together, up the valley, beyond where I'd stopped.

We had gone about three miles beyond where I'd turned back when the cattle tracks began to separate. The herd seemed to have been allowed to mill, and small group's had broken off from the main herd. As we sat and studied the tracks, Jacob reached over and touched my shoulder.

"Look in there," he said.

I looked into a grove of small spruce to see a group of eight of my cows quietly grazing. Two of them were even lying down. Jacob went to gather the small bunch. By dark we had thirty-four head in a small meadow we'd found among the trees on the west side of the little valley.

We made a cold camp along side the meadow and were up and around before the sun.

I left Uncle Buck to watch the cattle while Jacob and I searched out the remainder. I rode over a small hill and almost into the dooryard of a small cabin. There was smoke coming from its chimney and three cows in a corral. There was even a fresh hide laid out on the roof of a lean-to shed beside a small barn.

I backed quickly into the trees and sat watching the setup. I immediately went back to the meadow where I found Jacob and Uncle Buck. Jacob had found five more head.

I explained what I had found. When Jacob asked how many men I thought might be in the cabin, I had to admit I had no idea. The only explanation I could offer was their horses must be in the barn.

I asked Uncle Buck to stay with the herd while Jacob and I went back to the cabin. He didn't much like it, but he reluctantly agreed.

We stopped in the trees where we could see the cabin and barn without being seen.

"I know there has to be at least three in there," Jacob said. "There were the tracks of at least three different horses driving that herd. There may be more in that cabin."

"Let's leave our horses here and see if we can sneak up to the backside of that barn. Maybe we can find out how many horses they have," I said.

We went back into the trees and found we could circle around and put the barn between us and the cabin.

It was easy to get to the barn without being spotted. Inside we found four horses, but only three saddles. No wagons, buggies or harness.

As we stood, watching the cabin, the door opened and a kid came out and headed for the barn. He didn't look much older than Bud.

He was headed straight for the barn. So, Jacob and I stepped aside so that when the door was opened, we'd be behind it.

The boy was whistling some tune I'd never heard as he came across the yard and into the barn. Jacob grabbed him from behind and I threw a saddle blanket over his head to muffle any outcry.

Jake quickly tied his hands with a piggin string and I slowly removed the blanket from his head.

"Make one sound, kid, and it'll be your last!" I said.

His eyes were about the size of silver dollars and he had turned white as a sheet.

"Don't shoot me!" He whined. "I ain't done nothing."

"What about the cattle in your corral and that hide stretched across that shed roof?" I demanded.

"Cecil claimed rustling was done all the time out here. He said if we was careful, we'd be all right."

The boy had an accent I couldn't place. He also had the look of a rat. No other way to describe it. He looked just like a cornered barn rat.

"Where you from, kid?" I demanded.

"Me and Cecil come from New York. Gene is from New Jersey."

"What in the sam-hill you kids doing clear out here stealing other peoples cattle?" Jacob asked, stepping in front of the boy.

I glanced down and saw he had a pistol stuck in his belt. When I pulled it from his waist, it was a short barreled .32 caliber. A woman's gun!

"What's your name?" I asked.

"Allen Doyle."

"All right, Allen Doyle, what are you supposed to be doing out here?"

"I came out to get some meat off that cow carcass hanging yonder."

I looked over to see three quarters of one of my heifers hanging from a rafter. It was covered with green flies.

"Don't any of your bunch know how to take care of meat?" Demanded Jacob.

"Ain't nothing wrong with that!" He said. "We was real hungry, and Gene says his uncle worked in a slaughter house. Said he knew how to take care of it."

"Tie him to that stall," I told Jacob, "and, put a gag in his mouth. You and I are going to have a talk with Cecil and Gene."

We made no attempt at stealth. We simply opened the cabin door and stepped in.

The two young desperados were at a broken table drinking coffee.

"It took you long enough!" One said turning to see Jacob and me standing inside the now closed door. We both had drawn and cocked our pistols.

Both of the young boys stood and took a step backward.

"Don't move," I said. "Just stand still. You make one false move and you will hurt for a long time, or never again."

Jacob stepped over and found both to be unarmed. We found two ratty old shell belts and holsters hanging on one of the bunks. Both held, almost brand new, Colt revolvers.

"Little better fixed than Mr. Doyle," Jacob said.

I asked both their names. One was Cecil Green and the other, Gene Cable. Both had the heavy accent first voiced by Allen Doyle.

"I got just one question for you two hard cases," Jacob said. "Just what in the world are you three doing in this country?"

"We came out here to start a ranch," Gene, the smaller of the two said.

"With what?" I asked. "An abandoned cabin and someone else's cattle?"

"Well, we read where lots of the big ranches got their start that way," said Gene.

Oh, no! I thought. "Here we go again."

I turned slightly to Jacob and briefly explained my previous experience with this attitude.

"Kid, I've been through this before. Some greenhorns from back east thinking life out here is like it is in the dime novels. The last time I tried to be easy with those folks. It was a mistake. You know what we do with rustlers out here?"

"You ain't gonna hang me!" This from Cecil.

"So, you do know what your stupidity can cost?"

"That don't matter. You ain't hanging me!"

"Now, just who do you think is going to stop me?"

"The law! They won't let you do it. And, if you do, they will get you!"

"What law, punk?" Jacob asked. "There's not a lawman within a week's ride in any direction. We hang you and my great grand kids might find your skeletons. Maybe not."

Gene began sniveling, "We're sorry, mister. We didn't mean no harm. We was just trying to get us a ranch."

"I've heard enough," I said. "You keep an eye on them while I tie their hands."

I stepped around Gene to get at Cecil's hands. I reached for a length of rope hanging over the back of one of the chairs at the broken-down table.

"Look out, Will!" I heard Jacob yell, just as I felt the searing pain in my left shoulder. Then the cabin was filled with the roar of pistol fire.

I was on my knees holding onto the seat of one of the chairs, when Jacob got to me.

"Be still, Will. That punk stuck a butcher knife in you. From the looks of it, it's the same one they used to skin that cow."

When Jacob pulled the knife from the top of my shoulder, just outside my neck, it hurt almost as much as when I'd been stabbed.

"You stay right where you are, Will," Jacob said. "I want that to bleed out some, as filthy as that knife was. Maybe the bleeding will cut down on the infection. I'll go get a bucket of water and clean you up."

It seemed Jacob was gone a long time but I wasn't sure because I passed out and the next I remember, I awoke on one of the cabins bunks.

Uncle Buck was there, along with Jacob and Allen Doyle.

"Where's the other two?" I asked.

"How you feeling, son?" Uncle Buck asked.

"Real light-headed, but not too bad. 'Course, my shoulder hurts. Where's Cecil and Gene?"

"They're out in the barn," Jacob said. "They won't be doing any more rustling."

"Both dead?" I asked.

"Yep, just as dead as I could make them. I don't know what they were thinking? Stabbing you with me holding a gun right on them."

"Sounded like a war up here." Uncle Buck said. "I came a running, but it was over by the time I got here."

"We got to get you out of here and back home where you can get better care," Jacob said.

"What you gonna do with me?" Allen Doyle asked.

"Maybe you don't want to know, kid," Jacob responded.

"You ain't going to hang me, are you?"

"No, kid." Uncle Buck said standing and turning to face the boy. "We're going to do worse than that."

"What . . .?"

"You have a horse in that barn, out yonder?"

"Yes sir."

"All right, we're going to go saddle that horse and put you on it. I'm then going to let you start riding northeast. I'll give you a slow count of ten. Then I'm going to start shooting. If you ride hard enough, maybe I won't hit you." So saying, Uncle Buck took Doyle by the arm and shoved him out of the cabin door.

A few minutes later we heard a horse leave the yard at a gallop. A few seconds after that we heard the boom of a rifle. Eight shots later, we then heard five pistol shots.

Uncle Buck came back into the cabin with a wicked grin on his face.

"Did you hit him?" Jacob asked.

"Shoot no," Uncle Buck said, "wasn't even aiming at him. But, I'll bet he don't get that pony stopped much this side of the Kansas line. I never seen any one flog a horse like that. That kid will think a while before he tries another stunt like this."

I was able to ride, so Uncle Buck went on toward home with me while Jacob rounded up our cattle to herd them on back.

By the time we got home, I had a raging fever and my shoulder was badly swollen.

Clatilda had me in bed within minutes and I remember little of anything, for what I was told later was several weeks.

Chapter 28

I had been fully awake and up and around for almost two weeks when one morning I was sitting on the front porch when I noticed smoke over the mountains northeast of the barn.

Uncle Buck was coming out of the barn, leading his saddled horse. I called for him to come to me.

"You have any idea what that might be?" I asked, pointing toward the smoke.

"Never knew smoke to be good news, unless there was a chimney at the bottom," he answered.

"Uncle Buck, saddle me a horse, while I get a jacket. Might be we'd better look into that."

"You sure?"

"That we'd better look into it?"

"No, you sure you're up to riding?"

"It's about time I did something. You saddle me a pony and we'll go see."

I went into the house for a coat and was met by Clatilda.

"What are you doing?" she asked.

"There's some kind of fire over east of here. Uncle Buck and I are going over to check it out."

"Are you sure you should? You're still awfully pale."

"That's because I've been sitting around for over a month, mostly inside."

"You be careful, then. Here, I'll make you two some food to take with you."

She shortly handed me a plump package and a brief hug.

I went out just as Uncle Buck led our horses up to the porch.

"You all right with this, girl?" he asked Clatilda.

"Not really, Uncle Buck, but I've expected him to break out for a week now."

We rode out of the yard at a shambling trot until we had just cleared the barn. I happened to glance up at the smoke column to get my bearings. As I did so, a larger puff of smoke pushed the column higher as if some larger fire had erupted.

The urgency I felt was unexplainable for what ever was happening was clearly beyond my control and even if I had been at the fire site there would be little I could do but watch.

Nevertheless, we spurred our horses into a sharper pace as we headed up the side of the mountain.

I was more afraid of a wildfire or even a forest fire, than anything else. Although it seemed far too early in the spring for either. The ground over which we rode was still mostly muddy.

It took us almost an hour to reach a ridge where we could look down on the source of the smoke.

We sat staring down trying to distinguish the fire.

"Well, I'll be!" said Uncle Buck. "You know what's burning?"

"Not sure. But from the direction, do you suppose it's that old cabin and barn?"

"I'd bet a dollar that's exactly what it is. Let's just go make sure."

We rode the rest of the way to the fire at a much slower pace. Even so, I was feeling the effects of being horseback for the first time in over a month.

We slowed to a walk while still in the trees before we reached the fire. We could, however, see that the conflagration was indeed the cabin and barn.

We pulled up at the edge of the tree line.

"Rock bound cinch that fire didn't start itself," I said.

"How you figure?" Uncle buck asked.

"Wind's blowing away from the barn. Cabin fire started first. It's just a bunch of embers and ashes. That barn's no more than half burned. Someone started both those fires."

"Why?"

"I don't know, but we'd better watch ourselves. Whoever set those fires may just still be here."

We carefully rode round both the barn and burned out cabin. There were at least two sets of horse tracks, but no footprints that we could find.

We stayed around until a while after noon. The barn had fallen in on itself leaving only smoldering embers of both the cabin and barn. Both had been so dry they had burned like a tinderbox.

When we left, there was no fire, few sparks and little danger of either spreading.

That the fires had been set, I had no doubt. But, as we rode home, we couldn't figure out why.

We had just topped the ridge and headed down into the valley when we heard a rider in the trees ahead. We stopped and waited. Soon, Aaron Blalock burst into the open, riding much harder and faster than he should have been.

"Whoa, up," I said as he came toward us.

"Uncle Will!" He began shouting. "You gotta come to our house!"

"What's wrong, son?"

"Pa says there's trouble at your place and you're to come to our place before you go home."

"Just exactly what's wrong, Aaron?" I asked. "And how did you know where to find us?"

"Dan seen you and your Uncle Buck riding toward the fire, and Pa sent him to your place to see if we could help. He got there just as these two fellows rode up to your dooryard holding guns on Mr. Webber and Bud. They made them go into your house and then went in after them. Dan came home, and after a bit Pa sent me after you folks. I had some trouble finding your trail."

"Don't surprise me none, boy. Next time you're looking for a trail, slow down. It'll help," Uncle Buck said.

"Why does your Pa want us to come to his place? The troubles at my house," I said.

"Pa just didn't want you riding into a surprise."

"Well, you go tell your Pa to sit tight. Uncle Buck and I'll come to your place if we see we need help. In the meantime, you ease on back and come into your place from the north. That way you can't be seen from my house."

Aaron was reluctant to leave without us but did as he was told.

I turned to Uncle Buck "You know, there's been something in the back of my mind ever since we came upon that burning barn. I believe that fire was deliberately set to lure someone away from our place. I'm not sure they thought it would be me. I'm wondering if they thought to catch me still in bed."

"Yeah, but who in the world would pull such a stunt, and why?"

"Well, just think about it a minute. Who knew where the cabin was? Who knew where we lived, and who knew I was bad hurt?"

"Will, that boy was so scared, I'll bet he's still running!"

"He might have been scared, but I don't believe he's still running."

"But, what would he hope to gain by such a fool stunt?"

"I don't know, Uncle Buck, but there's at least two people in my home with no good on their minds. I think one is that Allen Doyle and I don't know who the other is, but before the sun rises on another day, I'll kill them both for going into my home with drawn weapons."

"Only if you beat me to them, son. Only if you beat me to them."

We went down off the mountain in a rush. Always careful, however to keep timber between us and the house.

We stopped just short of the old barn, and I showed Uncle Buck how, by using the old barn and cabin as shields, we could reach the back door of the new house, on foot, without anyone in the house being able to see us.

As we left our horses and headed toward the north side of the old barn, I felt a rage building inside me. It was not the anger I'd felt upon finding the worthless slaughter of yearling calves, those years ago. It was not even the hot flash of rage when that shyster lawyer had insulted

Clatilda that time in Alamosa.

It was, rather, a feeling that seemed to build inside my mind. White hot in its intensity. The rage was in itself frightening

I cared not for anything but the thought of someone in my home with my wife and children, with guns and the obvious intent to do harm to someone of mine.

As Uncle Buck and I stole our way to the back of the new house, it was almost as if I was outside myself. I knew what I was doing and I knew what to do next, but I had only one thought in mind. I did not wonder whether what I was going to do was right or wrong. I only knew, and that for an absolute fact, that soon I would kill anyone I found in my house that did not live there. And, I would do it without fail.

We eased up to the back door and as I reached for the door knob, I felt it turn in my hand! I stepped back and drew my pistol only to see Anna Laura slip out and ease the door shut, behind her.

She jumped back as she turned to face me and my pistol.

"Papa!" She whispered wrapping her arms around me.

"Papa, there are two men in there that say they are going to kill you and all the other men and take our ranch. They say they will even kill Bud, after they kill you and Mr. Webber. But. Papa, they say they are going to kill you first!"

"Is one of them just a boy, a little older than Bud?"

"I think so, Papa."

"Does he talk with a funny accent?"

"They both do Papa. The other one claims he's a gunfighter and he's going to make you draw against him. He claims he'll kill you before you even get your gun out."

"What's Mr. Webber doing?"

"He's mostly just laughing at them. Papa did you know Mr. Webber carries four pistols and a whole bunch of knives?"

"They searched him?"

"Yeah, they weren't going to until the young one felt the knife hanging down behind Mr. Webber's neck. Then they searched him from his hat to inside his boots. He still just laughed at them. The 'gunfighter' was going to hit him once but Mr. Webber just stood up and looked him right in the eyes. He didn't hit Mr. Webber."

"Where is everyone?"

"They are all sitting at the dining table, except the gunfighter and the young one. They are standing where they can watch the table and also see out front."

"Where do they think you are?"

"I told them I had to see after the twins. They let me go easy."

"You run as hard as you can up to the Blalocks. You stay right there until Uncle Buck or I come for you. And, Anna Laura, you pay attention to me. You don't tarry along the way and you don't leave 'til we come for you. Do you understand?"

"Yes, Papa."

"Promise?"

"Yes, Papa."

"Then you go now. Go around behind the old cabin then keep the old barn between you and the new house. You understand?"

"Yes, Papa."

I swatted her behind as she turned and scooted away, completely intent on her new errand.

I turned to Uncle Buck.

"We'll go down the hall to Clatilda's pantry. You step into the kitchen so the dining table will not be between you and those two. I'll go through the Pantry and out into the front of the kitchen. That way I'll be behind them. Uncle Buck, don't shoot unless they do."

"What about you?" he asked.

"Uncle Buck, I intend to kill them both. Inside my home, or out. It doesn't matter."

Uncle Buck looked at me for a moment.

"Don't get yourself hurt, boy, I'd miss you a lot."

We eased into the hallway. When we were inside I could hear both interlopers talking. I recognized Doyle's voice. He was telling the other that I should be back by now and they had better keep a sharp eye.

I eased through the pantry and was in the kitchen, behind the two when Uncle Buck stepped out.

I could see both the men stiffen. Both had holstered their pistols. Doyle made as if to go for his.

"Touch that gun and I'll blow the back of your head off!" I said.

Both seemed to solidify their stance. It was as if they had been covered with ice. They stood stiff and still.

"Bud," I said, "go around and get their guns. Don't get in front of Uncle Buck or me. Jacob, why don't you collect your arsenal!"

Both moved with speed and alacrity. I then stepped out in the dining room to confront the two.

"Doyle," I began, "you were warned. What are you doing back here?"

"I came back to get me a ranch. And I'd have made it too, if you hadn't taken the 'Kids' guns away from him."

"What are you talking about, 'get you a ranch'?"

"Well, the 'Kid' was going to face you in a gunfight then we'd kill the rest of the men."

"What about the women, stupid?" Jacob demanded.

"They'd be no problem. The 'Kid' says western men don't pay much attention to women. Whatever they said, we'd have just said they were lying. The 'Kid' said folks would believe us, not them."

"That's enough! Outside, both of you!" I said.

"Clatilda, you and Bud stay in here!" I said.

"Will, we were not hurt in any way."

"We'll discuss it later."

I herded the two out and around behind the barn.

Jacob had brought their pistols.

"Jacob, step around behind them and put their pistols in their holsters."

"Will, you know what you're doing?" Uncle Buck asked.

"Exactly! I told you I'd not allow anyone with guns to hold my family hostage inside my own home!"

Jacob stepped away from the two.

"All right you two. You said you figured to kill me and take my ranch. Have at it!"

They looked at one another then at me.

"That ain't fair!" Doyle whined. "Even if we get you, your friends will get us."

"You're probably right. Draw!"

Neither moved.

"Come on, 'Kid.' I heard you were the big bad 'gunfighter.' What's wrong, yellow?"

As I stood there, one moment ready to shoot both down like mad dogs, I felt the rage leave me. I could not; would not, murder the two.

"Unbuckle and drop your gun belts and step away from them."

"Mister, you wouldn't shoot an unarmed man, would you?" These, the first words from the 'gunfighter.'

"Armed, unarmed, don't matter."

Something in my voice convinced both to drop their belts suddenly.

"Jacob, do you remember that stirrup leather you and Bud brought back from town last week?" I asked.

"Sure do, and I know right where it is!"

"Go cut me off a four foot piece."

"Right away!"

Jacob was back in minutes with the thick, three inch wide piece of leather.

As he handed it to me, I turned to the two desperados.

"Drop your britches and grab your ankles!" I demanded. "If you're going to act like a couple of snot-nosed kids, that's the way you'll be treated!"

The 'gunfighter' turned to me, "you ain't whipping me mister!"

I simply stepped over to where his holster lay. I removed his pistol and taking it by the barrel. I extended it to him while placing my hand on the butt of my own holstered gun.

"All you have to do is grab your pistol and shoot before I can draw mine. You got the guts, 'gunfighter'?"

He backed away from the offered weapon as if it were a coiled rattler.

I tossed the gun aside and retrieved the leather strap.

"Across the face as across your backside, punk, and it don't matter to me, which it is."

It was a bad situation, out behind my barn, that late afternoon. Not one I'll remember with much pride. Somehow, though I'm happy not having to remember killing those two.

We tied them in the barn that night, then Jacob and Uncle Buck left the next morning for Alamosa. I sent a letter along explaining everything to Jamie Nava. He later told me it would be a long time before either got out of prison.

The entire incident was put aside by all but Anna Laura. She was forever sorry she did not get to see the 'gunfighter' get his britches spanked. Somehow, to her, the punishment was exactly fitting and deserved. She had heard the expression "spanked until one couldn't sit down." Somehow Jacob's recounting both the young men riding all the way to Alamosa standing upright in their stirrups gave new meaning to the saying. at least in Anna Laura's understanding.

Chapter 29

My health steadily improved and by the fourth of July celebration, I was as well as I'd ever been.

While Clatilda and Anne Blalock were going around looking at some of the things other ladies were showing off, I stopped by the store to chat with John Terry about our bank.

"I suppose you've heard about the big doings at the church, next Sunday?" John asked.

"No, what, 'big doings'?"

"Some of the brethren are coming out from Salt Lake City. I expect we might see some changes."

"In what?"

"The church leadership. Maybe even a new Bishop."

"What's wrong with Bishop Terry. He sick or something?"

"No, but every once in a while the church replaces Bishoprics."

"I didn't know that. I just thought Bishop Terry was there as long as he wanted the job."

"No, it's not a lifetime job. Sometime bishops serve ten or twelve years. I heard there was a brother down around Manassa who only served a little over a year. There was some sort of mess. The only thing I know was that four members of the ward rode all the way to Salt Lake City to complain."

"Who's going to take Bishop Terry's place if they release him?"

"That's the big excitement. No one knows."

"Who do you think?"

"Well, if he was twenty years younger, I'd bet on Jess Turner. But, I don't think they can overlook his age."

"He'd be a good choice."

"There are a couple of brothers that have gotten right chummy with Bishop Terry lately. I guess they think the Bishop might put in a good word for them."

"Who?"

"I don't think I'd care to name them. Enough said that there is some politicking going on."

"Why in the world would anyone want to be a bishop?"

"Oh, Will, it's quite a blessing to serve as 'bishop'?"

"I'm sure it is, but from what I've seen, the responsibility would just about wear a man right down to nothing."

"Well, we'll just have to see. It will be exciting."

"I suspect so. We'll just have to see next Sunday."

That next week proved to be one of the most troublesome weeks of my life.

Tuesday afternoon, Jacob and I were over on the west stream clearing a couple of blown down trees that threatened to dam the stream.

Bud came galloping up and told me there were two men at the house that wanted to talk to me.

I left Jacob and Bud to finish clearing the stream.

When I rode up to the house, there were two strange horses tied at the hitch rail. Both had come some distance. I went in to find Jamie Nava and a stranger seated at the table with milk, bread and honey in front of them.

Jamie introduced his companion as a U.S. Marshal, out of Pueblo. His name was Carter James.

"Will, we've come a long way with a proposition for you. Hear us out before you answer."

Mr. James explained that he covered the southeastern part of Colorado and the San Luis Valley. He said he'd recently been authorized to appoint deputies in Trinidad and the San Luis Valley. He said he'd gone first to Jamie to offer him the badge. But, obviously Jamie's position would not allow for such a dual role. Jamie had suggested me, and Mr. James said he was there to offer me the job of Deputy Marshal for the San Luis Valley. I would report to him, but actually work for Jamie, as Jamie's court was being tied in with the federal court in Denver.

My initial reaction was to turn them down. The idea of being a lawman held no appeal.

"Will," Jamie said, "before you turn us down, think about it. This country is not what it once was, so a Marshal's job is not even what it was when I carried a gun."

I told them I would not give them an answer right then, but I would get word to Jamie in ten days to two weeks, one way or the other. This was not what they wanted but they agreed.

Clatilda invited them to stay the night and by mid-afternoon, had won over both of the men.

Jamie commented that he had lost his wife some twelve years before and while his daughter kept a nice home for him, he had forgotten what a wife could bring to a home.

Jamie and the Marshal left the next morning, after an early breakfast.

After they had left I saddled my horse and rode up the mountain to the little flat, from which I'd first seen the ranch.

I tied my pony and walked over to a big rock and sat down.

I thought of how good life had been to me. Admitting to myself that I had done little to really deserve the bounty that had been placed before me, I wondered at what I might have become.

I'd never been one to sit and reflect on my life. Shoot, most times I didn't even think about what was happening at any given moment And, usually before one situation had been taken care of I would be knee-deep in another.

It was good Clatilda had come into my life, for without her I would, at best, have wound up punching cows for someone else, and at worst, being carried out of some saloon on a shutter.

I thought of Bud, now beginning to fill out, his voice already cracking, sometimes the tinny high pitch of a boy and then filling out in the timbre of a young man. And Anna Laura; oh, there was trouble on the horizon for some young man. Already she was so much like her mother it was scary.

The twins were now running around and into everything.

I thought of Robert and Sarah, sleeping there on the knoll directly across from where I sat.

It came to me that I had taken much from the world. Had I given anything back? Had I really done anything that would live beyond the memory of my children? I could think of nothing.

I thought of that quiet, hard man, that U.S. Marshal, I seen arrest that old boy, in Amarillo, so long ago. He'd seemed a lonely person. But, then those were different times. Very few people, I knew, regularly carried a firearm any longer. That is, excepting Jacob.

I wondered how Clatilda would really take it if I accepted that badge. I somehow felt she would support any decision I made, but how would she really feel?

I stood up and headed for my barn.

I thought to myself, "Well, stupid there's one sure way to find out how Clatilda would feel about anything. Ask her! She'll tell you. You might not like the answer, but you'll get her truth, and right now!"

As I rode down off the mountain, a vague idea seemed to come to the front of my mind. By the time I reached the barn, I was amazed at the wild thoughts that had come into my head.

I put up my horse and went into the house. Clatilda and Anna Laura were busy at some kind of sewing project.

"Anna Laura, could you go outside for a bit? I need to talk to your mother for a while."

"Sure, Papa. Mama, is it all right if I go up to see Sister Blalock?"

"Go ahead," Clatilda said, "but when they start dinner you come on home. We need to finish this dress today."

Anna Laura left the house in a rush, and I turned to sit at the table.

"I have fresh bread," Clatilda said. "How about some bread and honey?"

After she had sliced the bread, she seated herself across the table from me.

"Did you get it all sorted out?" She asked

"Yes, and no. I may have come up with more problems than

solutions."

"Do you want to be a Marshal?"

"No, I don't think so. Jamie and that Marshal tried to convince me that the job would be quiet and straight forward. I don't think so. From what I've seen, and what I know about Deputy Marshal's, they are pretty much hired guns. I think for me to get involved with that at this time is not to be."

"I was praying that would be your decision. But what problems have you come up with?"

"Clatilda, this country is growing and at the same time, becoming much tamer than even it was when we were married. I think I want to leave a mark on it. That is, besides just being a rancher."

"You're not 'just a rancher,' cowboy. We have four children, you have your bank, you are more well thought of in this area than you know. What more do you want?"

"To know that I've had an effect on the world. That when I die, what I've done will live beyond the memories of my children."

"Well, cowboy, like you told me once, 'you're taking a lot on your self'."

"I don't know, maybe I am. I know that given who I am and what I have, with you and the children and considering where I came from, I should be more than satisfied."

"What is it, then, Will?"

"Clatilda, I've got a crazy idea in my head. It's a new thought for me, and I'll admit I've not thought it through yet. But, I'd like to talk to you about it. Only if you'll promise not to laugh."

She just looked at me in that direct way of hers.

"You promise?"

"Of course I do!"

"I want to be a lawyer, then I want to be a judge."

"Is this the cowboy who once told me not to use big words?"

I looked at her for a moment. Of course, she was right. What was I thinking.

"Oh, Will, I'm sorry. You took that wrong. But, I shouldn't have said that!"

"You're probably right. Besides, like you say, I should be happy with what I have. Most men would."

"No! Let's talk about your dream."

"It's not a dream, Clatilda. It was only a thought, and not a very good one at that."

As I rose to leave, she stepped around the table.

"How long have you really been thinking about this?"

"Like I told you. Probably no more than an hour."

"I know you better than that, cowboy. For you to bring it up at all, it's been at least in the back of your mind for awhile."

"Do you think I'm stupid for thinking of such a thing?"

"No, I do not. But, I have a couple of questions for you. Do you realize how hard it will be to get where you want to go? And, have you thought about how long it might take?"

"I know it would probably be the hardest thing I've done and it really doesn't matter how long it takes. John and I have a good man running the bank and it's making money. Jacob could easily run the ranch by himself. With Uncle Buck, they're both looking for something to do about half the time. I have the time, and we have enough money. The only thing that worries me is if I am smart enough."

"Do you have any idea how to get from where you are now to where you want to be?"

"Not really. What I thought to do was to get Uncle Buck to go back to Cimarron with me. There's a Judge Wagner there, I told you about him. He was a lawyer before he became a Judge. Then I thought to stop in Alamosa and talk to Jamie Nava. He wasn't a lawyer before he became a Judge. I think the two of them could give me all I need to know to make a final decision."

"When are you leaving?" Clatilda asked.

"You mean you don't think I'm crazy to want to check out this thing."

"Cowboy, the only time I've ever thought you were crazy was that time you quit and was gone all that cold fall day. By the way, did you ever give me back that forty dollars I gave you that day."

"Did I give it back! You wouldn't feed me until I did. Don't you remember? Oh, of course, you do. You're just trying to do me out of my hard earned money."

"Hard earned! I don't remember the last time you put in a hard day's work! Bud works harder than you."

"He is a good worker, isn't he? I was watching him and Uncle Buck the other day. That boy's going to make a good hand someday."

"And, why not," Clatilda said coming around to stand with her arm laid easily across my shoulder, "his father's about the best."

Chapter 30

Uncle Buck and I had planned to leave for Cimarron on Thursday of that week, but one thing led to another and Saturday morning found Jacob and me in the barn working with Uncle Buck's Jersey milk cow who was having trouble with her calf. We were all about worn out; Jacob, me and Uncle Buck's Jersey.

Clatilda came into the barn and over to the stall where we were working with the cow.

"Will, there are some men to see you. I think you best come."

"Ma'am, they are just going to have to wait. If I go now, we might lose both the cow and her calf!"

"I'll ask them if they can wait."

As busy as Jacob and I were, I thought little more about anything or anyone except the task at hand until I looked up to see John Terry, Seth Blalock and three other men I didn't recognize, standing just outside the stall.

"Howdy folks," I said, "I'm a little tied up. Can you wait a while?"

John said for me to go ahead, they could wait.

It was a good half an hour before we were through. Mama Jersey and little heifer calf were fine, and Jacob and I looked like thirty miles of muddy road. We both went outside to wash up, followed by the visitors.

When I was a little more presentable, I invited John, Seth and the others in for something to eat. While all, at first, declined the food, they all ate heartily of Clatilda's ham sandwiches and cold milk.

After everyone settled down, one of the men, introduced to me as Brother Written, asked if there was somewhere he and I might have a private talk.

I took him out on the front porch. We talked of many things: what I believed, what I did not believe and what I was doing in my life.

I did not know where all this talk was going, so I asked.

"Brother Written, I 'spect you now know as much about how I feel about some things as anyone, up to and including my wife. Where is this going? It's only because you've been introduced as one having authority in my church that I've answered all your questions. Now, answer one of mine, what do you want from me?"

He looked at me for a moment. I don't believe he was right pleased with my bluntness.

"Brother Jackson, we've come here today to discuss your worthiness and strength in the Church."

He stopped. I didn't know whether he was through, just catching his breath, or what. When he didn't continue, I was a little put off by his attitude.

"My strength and worthiness are something I cannot judge. I can only say that in the few years I've been a member, I've learned and believed what I should be, and became what was expected. I've done as I was advised to do, and as far as I know, those things will continue."

"Brother Jackson," he began, sitting back in his chair, "how do you feel about callings you've had in the Church?"

"I've taught a Sunday School class for young men and I helped out for two falls in the Bishop's storehouse. I liked both jobs just fine."

"Do you think you might be able to serve in a more responsible position?"

"Friend, I don't know what you've been told about me, but there is one thing that I'm pretty sure got missed. I don't beat around the bush and I ain't just real patient with them that do. You got something stuck in your craw, spit it out. Or, as far as I'm concerned, this talk is over."

"Well, Brother Jackson, maybe that's just as well. Why don't we join the others?"

We went back inside and it was not long before everyone left. After they were gone and Clatilda and I were standing on the porch, after the good byes, she turned to me.

"Will, what did Brother Written want?"

"I don't have any idea. He hemmed and hawed around about what I felt about the Church, what I'd done and how I felt about more responsibility. I tried to get him to come to the point, but when I told him I had no patience with beating around the bush he seemed to be through talking. That's when we came back inside."

"He never said what he wanted?"

"No, and that's what rubbed me the wrong way. When Bishop Terry ever wanted me to do something, he'd spit it right out, and then we talked about my worthiness and such. It was like telling a man what you wanted. None of this asking him if he thought he was up to the job. I'm not real comfortable with that. It's this round and round the barn that I can't deal with."

"Cowboy, you constantly amaze me. You can be asked to move a mountain, but don't talk to you about how it could be done!"

"Well, ma'am, I guess I have a lot of shortcomings, but by you and the Church, I've always tried to do right."

"And, let me tell you something, Will Jackson, I'll take a buggy whip to the man or woman who says you've failed. Come on cowboy," she said taking my arm, "I saved an apple pie from those 'not hungry' folks. How would you like a big piece with a little cream on top."

"Right now!"

Clatilda laughed, and we went into the house, arm in arm.

Uncle Buck and I decided to leave Monday morning, so Sunday, we all went to church. Uncle Buck had been in the habit of coming with us since Aunt Gladys died. So, that morning it was Clatilda, the kids and me in a buggy and Bud and Uncle Buck on horseback.

When we pulled up to the chapel, John Terry was out on the steps. He came walking fast to our buggy and reached it before I had time to tie up the team.

"Will, I need to talk to you."

"Sure, John, when?"

"Right now. Let's go over there by the building."

We walked over to the corner of the church, away from the crowd gathered at the door.

"What did you say to Brother Written, yesterday?" John abruptly demanded.

"Why? What did he say I said?"

"He said you were real short with him and wouldn't let him talk."

"You figure that sounds like me?"

"Not really, but I would like to know what went on."

"Not much, John. He wanted to know lots of things about me and my attitude toward the Church. I told him, and asked him why he wanted to know. He seemed real shy about telling me. So, I told him if there was a point to the talking, I'd appreciate it if he got to it. That seemed to bother him so we went back inside the house."

"Is that all there was to it?"

"Yeah. You still haven't told me what business, all this is, of your's."

"That's all right, Will, I expect you'll know soon enough."

We went on into the church which, by now, was packed.

This Brother Written and his two friends were seated up by Bishop Terry.

When everything got started you could tell something was going on.

Bishop Terry was released, along with his two counselors. John Terry was called as bishop with Seth Blalock as his second counselor and Jack Turley, who farmed a little place south of town, as his first counselor.

I was right proud to have Seth Blalock in the Bishopric. He was, I thought, a real good man, a little stubborn but a good man.

As we walked out after the special service, we all stood around to shake hands with both the Bishops Terry. I especially wanted to see Jess Turner and thank him for his years of service to the Church, and most particularly his help to me.

When I approached him, Hester was by his side.

I shook his hand and greeted Hester.

"Will Jackson," Hester said, "there are times I could just spank your britches!"

It was like walking into a cold rain.

"What have I done, Hester? I surely am sorry, whatever it was."

"Oh, that's all right, Will. Clatilda, let's you and I go over and see the new bishop while these two men talk."

As they walked away I turned to Jess.

"I'll swear, I've never had so many people want to 'talk' to me in my life."

"What happened between you and Brother Written yesterday?"

"All right!" I said. "That's enough. What's the deal about my talk with this Written guy? You would think I cussed him out. What's this all about?"

"Do you really mean you haven't guessed?"

"Guessed what!" I demanded. "I've had about all of this jumping around I can handle. Just what exactly is going on?"

"You still don't know what Brother Written wanted with you yesterday?"

"No, Jess, and I'm getting real tired of these riddles!"

"You know, Will, I believe you. Brother Written, John Terry and the rest came to your house yesterday so that Brother Written could see if he felt right about you serving as John's first counselor in the bishopric."

"Me! In the bishopric? Jess, you've got to be mistaken. No one in their right mind would think of me for that position!"

"Why not, Will?"

"I could probably give you a couple of hundred reasons. It's good enough, though, to look at where I came from and who I've been. Why, Jess, I'd think they'd just as soon turn a bobcat loose in the school house, as let me in the bishopric."

"You really believe that, don't you, Will?"

"Absolutely. I understand, now, why Written was so edgy. I'll bet he took one look at me and wondered why he'd taken the long ride out to my ranch."

Jess took me by the arm and we headed over to where the ladies were.

"Will," Jess began, "I want you to do me a favor."

"Sure, Jess, I'd do anything for you."

"When I die and go before that judgement bar, is it all right if I tell them I'm your friend?"

"That will always be a fact, Jess. But, I don't figure it'll ever be of much trading value."

We joined the ladies and everyone stood around for an hour or so visiting back and forth.

When we finally started for home, we were not out of town before Clatilda turned to me.

"Will, I'm proud of you."

"Oh, oh. What now, Another bedroom set or is it another wagon load of goats?"

She punched me on the shoulder.

"No, cowboy, I'm proud of your lack of guile."

"I guess if I'm gonna be a lawyer, that's another word I'm going to have to learn what it means."

"You honestly never guessed what Brother Written wanted yesterday, did you?"

"You and Hester been talking again?"

"She said Jess couldn't believe Brother Written when he and John Terry came back to the church yesterday evening. She said Jess told them there must be some mistake. But Brother Written and John went out last evening and saw Brother Turley. Hester was right upset. But, you want to know something, cowboy? I think I was never quite so proud of you as I was while Hester was telling me the story."

"I suppose it'll be all over how dumb I was?"

"No, it won't be 'all over,' and besides I don't know anyone who will ever think you dumb. Hardheaded, stubborn, maybe even impatient, but, dumb, I hardly think so, cowboy."

Chapter 31

Uncle Buck and I left that Monday morning at daybreak. Off to find out what I could expect of myself for the rest of my life.

Our ride to Cimarron was without incident. We rode into town just as folks were lighting their lamps and lanterns. I didn't mind early evening on the trail, but when I was in a town or around folks, it was the loneliest time of the day. There was something about the activities going on at that time of a day that made me want to be in my own house with my feet under my own table, with my own folks around me.

Uncle Buck and I checked into the hotel, stowed our stuff in our rooms and headed to the dining room. There was not a big crowd, but there were, maybe, a half dozen people there, and seated alone in front of a window was Judge Wagner.

Uncle Buck and I went over to the Judge's table.

"Evening, Judge, remember me?" was Uncle Buck's greeting.

"Yes, I do! And, how are you Mr. Harris. And, you, sir, I believe it's Mr. Jackson, isn't it?"

"Yes sir," I said. "Are you waiting for someone?"

"No, sir, I dine alone. At least unless I can find someone to join me.

Would you gentlemen care to sit at my table?"

We sat, and gave our order to the waitress.

"Well, how have you been, Mr. Harris? And, how is Mrs. Harris?"

Uncle Buck told him of Aunt Gladys' death.

We sat and discussed weather, range conditions, and other small matters. At a lull in the conversation, I spoke up.

"Judge Wagner, you are the person we came here to see. I have several questions I need to ask you. I can ask now or if you'd rather, I could come to your office."

"Has this to do with a legal matter?"

"Well, yes and no."

"Maybe you'd better explain yourself, Mr. Jackson."

"Well, putting it as straight as I can sir, I want to be a lawyer and I don't quite know where to begin."

"I understood you enjoyed some success as a rancher up in Colorado."

"Yes, I own a ranch, but I have a real yen to go into the lawyering business."

"Are you sure, at your age, you want to take on the workload you'd have in front of you?"

"Sir, I don't know. That's mainly the reason I'm here. I know so little about the law, I don't even know if I have what it takes. I don't even know what it takes."

"Well, Mr. Jackson. Why don't you come over to my office at eight tomorrow morning. I have a very slow day tomorrow. I can, at least, show you what you might be getting yourself into."

The next morning, Uncle Buck left to spend the day at John

Hennessey's place. He said he might not be back until the next day and I was not to worry if he didn't get back that night.

Judge Wagner was waiting for me. He showed me into his office where one whole wall was lined with bookshelves full of books.

"Do you read much, Mr. Jackson?"

"I do now, but that's my wife's idea. Ten years ago I had some problem reading the label on an air-tight."

"What do you read, sir."

"Everyday, the scriptures. Also my wife sees to it that I have a new book every three or four weeks, depending upon my workload."

"What kind of books, sir?"

"Everything from Ivanhoe to Plato. I'm trying to get through a book about a fellow called Hercules. It's mostly poetry, but interesting."

"Do you enjoy reading, sir, or is it something you do because you feel you should?"

"I guess you could say, some of both. Honestly, I've read some things I thought were stupid, and useless."

"And what might that be."

"Oh, nothing particular. It's just when I get into a story and the writer goes into a lot of detail about stupid things; like how a flower looks or the way the sun strikes a tree, or a rock or how someone says something instead of what that person says."

"I take it you're more literal than some writers."

"If you mean do I like to keep things simple, you're right."

"The law is anything but simple, sir."

"Well, it's about justice, isn't it?"

"In some instances as it accompanies the law's main purposes. Many people have written flowery things about how the law guarantees justice for all and is there to protect the innocent. Just remember this, Mr. Jackson: the law and laws exist primarily to protect property."

"What about when one man hurts another, physically. Doesn't the law punish the wrong doer?"

"Of course! But, basically the punishment is based upon protecting society from the wrongful acts of a person or persons. It is my opinion, sir, even that has as it's bed-rock reasoning, the need to punish those who, having injured one person might, in some way, damage any property."

"Judge Wagner, there is one word I know, that seems to apply here. I believe, sir, that you are a cynic."

"Mr. Jackson, should you go ahead with the law, you will find there are basically three kinds of professionals in the law: the cynic, the greed driven and the buffoon."

"You may be right, but I guess the big questions for me are what do I have to do to become a lawyer, and how long will it take?"

"All right, Will; may I call you Will?"

"Of course, sir."

"All right. First, get yourself a copy of Blackstone's works. It comes in two or three ways: one single volume or two or four. If I were you I'd be getting the two or four copy version. Some eastern states are now requiring you to have read law with a practicing attorney. Some even require you to have studied at a university. A few of the western states still allow you to declare yourself an attorney by stint of your own personal study. If you then can competently handle yourself before a Judge you may become accepted as an attorney. If you don't train yourself carefully, you will soon be unfrocked by other lawyers and judges. Then, it won't matter whether you call yourself Lawyer Jackson or Farmer Brown. You won't have anyone requesting your services, either in the legal profession or out."

"Is Blackstone all I need. What about all these books you have?"

"The majority of those books I've picked up one at a time. You will need the statutes for your state. You will need to obtain each year's federal statutes: those are laws passed by the federal legislators, and you will need each year's Supreme Court rulings. From there on my friend, you read. You read and you remember what you've read. How does it sound so far?"

"Have you read everything on that wall?" I asked.

"Absolutely not. But, I can find anything in any one of those books I need to. Learning the structure and content organization of your reference books is absolutely necessary. Also, in some metropolitan, or city courts, rules of evidence are being developed. If and when they become necessary, or become the law in your locale, they will be published in a book. You will then have to know those as well as you do your name."

"Do you think it's possible for a cowboy, such as myself to become a lawyer?"

"Absolutely! We recently had a president who was a lawyer, and who started out as a young man splitting fence rails for a living."

"All right, very simply, what must I do to become a lawyer?"

"Read."

"That's it?"

"Simply put; yes. But, you've got to have the right books and you must get to the point where you understand what you read."

"How do I do that?"

"The best way is to read some, then discuss what you've read and your understanding of it with a practicing attorney."

"Given where I live, that's going to be the most difficult part," I said.

"Mr. Jackson, if, after you've thought about this for awhile and read Blackstone from front to back, you're still interested, you come back to see me. I'll sit down for an afternoon, possibly also the evening. By the end of that session, I'll be better able to advise you whether or not to continue in your studies."

"You'll do that?"

"Absolutely!"

"Where do I find a copy of this Blackstone?"

"I have two sets. I will give you one, on your word you will return it to me."

"If you'll let me borrow it, I will return it when I come back to see you in the spring!"

"Fair enough!"

Uncle Buck didn't make it back in that night, so after supper I sat down in the hotel lobby and opened up Blackstone.

It took about five minutes to find this was not to be an easy thing. I read until after midnight when the night desk clerk started turning off some of the lamps.

After breakfast the next morning, I had nothing to do until Uncle Buck got back, so I took up my place of the night before. I was deep into it when a shadow fell across my face. I looked up to find Judge Wagner standing in front of me.

"How does it go?" he asked by way of greeting.

"Slow, mighty slow!"

"Do you still think this may be for you?"

"Oh, yes. It's going to be tough going, but I'm nowhere near ready to quit. I'll see this part through. Then you and I will decide if I have what it takes."

"It may just be that decision is already nearer than I thought!"

"I doubt that. We'll just have to see."

"I usually take a break about this time of morning, when court is not in session. Will you join me for a cup of coffee?"

"I'll join you, but I think I'll have milk."

"Good! Lets's go, then."

I'd had my milk, and the Judge his coffee, before Uncle Buck got back to town.

"Got your visit over?" I asked as he came into the lobby.

"Yeah, and it was right nice to see the Hennessey's again. But, it just wasn't the same without Gladys. I figure that will be the last I see of the Hennessey's. Lately I seem to have more in common with Bud and Jacob. You get your lawyering done?"

"Yep, I'm ready to start back whenever you are."

With our late start from Cimarron, we spent our first two nights on the trail back, out in the open. I didn't try to read any by the campfire.

We got into Alamosa just at noon. After my talk with Judge Wagner, I felt I'd need no more than a few hours that afternoon with Jamie Nava.

We found Jamie in his office right after dinner.

He seemed some disappointed that I would not be taking the Deputy Marshal's badge.

"No, Jamie, I have something else I'd like to visit with you about."

"Good," he said, "it's a slow afternoon. I'll welcome your company. Although I must admit it would be more pleasurable if that wife of yours was here."

"She does brighten a room," I said.

I explained what I was planning to try.

"I wish that was the way I had done it. Oh, I had a lot to do with the law before I got this job, but not enough. Many's the night, I'm up until midnight studying to make sure I don't make a fool of myself. And, believe me, that happened a time or two, even with my studying."

"Have you ever thought of trying to go ahead and study the law more?"

"Oh, yes. But, I haven't the time now. I'll just have to be happy as a small town magistrate."

"Well, aren't you going to have something to do with the federal Courts?" I asked.

"No, that fell through when the folks in Denver found out I had no real background in the law. When they found I'd only been a sheriff they dropped he idea."

"I'm sorry about that, Jamie. You're a good hand."

"Yeah, but I'll tell you, Will, I was scared to death over the idea."

I laughed. "I don't see you being scared over much of anything."

"Nothing I can grab hold of, but this law backs me into a corner, often."

We spent a pleasant afternoon, but I really learned little from Jamie. I did learn an important thing. That was before I went anywhere, I would be a lawyer first.

Uncle Buck and I left Alamosa in the middle of the afternoon and made it almost to Saguache before camping.

It was late in the evening before we got home. Clatilda fixed us a late supper and Uncle Buck went immediately to bed.

"Well, cowboy, tell me all about it." Clatilda said almost before the door had closed behind Uncle Buck.

"It will be hard to do what I told you I intended."

"Too hard?"

"I don't yet know."

I told her of my meeting with Judge Wagner and showed her the books he had given me.

"I must study and understand them by spring. Then I'm to go back and discuss what I've learned and what I understand with Wagner. He says at that time, we will both be able to make the decision to continue my studies or quit. He did say I'd do better if I could read law with another lawyer. I told him we had none close. He said I'd just have to try it another way."

"Will, how are going to have time for all this studying, with all you have to do?"

"I thought about that a lot on the way home. I have an idea how I can do it."

"Let's hear it, but be aware, cowboy, I'll not herd cattle!"

"Aw, well, that shoots my idea," I said.

"How will you handle everything?"

"I'm thinking of working the ranch Monday through Wednesday, then studying Thursday through Saturday. I thought to take over that big back room, the one with the outside door, as a kind of office. That way, I'll be available to Jacob or Uncle Buck, if needed."

"Can Uncle Buck help much. I noticed he was very tired tonight," she said.

"I don't know. I know he will try and he's savvy enough to pace himself. But then, there's Bud and if needs be I'm sure I can get Dan and Aaron Blalock to help out part time."

"Could you hire someone to work with Jacob?"

"I don't know that we could afford another full-time hand."

"Oh, that's right, we are close to having to ask for help from the Bishop."

"I know we're not bad off, but to hire another hand would cost and would put more work on you, cooking, and all."

"Will, do you have any idea of our steady income?"

"I've got a fair idea of what the bank brings in, but I know it will be at least two more years before I'll be able to sell any cattle."

"Let me tell you something, cowboy! The store has made us so much that I no longer bring our share to the ranch. I have John keep it in the new bank safe. We have, on deposit, in your own bank, more than four times what you sold your herd for. And, I have more cash in our bedroom than I'd care for anyone other than you to know."

"The store money is, and has always been yours."

"Oh, Will Jackson, unbend that stiff-neck of yours. Let me suggest what we do. You take that back room. We'll order you a desk and chair. Hire a good hand to help Jacob and you go out on Monday and lay out the week's work. Then you can devote yourself to your studies. Next spring, if you decide not to continue, buy more cattle and ranch bigger. Think about it."

"Let me go in and sit down with Abraham and John and see how the bank's doing. If there's enough there to pay for operating the ranch, I just might sponge off my nice wife, at least until next spring."

"That's fine. Let's go first thing tomorrow. You can talk to John and Abraham and I'll check the catalogs and get your desk ordered."

"Let's not get too fancy. I was thinking maybe a table and chair would be fine."

"All right. Let's go to bed so we can get an early start."

Chapter 32

I didn't get a table and chair. I got a great big old roll top desk, a bookcase, table and four chairs. One chair even had arms on it, swivelled around, and even leaned back. Anna Laura spent one whole afternoon in that chair the day we brought my "office furniture," as Clatilda called it, home.

She and Anna Laura spent two whole days getting everything set-up to their liking. Clatilda had even ordered pictures for the walls. John had picked up a big Navajo rug someplace and Clatilda got it, and instead of putting it on the floor where it belonged, she hung it on one wall. I never quite got used to having a rug on the wall. Jacob would hardly come into the room at first, said he felt like he should take his boots off before he came into my office. I bought a small wood stove, and that completed the room I might only use for a few months.

Clatilda was pleased and the work arrangement seemed to work fine. Uncle Buck sent for John Hennessey's nephew, Jim Ballard, and we had our hired hand. He was about the shyest boy I'd ever met, but a right good hand and a worker from who flung the chunk. His folks had been killed in a run-away. Their buggy had flipped into an arroyo. Their place had been heavily mortgaged and Jim had wound up with little but the clothes on his back. That's how he had come to be living with the

Hennessey's. He was glad to be out on his own, working for us, and we were just as pleased to have him.

Fall quickly faded into winter. I had only one major interruption of my studies. In early December, we had a real cold snap. It took all of us, including Bud, to keep the ice chopped out of water holes for the cattle, and feeding was a chore because a heavy wet snow had been frozen into an ice blanket over the hay stacks. We were going from daylight to after dark, everyday. The only time off we had was to go to church on Sunday. Clatilda didn't like it, but we had to come home on Sunday afternoon and go right back to providing water and feed to our herd.

Jim got to going to church with us and the first thing we knew he was spending a couple of nights every week up at the Blalock's, talking to Seth.

Christmas was a right good old time. Clatilda and Anne Blalock made it up that we should all have Christmas at our house.

The ladies, including Anna Laura, spent almost a week fixing up the place. Seth, Anne, and their two boys came down Christmas Eve afternoon. All work stopped and we all sort of congregated in our living room. Of course, with the three rooms: living room, dining room and kitchen, being open as they were, it didn't matter where you might be. The ladies in the kitchen were able to join in conversations clear into the living room, and did. It was real nice.

Anne and Clatilda put on such a feed that night, I had to wonder if there would be anything left for Christmas dinner.

After breakfast Christmas morning, I was sure nothing could be left for dinner. We men generally went from the table to chairs only to waddle back to the table a few hours later.

Christmas morning, Clatilda and Anne woke us all up before daylight. We gathered around the tree and shared our gifts. Jim Ballard and Jacob seemed somewhat surprised to be included. Clatilda had ordered them both, heavy coats, from the store.

All in all, it was quite a celebration, one that became a habit and was to be repeated every year.

I was spending long hours studying. I found that the more I read and cross referenced, the more I was coming to understand, not only Blackstone's ideas, but also more and more of what Judge Wagner had said. I began to wonder, at the task faced by Jamie Nava. I also intended to see that he would have his own set of Blackstone if he had none.

I was involved in my studies one morning late in February, when I heard a big commotion at the front of the house. I went into the living room to find John Terry.

"Will, we've got trouble! The bank's been held up."

"When?"

"Not more than an hour ago."

"How many were there?"

"Only two, but they shot Abraham. He's all right; It's only a flesh wound. They didn't get much. Abraham wouldn't open the safe. They were surprised by the Carter brothers who came into the bank and being quick to recognize what was going on, they quickly left. They started yelling the minute they got out the door. That's when those fellows shot Abraham."

"How much, you figure they got?"

"Nowhere near as much as if they'd gotten into the safe. I'd just brought the store's receipts over. I'd guess about two thousand, more or less, including the store's receipts."

"Do you know which way they went?" I asked.

"I followed their tracks to where the west creek splits off. Then I came here."

"Do you know how well they were mounted?"

"Not well. I caught a glimpse of them as they left town. One was on a sorrel and the other a black. Both animals looked right poor."

"Hey, Will!" Jacob said running across the porch. "Someone's out in the west pasture trying to run down our horses!"

I grabbed a rifle from beside the door, and yelling at John that I was taking his horse, I ran out to join Jacob.

Jacob and I went through the gate, he'd left open, at a gallop. When we cleared the trees, I could see the two riders chasing our horses in the southwestern part of the pasture. If it had not been such a serious situation it would have been funny. Neither one was mounted well enough to get so close they could rope one of our animals. The funny part was that, if either of the riders had any sense, they would just have stopped running our horses, and then could have walked their ponies right up to any of the herd.

I sent Jacob around one side and I took the other. The two riders finally cornered the horse herd against an outcropping of rocks. We cornered the riders against the same rocks. We had them in a crossfire and as one started to step down from his horse, I fired over his head. They both turned toward me just as Jacob also sent a shot over their heads.

In a second, both threw up their hands. Their horses started moving around as untrained animals do when pressure on their reins is removed. Jacob rode up and grabbed the reins for both horses as I closed on the two men.

They were a sorry looking pair. Their saddles and tack were all but useless. Their clothes were in tatters. In all, a sorry mess.

"Where's the money?" I demanded.

"What money you talking about?" The older one whined.

"Friend, don't push it. I'd just as soon shoot you where you stand. Now, where's the money. I want it, and right now!"

The younger of the two reached back and tore his saddlebags loose and threw them to the ground.

"There it is, mister. Please don't shoot us!"

"Jacob, lead those horses aside and keep these two covered."

I stepped down and picked up the saddlebags. While I did so, I told the two to carefully unbuckle their gun belts and let them fall to the ground.

I opened the saddlebags to find them both stuffed with money. I had the older one step down from his pony and searched him carefully. I then took my rope, tied his hands behind his back then looped the rope around my saddle horn. I then did the same to the whiner.

"Mister," the younger one said, "if'n your horse spooks, we'll be drug to death!"

"Then stand real still so he doesn't spook."

Their pockets yielded only a broken knife, a few coins and a wad of string.

I picked up their pistols. I was surprised by the condition of both the holsters and pistols. The pistols were practically new Colts, and the shell belts and holsters were in excellent shape.

I remounted and told the two to head out to the north east.

"You ain't gonna make us walk far, are you, mister?" The younger one asked.

"Why you got something against walking?"

"I got new boots and they are tight."

"Well, a nice little stroll will break them in real good." Jacob said urging his horse in against the younger one. They slowly began trudging across the pasture.

It didn't take us long to get back to the house. We were watched for the last several hundred yards by quite a crowd, standing on the front porch.

When we walked the two up to the house, Uncle Buck took them onto the porch and tied each to a porch column.

"That was almost too easy!" John Terry said.

"That pair of trash wouldn't have caused anyone trouble," said Jacob. "I'm surprised they had enough sense to know a bank had money."

"Speaking of which," I said, "let's go inside, John, I want to show you something."

We went inside and I dumped the contents of the two saddlebags out on the dining table.

"There's a lot more than two thousand dollars there!" John exclaimed.

We counted the money and found there to be a few dollars under five thousand. Mostly paper, but some gold.

"Abraham and I might be off a few dollars but no way did those two get this much from our bank," John said.

"Then, let's go have a talk with our two desperados. It seems they've been busier than we thought."

I went up to the younger one who had, I noticed, actually been crying.

"Boy, you've got more money than you took from our bank. Where did you get it?"

"That ain't none of your business!" Said the older one.

"Jacob stick a gag in that one's mouth!" Uncle Buck said. "I'll get this punk to talk!"

He then stepped around in front of the young man, put his cocked pistol right at the end of the man's nose, and said, "Fellow, you've got 'til I count to three to tell us where you got that money, or I'm just naturally gonna blow your head off! One . . .."

"We stole it, mister! We stole it! Please don't shoot!"

"Where did you steal it, boy?" Uncle Buck demanded.

"We stole it in Monte Vista, mister. We robbed their bank!"

On a hunch, I stepped closer, "and, where did you get those new boots and your gun belts?"

"We robbed a saddle maker in Walsenburg. We was gonna get new saddles but a lady came in and started screaming. Clifton shot the saddle man and we high tailed it outa there."

The older one was staring at the kid as if he could kill him, and probably would have, if able.

"That's an awful lot of money for a bank in Monte Vista to have," John said.

"Clifton made the banker open his safe there, like he wanted to in town before those two men came in."

"Did he shoot him, also?" I demanded.

"No, he just knocked him in the head, and we went out the back door. Nobody even chased us."

"Will, what do you think we ought to do with these two?" Jacob asked.

"I suppose we could take them down to the stack-yard. Those big cottonwoods would be just right for a hanging party."

"Will . . .!" Clatilda gasped.

I looked at her to explain, expecting to see a look of horror. Instead,

I could tell, she was suppressing a laugh, and staring at the younger man. He had just wet his britches.

That afternoon, the decision was made that Jacob and I would take the men to Alamosa and turn them over to the gentle graces of Jamie Nava. I was sure, the punishment he would mete out would be fair and severe enough to take care of the two.

Our ride to Alamosa was without incident. The younger one sniveled the entire way and the older one said not a word. We gave Jamie the money from the Monte Vista Bank to return, and also the pistols, shell belts and holsters.

I was somewhat curious to see how it all turned out, but in no mood to hang around Alamosa for the month or six weeks it would take to sort everything out. John Terry had given us a sworn and witnessed affidavit representing the bank, and Jacob and I both gave depositions as to what we knew and had done.

I told Jamie I would stop by in the spring to find out how it all turned out.

The morning we left Alamosa was the coldest I'd ever experienced. We did not stop before we reached the Medina's ranch. We were afraid to. Afraid that to stop would be to freeze to death.

We spent a pleasant afternoon and evening at the Medina's place. The next morning when we left, it was not so cold.

As we were riding back to the ranch, I asked Jacob how much money he had. I guess the bluntness of my question surprised him for he didn't answer for a minute or so.

"I've got enough, I think," he finally said.

"No, I mean exactly."

"Why do you want to know?"

"Well, Jacob, your too good a man to always be working for

someone else, and your loyalty must have it's reward."

"I'm doing fine. You and Clatilda have always treated me like family. And, partner, outside of Buck and Gladys Harris, I ain't never had family. Wasn't for you, I'd probably be dead by now or, at the best, on some owl-hoot trail."

"That's fine, Jacob, but what I had in mind was a set-up like I have with Uncle Buck. If you have a hundred or so, we could cut out twenty of this year's calves, and you could start your own brand."

"Ain't got no place to run them."

"No? Just several thousand acres of some of the best range land I've ever seen."

"You mean run them on your spread?"

"Yeah, but don't worry. I'm sure Clatilda will think of some way to make you pay for the privilege."

"Huh!" he said. "Somehow when it comes to a business proposition, I think I'd come out better dealing with you."

"Trust me, friend, if you take out your money around that sweet thing, count it coming out and going back in."

"You know, there's something I been meaning to ask you. You don't have to tell me, but Miss Anna Laura told me right after Christmas that you folks own part of John Terry's store. She was admiring my new coat. Don't be upset at her."

"Clatilda does. She had it when we got married."

"You're pretty well fixed, ain't you?"

I looked over at him, only to find him grinning at me.

"That kind of makes us even! 'How much money you got Jacob.' Man, I almost fell out of my saddle when you asked me that."

"Well, what do you think of my idea?" I asked.

"Why wouldn't I jump at it. I don't see how I can lose."

"All right, when we brand, you get you an iron made up and we'll brand out your string."

"Why you doing this, Will?"

"I'll be honest with you, Jacob, I have two reasons. The first is that if you ever decided to leave this country. I'm afraid Anna Laura would just up and leave with you. I'm not so sure about Bud, but he might go too. The second reason I want to do it is Clatilda and I owe you, Jacob. We owe you the kind of debt that cannot be repaid. But, we're obliged to try."

We rode along for close to an hour before Jacob said anything more.

"Rosebud!" Jacob said, right out of the blue.

"What rosebud?" I asked.

"That's going to be my brand!"

"Why, rosebud?" I asked.

"Rose for that sweet little flower, Miss Anna Laura and bud for Bud."

"Well, Jacob, I never knew you were so sweet!" I laughed. Then I had to grab for my saddle horn for he switched the rump of my pony with his quirt.

I laughed most of the rest of the way home. Jacob would growl and threaten me with dire circumstances if I didn't shut up.

I never told anyone why Jacob had chosen the Rosebud as his brand, not even Clatilda. But, Jacob sent away to Pueblo and had two irons made by an iron monger there. Best looking branding irons I'd ever seen. He took care of them as if they were pieces of jewelry. The only one I ever saw him let use the irons was Bud. Somehow that seemed right.

Chapter 33

Winter that year seemed to disappear into a rainy spring that suddenly, in early May, turned to summer overnight.

I awoke one morning to two facts. I had gone far enough with Blackstone's comments on law to allow me to discuss what I'd studied, with at least some understanding. The second fact was that whatever spring we were going to have that year, had come and gone, and it was time for me to be in Cimarron. I asked Uncle Buck if he wanted to go with me and he declined. He said he didn't feel like that long ride. But, I suspected the truth of the matter was that he was missing Aunt Gladys more as he got older.

I started to go alone until one evening during supper Jim Ballard spoke up and asked if he might be allowed to go with me. He said he'd be right pleased to see his aunt and uncle again. I liked that idea a lot so Jim and I left for Cimarron two days later.

It was a pleasant trip, all the way into Cimarron. Good weather all the way.

We rode into the town, again right at supper time. Jim said he was just going to ride on out to the Hennessey's place and we arranged to meet back at the hotel two days hence.

As I had hoped, I found Judge Wagner at his usual table in the hotel dining room. He seemed genuinely pleased to see me.

He began, almost immediately to talk about Blackstone's commentaries on common law, specifically the spoken and written contracts between two parties. I could tell, right off how much more I had to learn, and I said as much.

"Don't sell yourself short, Will. We are talking about my decades in the law and your six or seven months of study."

We sat and talked until long after all else had left the dining room. Suddenly Judge Wagner looked at his watch and apologized for keeping me so long. I quickly excused him of any delay and we both went our separate ways with my promise to be in his office the next day by eight in the morning.

We had breakfast together the next morning and walked to his office together.

"I'm pleased you came down at this particular time," he said, hanging up his coat and hat. "I have two trials scheduled this week. One involving a man who killed his wife and her paramour in the man's own house, and the other over an alleged breach of contract involving the sale of land and cattle."

"Sir, I'm right sorry, but what's a paramour?"

"His wife's, how can I put it? Her boy friend?"

"I'm sorry. That's what I thought, but I wanted to be sure."

"Don't ever apologize for learning, Will. Apologize when you become so arrogant you think you know all."

"I don't really expect that time to ever get here."

"Let's hope not."

Judge Wagner discussed briefly the first trial and what I could expect and what I should particularly look for.

The trial recessed at noon and Judge Wagner invited me to have dinner with him, in his office. He had sandwiches sent over from the hotel dining room.

After we had started eating, he sat back and looked at me.

"All right, Will, what was the biggest mistake made this morning?"

I momentarily went blank. I just sat and stared at him.

"Oh, come now, Will, surely you noticed. If you didn't, I shall be very disappointed."

I thought, for a moment, back over the morning activities.

All of a sudden, I remembered my amazement at the failure of the defense attorney.

"That lawyer from Raton. That Mr. Bellow, who's defending Dexter, he messed up in his cross-examination of that old lady who lives next door to Dexter. She said she heard a ruckus and jumped out of her bed and ran to the window."

"She said she saw Dexter throw his wife on the bed, then shoot her."

"How did he mess-up, Will?"

"I could see, from where I sat, that old woman wore real heavy glasses. It's not reasonable to think that an old woman awakened, as she said she was, would have thought to put on her glasses. She may have, but it would have been a good chance to challenge her, and I believe make the challenge stick. And, as she was the only, so-called, eye witness, it seems to me Bellow missed his best shot."

"What would you have done? Called the old woman a liar?"

"No, sir, I would have just ask her to take off her glasses and then tell me how many men in the room wore mustaches."

"Ha! It looks like even you are developing a slight case of cynicism after all."

"I don't know, but that just seemed so clear to me, I couldn't believe an established lawyer didn't catch it."

"Do you remember the three kinds of lawyers I told you about?"

"Yes, sir."

"Well, Mr. Bellow seems not to be very cynical. He's not making that much money on this trial, so he can't be too greedy. It would appear there's only one description left."

"But he seemed to handle all the rest pretty good."

"All the 'rest' could have been handled by you, this morning, with about thirty minutes instruction. The one point upon which he could have turned it all in his clients favor, he missed completely."

"Will he lose the case because of that?"

"Think back on your studies, Will he?"

"No! Dexter was defending his home and property. I hesitate to call his wife his 'property,' but that's what it boils down to, doesn't it?"

"Let's see what happens this afternoon. I expect the trial will go to the jury by mid-afternoon. I would imagine you and I will be able to discuss the verdict over supper this evening."

It was; it did and we did.

"I'm not sure I thought they would acquit Dexter. I sort of thought they might at least punish him for killing his wife."

"Remember one thing, Will, If you ever go to trial, to know your jury is to have your case half won. You noticed that all the men on the jury, but one, were married?"

"Yes sir, I noticed that. If I had been Bellow, I would have challenged him too. He only challenged that preacher."

"Right. He was lucky, for that one person could have hung the jury."

"A hung jury means you have to start all over doesn't it?"

"Yes, and it creates all sorts of problems. Both for the prosecution and the defense."

We sat and talked again, long into the evening. Judge Wagner went over the entire trial, step by step.

We parted that evening, agreeing once again to meet at breakfast.

The next morning, Judge Wagner seemed excited.

"Will, I want you to pay close attention this morning. This trial involves Daniel Blair of the Ladder ranch and Bennet DeChamp, of the Spoke outfit. The dispute is over DeChamp's claims that Blair contracted to sell him one hundred head of cattle and fifty acres of land. The land transfer is not in dispute, as the land lies in a small area completely surrounded by DeChamp's land. Blair claims he only agreed to sell DeChamp fifty herd. There is no written contract. A verbal agreement with no witnesses. The land's been paid for by DeChamp and subsequently fenced. The cattle have not been paid for or returned to Blair, by DeChamp. Blair want's his cattle and land back."

"That should be interesting, but I don't see how either one can prove the other is wrong."

"Just watch and we'll talk at dinner."

The trial was marked by both men challenging the other, out loud, and in the courtroom. Judge Wagner finally told them both to shut up or he'd have them jailed, and hold the trial without them.

At noon, Judge Wagner ask me what I thought.

"Well, it's nowhere near as clear as it was yesterday. It seems to me the lawyers have taken all morning to say what you told me in ten minutes at breakfast."

"One small difference."

"Uh oh," I said, "I didn't catch it."

"Oh yes, you did. You just think back over this morning, you'll remember it."

That ruined my dinner. Judge Wagner ate his, with relish, but all I could do was go over and over the mornings testimony.

Judge Wagner had finished his dinner and was almost done with his coffee when I remembered.

"I think I know what it was," I said.

"All right. Now, just remember what you heard, and pay close attention this afternoon. If neither party is able to explain that one point, I know already what my ruling will be. Let's see if we're both right."

As there was no jury, Judge Wagner would rule on the case. As he told me, he could hand down his ruling immediately, or take about as long as he pleased. I suspected he would rule immediately if nothing happened to correct the point made that morning.

The afternoon dragged by with both lawyers going over the same ground they'd covered that morning.

Finally, about four in the afternoon, the last word in the last summation was spoken.

Judge Wagner told them he was ready to rule immediately. He said he had only two questions.

"Mr. DeChamp, how many head of the stock Mr. Blair delivered were cows, and how many were steers?"

"Forty-three were cows and seven were steers." DeChamp answered.

"How many of those cows have dropped calves since you have had them?"

"Forty-two, sir."

Judge Wagner looked at Blair.

"Mr. Blair, you owe Mr. DeChamp eight head of cattle, case closed!"

He rapped his gavel and left the courtroom quiet, with all its inhabitants stunned.

It was only moments until an old man on the front row slapped his knee, then stood up and leaned over toward DeChamp.

"Solomon couldn't a done it better. Put that in your fancy pipe, and smoke it DeChamp."

A healthy chuckle went through the courtroom as all stood to leave.

DeChamp was still standing there when I left. I went back to Judge Wagner's office.

"It's a good thing that trial wasn't held in front of some big city judge," I said, as a greeting.

"Oh, I suspect there are many 'city judges' who know the length of the gestation period for cattle."

"When Blair said he'd picked out the best 'mama' cows he had, I'd have bet most were with calf. But I had to go back over the whole thing at noon, before it came to me," I said.

"Will, let's you and I have and early supper tonight. I'll be over in an hour."

Jim Ballard and I were waiting for the Judge when he came into the dining room. Jim having been sitting in the hotel lobby when I came back from the courthouse.

I asked the Judge if he minded Jim eating with us.

"Of course not. We're only going to spend a few minutes on the law tonight anyway," he responded.

"First, Will, I would like it if you would address me by my first name, Thomas. I believe that's acceptable for colleagues. Next I have here a list of books. They may all be obtained, or ordered, in Denver. I have written the name of a Judge, there in Denver, to whom I've also written for you a letter of introduction. This man will assist you in ordering and buying your books. You must understand these books will represent an expenditure of several hundred dollars. You can afford that, can you not?"

"Yes, sir, that and more."

"Good. Get those books; familiarize yourself with them. Start improving your understanding of words, and after another six or seven months of study hang out your shingle."

"My what?"

"Your sign, which should say Will . . . or is it William Jackson, Attorney at Law."

"You honestly think I should do that? And it's just Will, sir."

"I'll not tell you what you 'should' do, only what you can."

The rest of the evening was much a blur. It wasn't until we were well on the trail the next morning, when Jim rode up beside me and his question brought it all home to me.

"Are you really going to be a lawyer, Mr. Jackson?"

I studied on that for a few moments.

"Yeah, Jim, I guess I am. I'm really going to be a lawyer."

Suddenly I was very eager to be home.

By the time we got home, I had settled down somewhat. But, I was still excited.

I told Clatilda what had happened. She seemed not at all surprised.

"When do you want to go to Denver?" she asked.

"I thought I'd leave as soon as I could."

"Well, we can't leave for a few days. There are some things I have to take care of first."

"We?" I said.

"Yep! We. I'm going to see you have everything you need to do this properly. I know you. If you left here with ten dollars, you'd try to come back with eleven. No, cowboy! If my husband is going to be a lawyer, we're going to do it right."

"What's to do right. I'm going to Denver, see a man, buy some books, order some more, then come home."

"See, that's what I mean. Where are you going to get your 'shingle,' as Judge Wagner calls it? You will need at least two good suits, and not some hand-me downs from a general store. You'll need some nice shirts. You've got to have one of those leather satchels I seen men carry in the newspapers; paper, pencils, pens. There's probably no end to what we'll find in Denver that you'll need."

"Clatilda, I don't want you going to Denver with me."

She stopped her pacing for a moment, and stared at me with those piercing blue eyes.

"No?"

"No, ma'am. You are making too much of this. I'm excited, but Clatilda, what if after I get all those expensive books, I find out I'm not good enough or don't like the law. If I let you spend all that extra money on doo-dads, I'll feel obligated to go in to something I really might not like."

She stood for a moment, looking off out the front windows.

"I'll make you a deal, Will. I'll go with you; I won't buy anything. I'll just make a list of what you may need. Then we'll come home and if you decide against the law, there'll be no loss. If you go ahead, we, at least, will know what to order and where to order it. Will that be all right?"

I knew I was beat and I'd better grab what compromise that was offered.

"That'll be all right. Only if you promise you'll not buy anything except for you and the kids."

"What about Uncle Buck, Jacob, Jim and the Blalocks?"

"Clatilda, you know exactly what I mean."

"Yes sir. Can I go talk to Anne Blalock and see if she can take care of the kids?"

"Of course. But you better not include Bud. If he's not allowed to stay down here with Jacob and his Uncle Buck, he's liable to throw a fit."

"Do you really think he's big enough for that?"

"Yes ma'am, and past time for the apron strings to be loosened."

She stood and looked at me for a moment then turned quickly away, grabbing her shawl, thinking I'd not seen the tear slide out of her eye.

We left for Denver three days later. It was as if we were on a picnic instead of the deadly serious trip into our future.

We had no trouble locating Judge Wheeler when we got to Denver. He was well known, and after we had sent Judge Wagner's letter into him by his clerk, he became known to us.

In fact he came out of his office, himself, to greet us.

We talked at length about Judge Wagner. We found out that Judge Wheeler and Thomas Wagner were not just friends; Judge Wheeler had married Thomas Wagner's sister.

"How is Thomas getting along down there in New Mexico?"

"He seems fine, sir. I do not really know him that well, but he seems to prosper and he's well."

"My wife, his sister, and I spent the better part of one whole winter trying to convince him not to go down there. But, Thomas is a strong-willed man. Did he ever tell you why he went there?"

"No, sir, we really never had a personal conversation."

"That's strange. He writes of you as if you were good friends."

"Judge Wagner seemed to take a liking to me, sir. I guess because I'm so green and he probably felt sorry for me."

"I doubt that. But, the reason Thomas went down there was because he hates snow. He said he was heading south, and the first person that looked at him like they thought he was crazy when he asked how much snow they got, where ever he stopped; that person would be his neighbor. He's written us that there has been only one serious snow storm in the eight years he's been down there, and it melted and blew off in little more than a week."

We chatted for awhile longer, then Judge Wheeler said Thomas had indicated I needed help.

"Yes sir. I am studying the law and, Judge Wagner felt you could help me in obtaining the books on this list," I said handing the list to him.

He looked at the list for a few moments then taking his pen wrote on the bottom of the list.

"I am adding two more publications you will need. Can you afford these books, sir? A few are rather costly. Even more so than when Thomas and I acquired ours. And, this request for Supreme Court rulings for the past twenty years will, alone, cost several hundred dollars."

"Yes sir, I came prepared."

"Good. Have you found lodging yet?"

"Yes sir, we got in yesterday afternoon. We are comfortably settled."

"Good, then you go on back to your hotel. Leave your location with my clerk and I will see that he rounds up those volumes on this list that are available, and he will provide you the Publisher's names and addresses for those not easily available. He should have them all to your hotel by tomorrow afternoon at the latest."

"Sir, I really can't allow you to go to all that trouble. If you'll just tell me where I may get the books, I'll do the rounding up myself."

"'Can't allow?' Young man, you can't keep me from it. My brother-in-law has made exactly three requests of me in over twenty years. One that I marry his sister, one that we never name one of our children, Thomas; he hates the name. And now, he asks that I help you. You seem a nice enough young fellow and I might even do it for you anyway. But, a request from Thomas . . . Allow, indeed! I hardly think you could stop me."

He stood and extended his hand.

"Now you and your lovely wife go on back and enjoy your stay while we take care of your library needs."

He showed us out and we went back to our hotel.

We hung around the hotel that afternoon and evening. Clatilda enjoyed the dining room and seeing all the women, and what she called their "fashions."

To me, all the men looked overdressed, and the women looked as if you touched them, they would crush like a china doll. The old saying about a "silk purse out of a sow's ear" came to mind. I felt uncomfortable.

The next morning we went shopping. Clatilda had talked to one of the chamber maids and found out where to get everything she needed. By noon, I had to hire a Hansom Cab to take us back to the hotel. I then had to get two bellboys to help get everything to our room. I couldn't wait to start home. I'd be lucky if I didn't have to trade our buggy for a springboard wagon.

We had just returned to our room from dinner when there came a knock on our door. I opened it to find Judge Wheeler's clerk and two men pushing dollies loaded with books. When they came in and stacked the books, I was dumb-founded by the number and size.

"Mr. Jackson, I was able to find everything but volume four of the federal statutes and, of course, the Supreme Court rulings. But, I have here the names and addresses of those publishers who can provide them for you."

I thanked him very much and even offered to pay him, personally, for his services, but it was immediately clear that I'd insulted him. I quickly apologized and asked if he had brought an invoice for the books. He had, and handed it to me. I had expected about the total shown on the invoice. I counted out, in gold coin, the invoice amount plus a little extra.

"Please see your dray-men are shown my gratitude."

He seemed somewhat surprised. Whether that a cowboy, such as I, could afford the books, or that I would think to pay the dray-men.

At any rate, he left immediately.

Clatilda and I walked around those books like a bull around a strange calf. We were both overwhelmed.

"Will, how in the world are we going to get these home. There's hardly room in the buggy for the things I bought, let alone this mountain of books."

"Well, my lady, you like the stream cars so much, I guess we'll just ride the train to Pueblo. From there, I'll just have to get us a wagon and team."

"What about our buggy and team?"

Selling the buggy and team was easy. The market was good. And, I found a fairly well equipped carpenter's shop in the basement of our hotel. Two days later, we were standing at the depot waiting to board our train to Pueblo. Our crated books and other material safely in the baggage car.

In Pueblo, I found a broke teamster willing to sell his wagon at a giveaway price. The only trouble was that he had a four-horse team. By the time I had bought the wagon and sold two of the horses, I came out a few dollars ahead.

When we left Pueblo we were in high spirits. We had what we came for, we had good weather and we were headed home.

"I have enjoyed our trip, Will. But, I will enjoy, even more, our homecoming," Clatilda said.

Our trip was uneventful, and we were seen, by the children, as we came up our valley. They were all at the house to greet us, even the whole Blalock family.

Jacob walked around the new wagon and team.

"Not bad, but somehow, I don't see Clatilda going to church in this," he said, somewhat jokingly, and some serious.

"You know," I said turning to Clatilda, "I hadn't thought of that."

"I had," she said brightly. "John has the solution out behind his store."

"You mean that new surrey with the red wheels!" Bud popped in.

"That's the one," Clatilda said.

"Boy, pa, that's about the best looking buggy I ever saw. Dan and I were talking how we'd like to have that!"

"We'll see, son."

"Yes, Bud, we'll have to count our money to be sure we can afford it"

I looked sharply at her, and that hussy just winked at me!

We made quite a show that next Sunday in our new red-wheeled surrey.

Chapter 34

I spent that summer and clear into fall arranging and getting to know my new books. It was two or three months before I felt I was really getting the hang of what Thomas Wagner had told me about cross-referencing.

Christmas was great. Again the ladies staged the whole affair at our home. Anne had painted a funny picture showing me wearing two six-guns and a rifle strapped across my back, digging potatoes. It was really a good painting, but I was not about to tell her that, given the subject of the painting. Gifts were many and food, again, abundant. Much to my secret pleasure and public chagrin, Anna Laura insisted on hanging the picture in my office.

The new year came in windy, cold and snowing. It snowed for a week and then turned cold. Once again, I had to abandon my studies to help with the cattle. It felt good to be working. I thought long about the path I had chosen. It seemed right and felt right. But, I did get a kick out of working with the animals.

Winter was short that year, and by mid-March we had green shoots peeking through the rotten snow.

One evening, after supper, I was sitting at the table while Anna

Laura and Clatilda washed the dishes. Bud was long gone with his Uncle Buck.

"Will," Clatilda said, over her shoulder, "you and Jacob are going to have to build another house."

"You've grown tired of this one so soon?" I asked.

"No! It's for Jim and Lydia Todd."

"Why should I build a house for Jim and, who?" I was busy working on my tally book. I seemed to have more cattle than I should.

"Because they are getting married in June and we can't have them living in the barn."

Suddenly, what Clatilda was saying soaked in.

"Jim's getting married? I didn't even know he'd been seeing anyone."

"You'd have to be the only one in the valley, Papa!" Anna Laura said. "They started standing around after Sacrament almost a year ago!"

"Jim hasn't said anything to me," I said.

"He needs your permission?"

"No, but if I'm going to have to build him and his bride a house, it seems he would say something."

"Well, you'd best talk to him in the morning or you're going to lose a good hand."

After breakfast the next morning I asked Jim to come back to my office.

"Jim, I hear you're getting married?" I opened the conversation.

"Yes, sir. I was going to talk to you about it. I don't know what we're going to do about a place. Lydia and I have been looking at some ground just outside town. Her pa says we could probably pick it up right cheap."

"Be kind of a long ride to work every morning, wouldn't it?"

"Yes, sir, but for now it looks to be the best I can do."

"You going to stay with us, Jim?"

"Yes, sir if you'll have me. Cowboying is the only thing I know. I don't know I'll ever amount to much but Lydia is willing to take me as I am. It's just that this place to live is worrying me some."

"Well, I think we can solve that problem. Spring seems to have set in for sure. What would you say if we built you and your bride a place over north of the old cabin?"

"I don't rightly know what to say, Mr. Jackson."

"You going to continue working for me?"

"Yes, sir!"

"Good. Let's go get Jacob and we'll go mark off your foundation, and go up and see if we can find enough logs."

It took almost two months to finish the Ballard house, as it has always been called. We were very close to not getting it done by the wedding date. As it was, the ladies were working on the inside while we were finishing the porch the latter part of the week before the wedding day on Saturday.

Bishop Terry insisted the wedding be held in church but the ladies demanded the reception be held in the "Ballard" house. Before the evening was over there were three receptions going on simultaneously: one in the newlywed's home, one in the old cabin, and one in our new house. Mass confusion existed, in the midst of which Clatilda and Anne had the time of their lives.

I was sitting in my office early in July when Clatilda, Anna Laura and the twins returned from a trip to the store.

Anna Laura came running through the house and burst into my office.

"Papa, Papa! You've got a letter. It was at the store! Can I read it?"

"Whoa, let's open it first and see who it's from."

"We already know, Papa. It's from Mr. Nava, down in Alamosa. Can we read it, Papa?"

"Well, let me read it first. Will that be all right?"

By this time Clatilda and the twins completed my audience.

I briefly scanned the one page letter then went back and carefully read it again.

"Is it bad news, Will?" Clatilda asked.

"Well, yes, and no. Jamie wants me to come to Alamosa before the end of July. He says he has a case he wants to discuss with me."

"What could be the bad news about that?" She asked.

"What if he wants me to take the case? I may not be ready for that."

"Why, Will, you've already handled Brother Burton's estate for his widow and you rewrote the notes and contracts the bank uses. You've handled 'cases'."

"Not real trial cases, Clatilda. You can't believe how fast things can happen in a courtroom. You can win or lose in minutes, even seconds."

"Will, I've asked you this only once before in our life, Are you afraid?"

I thought for a moment, then I yielded to Anna Laura's persistence, handing her the letter.

"No, I'm not afraid. I guess it's time I quit being a student and see if I can be a real lawyer."

"Good for you! When do you want to go?"

"I suppose I might as well go tomorrow."

"Can you wait until Monday?"

"I suppose. Why Monday?"

"Well that will give me time to do the alterations on your new suit and wash your new dress shirts."

"Wait a minute. What's this about a suit and shirts."

"You made me promise to wait until you were a lawyer before we thought about suits and things. When you settled the Burton estate, I ordered you a suit and shirts from Denver. Upset John something terrible that I didn't buy from him. But, I told you I would not outfit you in hand-me-downs off some general store shelf. Your new clothes arrived last week and I picked them up today. Isn't that grand!"

I looked at this woman who had graced my life these years. How could I be angry?

I felt like an old maid at a quilting bee the next few days. Bud took my good boots and made them look new. Anna Laura spent hours trying to decide on which of the three ties, Clatilda had ordered I should wear, and Clatilda must have had me try on the suit a dozen times while she fitted pins, first here, then there.

Saturday afternoon, I was enduring yet another fitting when I turned to Clatilda.

"What if Jamie just wants to talk about some case he's hearing and I won't even be involved?"

"Fine! And while he's talking to you, he'll know he's not talking to some cowhand, but a real lawyer."

"You got something against cowboys?"

"You know what I mean, Will Jackson! And it's 'have,' not 'got'."

She had been doing that a lot lately and I'd finally had enough.

"Ma'am, I will never handle words as well as you, and I'd like it if you stopped correcting me as if I were one of the twins."

I looked down at her, as she knelt by my cuffs, measuring for a fit.

She looked up at me, right solemn.

"All right, Will," she said, real serious. "And it's 'was one of the twins,' not were."

Then she winked at me with that way of hers.

"You're not going to pay any attention to me at all, are you?"

"Yes, I am, cowboy, and to show you how much, I've a cherry pie fresh out of the oven. How's a big piece and some cream sound to you?"

Euchred again! I dutifully removed my new suit and went to the kitchen to enjoy my pie.

Monday morning found me on the way to Alamosa, new suit and all.

I stayed at the stage station in Saguache I had to promise Clatilda I would spend the night there. If these new suits, sleeping inside and ladies fussing over me all the time, kept up, I could see I was in some danger of becoming a real dude.

I got into Alamosa late in the afternoon and decided to wait until the next morning to see Jamie.

His daughter ushered me into Jamie's office.

"Will! I was afraid you did not get my letter."

"Yeah, the circuit rider calls on our little village fairly regular. I'm told we can now send a letter all the way to Denver and actually expect it to get there!"

"Sit down, sit down. I'm so glad you got here."

"It's my pleasure, Jamie. You said you had a case you wanted to go over with me."

"How are you coming along with your studying, Will?"

"Well, I've handled a couple of small things up our way. I'm getting a little more confident as time goes along."

"You think you're up to handling a bigger case?"

"How big?"

"Murder."

"Jamie, you have a way of dropping things on me, don't you."

"Well, we have only one lawyer here in town. At least, the one we have now is honest, not like Tim Johnson."

"Has this man been here long?"

"Yes, he's been here about six or seven years and is a good man. But the closest other lawyer is in Walsenburg, and he's a drunkard. There's a Circuit Judge comes through here three times a year, and he has three or four lawyers riding with him. But this crime occurred right here in Alamosa. So, I have jurisdiction. If I could get you to handle the prosecution, I could start the trial day after tomorrow. You game?"

"Prosecution? Aw, Jamie, I'm not sure I'm ready for that. Particularly taking on an experienced lawyer."

"Well, I don't have three or four inexperienced men to put you up against. But, seriously, Will, I'm willing to take a chance on you if you're willing to try."

"I don't know, Jamie, let me have a few hours to think on it. I'll give you an answer by three this afternoon."

I rode out along the river and sat there on the bank for the better part of three hours, new suit, and all.

I prayed some, I studied on my abilities, or lack of same, for awhile. I was no closer to a decision when, a little after noon, I climbed back on my pony and headed back to town.

I kept coming back to this 'prosecutor' thing. I felt I might be able to defend the man but to be the one responsible for prosecuting the man seemed too much like judging him.

I was riding along worrying the problem in my mind when it happened again.

As clear as a bell I heard a voice speak to me. "The truth will not be judged!"

I looked around, knowing full well I would see no one. I sat there remembering the other time I had heard such a voice. The prompting, then, had done well by me.

I sat there and tried to sort this out. If I took the available facts and if they pointed to the guilt of the accused, then to present these facts to a jury would not be judging. It would only be presenting the truth.

I walked into Jamie's office a little before two that afternoon.

"All right, Jamie, let's have a go at it."

"Good. Now, we have a new Marshal here, fellow by the name of Whitaker, Jack Whitaker. You'll want to get with him and he will fill you in on the case. You talk to him and whoever else you want, and let me know by tomorrow afternoon if you'll be ready to go to trial day after tomorrow morning."

"And, Will, as you probably know, from this point on it will not be proper for you and I to discuss the case without the defense attorney being present."

"All right," I said as I left his office.

"All right, my foot!" I knew no such thing. I began to get a grasp of what I did not know.

I sat down with Jack Whitaker in his office that afternoon and he told me all he knew of the case.

It seemed the accused man had been at a pie supper at the church hall earlier in the summer. He had bid on a pie against a young man, the son of a rancher out east of Alamosa. The accused, one Roy Payne had been drinking throughout the evening and after a couple of minor tiffs on the dance floor, had confronted the same young man and the young woman, who had baked the controversial pie, on the veranda of the hall. They had a few words and Payne shot both the girl and young Baker. Payne swore Baker drew first and the girl stepped in front of Baker. Many had seen Baker wearing a pistol when he arrived at the dance, and there was such a scuffle after the shooting that no one knew, really, what had happened. Baker's's gun was found on the veranda later. But, so was his shell belt and holster. Whitaker said he thought Baker had picked up his belt, holster and pistol from the cloakroom and was getting ready to leave when Payne shot him. Whitaker said he didn't believe Baker was even wearing his holster at the time of the shooting.

Whitaker said feelings were running high, as the girl was the very popular daughter of a local merchant. He said half the young men in the county would have liked to have been in Baker's place that evening. That is, sharing her pie and dancing with the young lady.

I asked Whitaker if he had any witnesses to the shooting.

He said he had a young couple who had been on the veranda when the shooting happened. And, also, a young man, Orville Rogers, a clerk in the local bank had been at the door to the veranda when the shooting happened. Those were the only three people who could tell anything about the shooting. That is except for Payne, himself.

Jamie had given me a small office, down the hall from his, to use during the trial. I told Marshal Whitaker to have all three of the witnesses in that office at nine the next morning.

Late that afternoon, I went over to the church and had myself let out onto the veranda where the shooting had occurred. Before I went to supper that evening I was thoroughly familiar with the physical location of the shooting.

The next morning when I got to my office, I found it was actually two rooms: a small waiting room out front and the office, itself.

Marshal Whitaker was waiting for me.

"All three of your witnesses will be here like you asked," he said.

"Do you know these people, Marshal?"

"I know Rogers well, and Carl Palmer is the son of a fellow I've known for years. Lloyd Palmer has ranched south of here for sometime. He's got a nice spread down on the Conejos. Carl's going to marry the girl he was with that night. Her name is Betsy Lanier. I believe that Betsy is short for Elizabeth. Her mother is a widow and runs a boarding house. Nice folks, living a little close to the bone since Betsy's dad died, but straight honest folks."

I had time to set out my paper, pencils and pens before young Orville Rogers came in. The Marshal asked me if I was ready to see him. I said to send him in.

After the introductions, I asked Rogers to tell me exactly what he'd seen.

"Well, sir, not a lot. I knew there were only two dances left and I figured Ken Baker would have the last, but maybe I'd get to dance the next-to-last with Jean."

I interrupted, "What was the young lady's name. I'm afraid I've never heard."

"Jean Story, sir. Her father owns the Story Mercantile."

"All right, son. Go ahead."

"Well as I said, I'd been looking for Ken and Jean all over the hall when I spotted that blue dress Jean was wearing, out on the veranda. Just as I stepped through the door I heard two shots, bang, bang, just like that. The first thing I saw was this fellow standing right outside the door. He had a gun in his hand, one of those big old Colt Dragoons. Jean fell first, and then Ken went down to one knee then just laid over on his side, sort of easy. The strange thing was that Jean seemed to be in front of Ken. She must have fallen that way, but I thought at the time that she must have been standing in front of Ken, but that didn't seem to make sense.

Two other fellows and I grabbed Payne and took his pistol from him. Looking back that seems a stupid thing to have done. He could have shot one of us, but he didn't even resist. He just stood there. Then Marshal Whitaker came out and took charge. I stood around and talked about it with everyone else for a while, but I had to go to work the next morning, so I went on home."

"Did Baker have a gun?"

"I heard later they had found his holster and pistol on the veranda but I didn't see it when I was there."

"It's claimed Baker drew first and Payne was only defending himself."

"I don't believe that. Ken would never have drawn with Jean there, and, like I said, I never saw Ken's pistol."

"Is it possible he dropped it when he was shot?"

"I expect anything was possible, but I saw Ken, one Sunday at a turkey shoot, draw and hit a whiskey bottle in the air. If he'd had his pistol, I'd have to believe he'd got off at least one shot."

"All right, Mr. Rogers. Can you think of anything else that might have any bearing on this case?"

"No sir, I guess I've told you all I know."

"Well, Judge Nava says he would like to start the trial tomorrow. Will you be able to be there?"

"Yes, sir! Mr. Beamon, he owns the bank, he says I can have all the time off I need. He says he wants to see this Payne hang!"

"We'll see about that. I'll have Marshal Whittaker come around the bank this afternoon and tell you when to be at the courtroom."

"Yes, sir."

I then asked Marshal Whittaker to send in Carl Palmer. I'd heard him and a young woman come in while I was talking to Rogers.

"Don't you want Betsy too?" Whittaker asked.

"No, just the young man."

Mr. Palmer was obviously nervous and kept fussing with his shirt sleeves.

"A little different than working a bunch of cattle?"

"Yes, sir. It sure is."

"Well, just calm down. All I want to know is just what you remember about that night. Tell me in your own words, and try not to leave any thing out."

"Well, Betsy and I had stepped out on the veranda to cool off before the final set of dances. Betsy's my girl."

"I know. Was anyone on the veranda when you went out there?"

"No, sir. Ken and Jean, that was the couple who were shot, came out a few minutes later."

"Was Ken wearing a gun?"

"No, sir!"

"Was he, maybe, carrying it in his hand?"

"I don't know. He did have Jean's coat. They said they were only going to dance one dance then leave early. Ken said they were going for a buggy ride down by the river. Betsy and I teased them a little about that, then we stepped over to the side of the veranda, to better get the south breeze. We'd just turned around when this Payne fellow walked out on the veranda. He told Ken that this would be the last time he outbid his betters. Ken had outbid everyone for Jean's pie. That Payne fellow had gone all the way to seven dollars, but Ken had bid ten. Can you believe that? Ten dollars for a pie? He told me later that Jean had put a special ribbon on the box so he knew it was hers. I guess that makes it all right."

"What happened then?"

"He pulled out this big pistol and began shooting. We heard Jean yell "Oh no!" then she and Ken were both on the floor."

"How did they fall?"

"I don't understand, sir."

"I mean where were they when they fell after being shot?"

"They were laying almost side by side, sort of an angle away from Payne."

"Not straight away or toward their killer?"

"No sir. They were both sort of slanted away to Payne's left."

"What then?"

"Well, Orville Rogers and some other fellow came running out and grabbed Payne and I stepped over and twisted the gun from his hand. It was easy. I could smell the alcohol on his breath. He must have been drinking."

"Anything else?"

"No, sir. Marshal Whitaker came out and took Payne away. I took

Betsy home and that's all I know."

"All right, Mr. Palmer. When you go out, will you ask Miss Lanier to come in?"

"She's real scared, Mr. Jackson. Could I stay in here with her?"

"No, you cannot. When she gets on the witness stand to tell her story, she will be all alone. It's time she gets used to it."

He looked at me with no friendship in his eyes.

Miss Lanier came in and sat down.

She was just about to twist a lace handkerchief in two, in her nervousness.

"Miss Lanier, are you afraid?"

"Yes, sir," she said not even raising her eyes.

"Were you afraid the night your friends were killed?"

"No, sir, not until after. It all happened so fast."

"Well, your young man did a pretty brave thing taking that pistol from Mr. Payne. You must be proud of him."

"Yes, sir, I am!"

"I understand you and Mr. Palmer are to be married."

"Yes sir, in September. Carl's building our house now."

"Where will that be?"

"Out on his father's ranch."

"Have you and Carl talked about what happened that night?"

"Yes sir."

"Do you disagree on any points that you're aware of?"

"No sir."

"All right then, why don't you go get your young man and have him go buy you dinner?"

"Is that all, sir?"

"Yes, I believe so. Is there anything you want to tell me?"

"No sir."

"All right, then, you go on now."

I told Marshal Whitaker I'd let him know when the trial would be and he could arrange to have the witnesses there.

I went to Jamie's office. I had to wait for a few minutes for him to return from an errand.

After we were seated in his office Jamie asked me where I was in my preparation for the trial?

"I'm as ready as I'll ever be, Judge. When will you set the trial?"

"How does tomorrow morning sound to you?"

"Just fine. You will want a list of my witnesses for the defense."

Jamie took the list and glanced at it.

"No Betsy Lanier?" He asked, looking over the list, at me.

"Nope."

He looked at me for a moment.

"All right. I'll notify Glen Stewart, he's Payne's attorney. If there are no problems we'll begin at ten tomorrow morning. You staying at the hotel?"

"Yes, I'll be there all afternoon."

"Very well then, I'll let you know if there are any problems. If not,

I'll see you in court tomorrow."

He stood, and I left.

Chapter 35

The morning of the trial dawned grey and overcast. The weather matched my mood. As I tied the string tie I'd slipped into my valise without Clatilda or Anna Laura noticing, I wondered at my presence here.

"My friend," I thought, "you are in the way of making a grand fool of yourself. How in the world did you ever get yourself in such a mess?"

I walked across to the courthouse much as one going to his doom. I'd eaten nothing. Feeling that to put food on my nervous stomach was to invite disaster of the worst sort.

I was somewhat surprised to see the crowd already gathering. I was shocked that I would be trying my first case in front of so many people. None of which I knew.

I had brought only a few pieces of foolscap and three pencils, so I was not long arranging myself at the prosecutor's table. Luckily Mr. Stewart and Payne were already seated at one table, for I feared to seat myself wrongly.

Judge Nava came in and after we were again seated, he looked at me and asked if the people were ready to proceed.

I was afraid I wouldn't even be able to speak, but the words came easily, to my everlasting surprise.

"We are, your honor."

"Mr. Stewart?"

"Ready your honor."

"So," I thought, "here we go, ready or not."

Jury selection went quickly. I did not know enough about any of the prospective jurors to make any peremptory challenges and found nothing objectionable. Mr. Stewart dealt with them likewise. Before eleven that morning, we were ready to try Roy Payne for the murder of Ken Baker and Jean Story.

In my opening statement I made it short and sweet.

"Gentlemen, it is a fact that Roy Payne did shoot and kill Ken Baker and Jean Story. Defense counsel will try to convince you that Mr. Payne shot in self-defense. I think they will not be able to prove that. There is no question that Miss Story was no threat to Mr. Payne. Think about that one fact as Mr. Payne's attorney tries to convince you that Mr. Payne is innocent by reason of self-defense."

Mr. Stewart then stood and spent over an hour explaining to twelve men the meaning and definition of self-defense. I'll swear, at least two of the jurors nodded off.

Judge Nava recessed the trial for dinner, after Stewart's harangue.

When we returned after dinner, Judge Nava asked me if I was ready to call my first witness.

"Yes sir, we call Orville Rogers to the stand."

After Rogers was sworn in, I did not even stand up from my seat at the table.

"Mr. Rogers, did you see Mr. Payne, the defendant, shoot and kill

Mr. Baker and Miss Story, on the night in question?"

"Yes sir," he answered.

"Did you see Mr. Baker draw or shoot a weapon?"

"No sir."

"No more questions, your honor," I said.

Jamie looked at me in wonder.

"Your witness, Mr. Stewart," Jamie finally said, after shaking his head, slightly.

Stewart took at least a half hour dragging out the story Rogers had given me the day before in my office. When he was through I stood and asked Judge Nava if I might redirect the witness. He agreed.

"Mr. Rogers, are you absolutely certain, beyond any question of a doubt, you saw Roy Payne shoot and kill Ken Baker and Jean Story?"

"Objection!" Stewart said jumping to his feet. "That question has been asked and answered!"

"Mr. Jackson, I believe he's right."

"Very well, your honor. Mr. Stewart took so long getting the same question answered, I just wanted to be sure the jury remembered the witness' answer when I finished asking the question."

"The objection is sustained!" Nava said. "Have you any other questions of this witness, Mr. Jackson?"

"Yes sir, only one more."

"Go ahead then."

"Mr. Rogers, did you see Mr. Baker draw or shoot a weapon?"

Stewart again jumped to his feet.

"Objection, your honor, and for the same reasons."

"May I offer the same response as a minute ago, your honor."

Judge Nava looked at me for a long moment.

"Do you have any other questions of this witness, Mr. Jackson?" Jamie asked.

"No sir."

"Then the witness is excused. Call your next witness, Mr. Jackson."

I called Carl Palmer, and once again we went through the exact same routine as we had with Rogers. Stewart was getting hotter and hotter.

After Palmer was excused, Judge Nava asked if I had any other witnesses.

I called Marshal Whittaker.

"Marshal Whittaker," I began, after he was sworn in, "did you arrest Roy Payne for the murders of Ken Baker and Jean Story?"

"I did."

"On what grounds, sir."

He looked at me for a moment.

"Because he did it."

"How do you know that, sir."

"I had three witnesses who saw him do it. I had the pistol that he shot them with. One of the witnesses took it away from him. And, after I got him to my jail, I asked him why he'd done it. He said, because Baker deserved it."

"Objection!" Stewart said jumping up. "That's hearsay, your honor."

"Sustained," Jamie said, "the jury will disregard the last statement."

"Very well, Marshal Whittaker, did you find Ken Baker's pistol?"

"Yes, sir, I found it on the floor behind Mr. Baker's body."

"Did you find his shell belt and holster?"

"Yes sir. It was about three feet further away from Mr. Baker's body."

"Let's see, then, the pistol was how far behind Baker's body?"

"I say at least three feet, maybe four."

"And the holster and belt?"

"Another three feet beyond the pistol."

"Was the pistol cocked?"

"No."

"Was the hammer sitting on a full or empty chamber?"

"Empty."

"Finally, Marshal, had Mr. Baker's pistol been fired?"

"No sir. It was as clean as a whistle."

I then turned the Marshal over to Stewart.

For a half hour we all listened to Stewart go over the Marshal's testimony again and again. Once more I saw a juror nod off.

When, finally the Marshal was excused, Judge Nava asked me if I had any other witnesses. I told him, no. I told him that the prosecution rested.

Stewart sat for a moment after being asked if he was ready to present his case. He turned and looked out over the crowd. Then he turned back to the Judge.

"Your honor, may I have a recess until tomorrow morning. I had a witness that seems not to be here."

"Can you have your witness here at ten tomorrow morning?"

"I'm sure I can, sir."

"Very well," Jamie said. "Court is recessed until ten tomorrow morning."

I was not real pleased with the recess but there was nothing I could do.

I went into the office Jamie had provided me, and sitting there, went over the trial in my mind. I traced my steps again and again. After an hour, I went over to the hotel and had a leisurely supper, then turned in early.

The first thing I noticed when I went into the courtroom the next morning was Betsy Lanier seated on the back row with an older woman that I assumed to be her mother.

After the preliminaries were over, Judge Nava asked Stewart if his witness was in the courtroom.

"Yes, your honor, the defense calls Elizabeth Lanier."

After she was sworn in, I could see she was much more nervous than she had been when she was in my office.

Stewart's first question set the tone for his entire examination of Miss Lanier.

"Miss Lanier is there a good reason you were not called as a witness by the prosecution?"

I thought, "This is an experienced lawyer?"

I stood, and objected.

"Your honor, how could the witness possibly know why the prosecution did or did not do anything?"

Jamie thought for a moment. "Mr. Stewart, where are you going with this?"

"I'm trying to find out what this witness knows."

"Then ask her, sir!" Jamie said.

"Miss Lanier, what did you see that night?"

Betsy told the same story that had been told by Carl Palmer. Every time Stewart prompted her, she jumped as if poked with a stick. By the time, he was through the girl was sobbing quietly and shaking visibly.

"Your witness, Mr. Jackson," Jamie said.

"I have only one question, your honor. Betsy, did you see Mr. Payne kill Mr. Baker and Miss Story?"

"Yes, sir," she said quietly.

Judge Nava excused her and asked Stewart if he had any other witnesses.

He leaned over and spoke to Payne. It was obvious they were having an argument. Finally Stewart turned back to the bench.

"Yes, sir," he said, "the defense calls Roy Payne."

After Payne was sworn in, Stewart walked over to the stand from his table, then walked back to the table and sat down.

"Mr. Payne, will you please tell the court, in your own words, what happened the night Mr. Baker and Miss Story were shot."

"Well, I went to this pie supper and I bid on this right pretty pie. I bid a lot of money, but this kid kept outbidding me. Every time he'd bid he'd look over to me with this smirk on his face. Afterwards he told it all around the hall how he'd outbid the dumb miner. All them cowboys and townees were having a big laugh at me. After a while I had enough. I tried to talk to him on the dance floor once, but some fellows dragged me away. I then went looking for Baker to make him quit telling stories about me. When I found him, out on the porch, I started to say something to him, but he drew on me. I had no choice but to defend myself. The girl stepped in front of Baker and I guess my first shot hit her. When she fell Baker still had his gun out, so I shot him. That's how it happened and that's all there is to it. I'm sorry the girl got shot. But, she threw herself into the middle of a gunfight. That was her fault, not mine."

He sat for a moment looking first at the jury, then at Stewart, then back to the jury.

Nothing else was said for what seemed a long time.

"Mr. Stewart, have you anymore questions for this witness?" Jamie asked.

Stewart sat for a moment before he answered.

"No sir, no more questions."

"Mr. Jackson?"

I started to decline to question Payne, but something prompted me to stand.

"Mr. Payne, had you been drinking that evening?"

"Well one of the boys had a jug out in his wagon. I may have had a nip or two."

"One or two, sir? Just how many, exactly?"

"I don't remember, exactly. It could have been more."

"Four, five . . . ten?"

"No, it wasn't ten. It could have been five or six, but it weren't no ten."

"You say Mr. Baker was telling other people you were a 'dumb miner,' just who did he tell?"

"I don't know. There was a bunch of them."

"Can you name one?"

"I didn't know all them people. There was lots he told."

"Again, sir, can you name one?"

He looked around, wildly, like a cornered animal. Suddenly his head stopped and fixed on the back of the courtroom.

"Yeah, I can! That there's Henry Young standing back yonder," he said pointing at a cowhand standing against the back wall of the room. "He told me how this Baker was laughing and telling everyone how dumb I was!" He leaned forward in his chair. "You can tell 'em, can't you, Hank?"

I stepped back and looked up at Jamie.

"Your honor, I believe Mr. Stewart might wish to examine this new witness at this time. I will not object if I may be allowed to continue my cross-examination after this new witness is heard."

"Are you sure, Mr Jackson?"

"Yes sir. If the truth can best be served by Mr. Young's testimony, by all means, let's hear it."

"Mr. Stewart?" Jamie asked.

"Yes sir, we agree and we would like to call Mr. Young."

After Young was sworn in, Stewart walked over in front of the jury, turning to face Young.

"Mr. Young, is it true that Mr. Baker was deriding my client in the hall that evening?"

"Sir, I don't rightly know what you mean."

"Was Mr. Baker telling people that Mr. Payne was a 'dumb miner'."

"Oh, yes sir. A lot of his crowd were laughing about it. Baker was saying he was just sorry Roy didn't have more money. Because he said he would have gotten a kick out of bidding higher, just to see the expression on Roy's face. He said no dumb miner was going to outbid him on his own girl's pie."

"Do you know if he said this to anyone else, other than you?"

"Yes sir, I expect there are six or seven fellows right here in this courtroom."

"How did Mr. Payne react to Mr. Baker's comments?"

"Well, as the night went on, Roy kept getting madder and madder. He braced Baker about it, once, when Baker and that Story girl was dancing."

"What happened?"

"Well, me and Shorty Wells went out to get Roy. Roy had been drinking a little bit, and we didn't want him to get in trouble. When we got out there on the floor, me and Shorty, Baker was just telling Roy if he didn't go outside and cool off he, Baker, would cool him off permanently."

"What did he mean by that?"

"Objection," I said. "The witness cannot know what Baker meant."

"Sustained," Judge Nava said.

"All right, Mr. Young, what did you think he meant?"

"I thought he meant what he said."

"And that was?"

"That he would settle the problem permanently. Beyond that you can paint your own picture!"

"Did you see Mr. Baker after that?"

"Not alive."

"Do you know if Mr. Baker was armed."

"No sir."

"Had you ever seen Mr. Baker carry a firearm?"

"Oh, yes sir. He was right proud of that tricked-up gun of his."

"What do you mean, tricked-up?"

"Well, it had fancy bone grips and he'd filed down the sear where it had a hair trigger. I've seen him out to the Palmer's showing off."

"Was he good, with that pistol."

"Yeah, he was some quick. But neither so quick or as good a shot as he fancied himself."

"He thought he was good?"

"Yes sir, he was always trying to get folks to shoot against him. He'd lay his holster and gun on a bench or table and want to bet you he could grab it and shoot a bottle on a fence post before you could draw and hit the same bottle."

"Did you ever see him do this, stunt?"

"I seen him try it a couple of times. Once he did it, but the other time he dropped the pistol and slung his shell belt and holster halfway across the yard."

"Was Mr. Payne good with a gun?"

"Roy? Not so's you could tell. Oh, once he got that old Colt Dragoon out, he was a good enough shot, but he carried the darned thing stuck in his pants, under his belt. Roy's a fair shot, but he ain't quick."

"Mr. Young, why haven't you come forward before now?"

"Weren't my business."

"Any other reason?"

"Well, yeah. I ride for the Palmer outfit, and Carl and Ken Baker was good friends. Didn't seem likely for me to say anything."

"Were you told not to testify or come forward?"

"No, sir. Ain't nobody gonna tell me what I can say!"

"Not even your boss?"

"I've had a lot of bosses and I 'spect I'll have some more. None of them gonna tell me I can't tell the truth."

Stewart sat down, turning the witness over to me.

"Mr. Young, were you around Mr. Payne most of that evening?"

"Pretty much."

"In your opinion, was he drunk?"

"No sir, we all had five or six nips out of a jug Shorty had, but Shorty was real frugal with his liquor. He'd not let you drink too much at a time and he put it away after the three of us had had five or six nips."

"Were you drunk, Mr. Young?"

"After five or six little old nips out of Shorty's jug? Not likely."

"You can drink more than that without getting drunk?"

"And you can bet on that. Come on down to Mama Santana's place any payday Saturday, and you'll see."

"I think I'll just take your word," I said as a ripple went through the crowd.

"Do you think Mr. Payne shot Mr. Baker and Miss Story?"

"Well, I 'spect he did. There's two or three has said they seen him do it. But, mister, I don't believe it happened like they're all saying."

"How do you think it happened?"

"I think Roy went looking for that Baker fellow to get into a fist fight with him. And, I believe Roy could have took him. But Roy Payne didn't go looking for no gunfight."

"Then you don't believe Roy Payne murdered these two people as he's charged?"

"No sir, I don't. I believe he shot that Baker fellow in a fair fight. As for that little girl, well, Roy killed her, and I 'spect he should be punished for that. But whatever you do to him, it hadn't ought to be for what he done to that Baker feller."

Stewart had no redirect for Young and I declined to continue my cross-examination of Payne.

My summation to the jury was brief. I asked that they only consider the facts and render their verdict based on those facts.

Mr. Stewart took most of the afternoon with his summation. It was four that afternoon before the jury went into the rooms I'd used as an office to consider their verdict.

I was eating an early supper when Jamie's daughter came into the dining room, looked around, then came directly to me.

"Daddy wants to see you, Mr. Jackson, right away, in his office."

"Mr. Stewart, too?" I asked.

"Yes sir," she said, "and he said for you to come right now."

Stewart was there when I got to Jamie's office.

"Will, we've got a problem," Jamie said without preamble.

"The jury foreman sent me a note. He wants to know if they can consider anything but first degree murder for the Story girl."

"What about Baker?" I asked.

"They said nothing in their note about that charge. As you know the charge is for two separate first degree murders. A guilty verdict on either will send Payne to the gallows. Strictly speaking, I should not reduce either of the charges but as you are the prosecuting attorney, I am making it your call."

"You can do that?"

"Yep."

"I can do that!"

"When I took your oath the other day you were vested with the power to do just that."

"Can we speak off the record, here?" I ask.

"No." Was Jamie's curt response.

"All right, then. You tell your jury foreman, he may consider a charge of manslaughter against Payne in the case of Jean Story. But, I want your signature on the order, Judge Nava. Right alongside mine."

Jamie grinned, "And was I in your shoes, so would I."

At seven-thirty that same evening, the jury returned their verdict.

Not guilty of the murder of Ken Baker and guilty of manslaughter of Jean Story.

Judge sentenced Payne immediately. Ten years in the state prison.

Interestingly there were only a few sharp remarks in the courtroom after the verdict. Most just quietly left.

As I walked across to the hotel, I was somehow at ease with myself. I didn't feel I'd won. But, somehow, I did not feel defeated.

When I came to the desk the following morning to check out, there was a note for me to see Jamie before I left town.

I went over to his office.

"I see you're dressed for the trail," he said as I walked into his office.

"Yeah, I don't think the coyotes and prairie dogs will be much impressed by my fancy suit and boiled shirt."

He grinned, "Will, I didn't want you to leave before I could talk to you. First, of all, thanks for your help, and here's a county warrant for twenty-two dollars and fifty cents. Your pay for your three days as a prosecuting attorney."

"You know something, Jamie? I hadn't even thought of pay."

"Enjoyed yourself that much?"

"No, not really. I was too worried to enjoy anything."

"Will, I wanted to talk to you about the trial. Why did you not question your witnesses more thoroughly?"

"After Stewart's opening statement to the jury, I knew he'd hound them to death. All I really had were the two questions. They were answered. I think the jury appreciated the briefness of my examination."

"You're right, but I would not have thought you'd be that savvy about a jury."

"Just lucked out, I guess."

"Maybe. The other thing, you effectively lost the case by allowing Young to interrupt your cross with his testimony. Do you realize that? You handed the victory to Stewart, a victory you had already won."

"I know that, but we got the truth, I believe. That's what it's all about, isn't it? It may not have been the best lawyering in the world, but it got the truth out on the table. That's what I was after."

"You're right, of course. Will, can I call on you again if I need you?"

"You'd want to?" I asked.

"Yes, old friend, I will. You may be having second thoughts but let me tell you something; only a truly good attorney could have done what you did. And only an honest man would have wanted to. Please come when I summon you, my friend, for I expect it may be often."

As I rode back towards home, I thought back over the past few years. Had it been worth the effort and money? I felt in my shirt pocket for the county warrant Jamie had given me: twenty-two dollars and fifty cents.

"Yeah," I thought, I think it was. Maybe not to some. Probably not to many. But, as I looked at the warrant, I thought, "There, cowboy, is the written proof of just how far a panhandle cowboy has come."

The warrant was made out to "Will Jackson, Esq. Attorney at Law."